SUMMERHILL

Kevin Frane

Summerhill

Copyright 2013 by Kevin Frane

Published by Argyll Productions
Dallas, TX
http://www.ArgyllProductions.com

ISBN 978-1-61450-103-9
First Printing, January 2013

Cover art by Kamui

To Jake and Seth

Who could have known that a silly online conversation on a slow workday would somehow take over the next three years of my life?

"Imagination will often carry us to worlds that never were. But without it, we go nowhere." —CARL SAGAN

TWO
Stowaway

The young girl with the long, dark hair and the tall, fur-lined ears smiled at Summerhill from behind the rim of her glass. At least someone in this circle had noticed how awkward it was for him to stand there listening to others argue about what exactly he was supposed to be.

"I tell you," the ankylosauromorphic cyborg said in its fluid, polished, robotic voice, "he's got to be some sort of wolf. Just on two legs, is all."

Summerhill kept his ears perked and his mouth shut. He lifted his own glass of golden, bubbling something-or-other to his lips and took a sip, his eyes meeting the little girl's for a moment of grateful acknowledgment.

"Oh, please. Have you ever *seen* a wolf?" asked the Crown Prince of the Akashic Realm, lines of disapproval appearing on his otherwise smooth, pale blue face. He and Summerhill had met earlier in the evening; the two shared a taste for fizzy beverages. "He's far too small, and the colors are all wrong."

The girl quietly begged pardon and broke away from the group. As she left, she offered Summerhill a tiny wave with her slender fingers, along with one final smile of sympathy and encouragement.

A being that looked like a pinkish cloud of gas with a self-contained thunderstorm rumbling all through itself chimed in. "No, I saw a wolf here aboard the ship just this morning." Blue tendrils of electricity crackled over its wispy form as it somehow created the sounds of speech. "He didn't look anything like this."

"I think he's very clearly a jackal," the Crown Prince offered, looking Summerhill over again. "Perhaps a mongrel of some sort, true, but with the overall body shape and the coloring of the fur, I don't see how—"

2

"My memory module contains information about jackals, as well," the cyborg dinosaur interrupted. "I can say with near-absolute certainty that he is not a jackal."

Summerhill rubbed his snout to conceal a smirk as the Crown Prince rolled his eyes. "Near-absolute? Then you at least acknowledge that your computerized deductive reasoning skills might be flawed," the blue-faced man said. "That's a start."

The gas-creature indicated Summerhill with a gentle burst of static. "All right," it said, its pink shade turning to a faint purple, the change in all likelihood representing some shift in demeanor that Summerhill couldn't interpret. "Can you settle this for us?"

With all this attention fixed on him at once, Summerhill looked around at the others, then cleared his throat with a soft cough. "I'm not sure there's anything to settle," he said. "As far as I know, I'm just Summerhill."

"Well, yes," the cloud of gas replied. "But surely you must know what you are."

"Other than Summerhill?"

"That is *who* you are, sure," the Crown Prince said. "We're asking *what* you are."

"Oh." Summerhill looked down at himself, a canine form dressed in a plain shirt and shorts. "I think it's pretty clear that I'm a dog." He wagged his long tail and flicked his pointed ears.

The ankylosauromorphic cyborg leaned in closer. "What designation do your people have for themselves?"

Summerhill took another sip from his glass, and didn't stop until it was empty. "Well, where I come from," he started, picking his words very carefully, "there's only us, so there isn't any need to call ourselves anything. I mean, as a people or a species or whatever." Technically, that was all true.

"Fascinating," the cyborg murmured. "There is some logic to that."

"Where *do* you come from, incidentally?" the Crown Prince asked.

3

Though there was nothing left in his glass, Summerhill brought it to his lips again, slurping at the melting ice in order to buy himself another second or two. He tried to banish the images that came to mind, memories of countless skyscrapers clawing at an endless sky. His pulse raced for a few seconds, but he managed to calm himself and return to the moment. "That's kind of a long story," he said, which wasn't quite as technically true as his previous half-truth. "Let me just refresh my beverage, here."

Excusing himself with a nod, Summerhill slipped into the crowd. Before he passed out of earshot, his keen ears picked up the Crown Prince of the Akashic Realm saying, "I still say that he's some kind of jackal-mutt." He looked around one more time to see if the girl with the furred ears was anywhere to be seen, but to no avail.

Really, trying to find any given individual here in the great ballroom of the *S.S. Nusquam* was close to futile.

The vast chamber echoed with the sounds of thousands of beings speaking almost as many different languages. Despite the lack of any shared tongue, they had no difficulty whatsoever understanding one another. Conversation flowed, vibrant and uninterrupted.

Massive chandeliers of crystal and gold hung from the ceilings, and the walls were decorated with expanses of colored drapery hanging between massive ornate frescoes. The room was illuminated by glowing tubes and orbs strewn amidst the chandeliers, and also from tall torchieres that crackled with what looked like real flame yet which cast far more light than any natural fire. One wall, in stark contrast to the old-fashioned décor, was comprised entirely of smooth panels that, with a simple touch in the right spot, turned transparent to offer a splendid view of the unbroken inky blackness outside.

Fully stocked bars were spaced evenly throughout the ballroom to ensure that long lines never formed. For those guests too busy dancing or making conversation, staff floated seamlessly through the crowd to provide refreshments. On the main stage, a live orchestra performed, its members playing a wide variety of instruments so eclectic that no one in attendance could hope to name them all. During some songs, a vocalist provided lyrics that were nothing more than pure and beautiful gibberish.

Far stranger than the music were the guests themselves. Some were flesh and blood, some circuits and steel. Others existed as beings of energy or gas, some bound into a discernible shape and others not. There were representatives from technological empires that spanned entire galaxies and individuals plucked from backwater villages and beings that had roamed solitary through the vastness of space since time immemorial.

The one thing they all had in common was that they had all been hand-picked to be guests aboard the great marvel that was the *S.S. Nusquam,* the one and only cruise ship that sailed in the gulf between realities in the very literal middle of nowhere. Whether they were chosen because they were influential or wealthy or special or interesting or because they were just plain lucky, they had all been chosen.

All of them, that is, except Summerhill.

Not that anyone could tell by looking that Summerhill wasn't supposed to be there. He didn't look any more or less out of place than anyone else, since everyone on board already came from a mind-boggling set of different worlds and realities. This allowed him to mingle without anyone being any the wiser.

It had taken some work, though, steering conversations to figure out just what the *Nusquam* was without sounding like a complete idiot. Luckily, one thing that sentient beings had in common, he'd noticed, was a propensity to want to talk about themselves when given even the slightest incentive to do so. He found it simple—and maybe a little fun—to just prompt, listen, and fill in the many missing pieces about where he was.

Summerhill had seen the ship from the outside, and it really did look for all the world like an enormous luxury liner, one that sailed through a gulf of pure nothingness instead of an ocean. One thing he still wasn't sure of was why a trip through the middle of nowhere was considered such an exciting thing. He decided to run with it, though, since everybody else seemed so eager to be along for the ride, and it behooved him to fit in for the time being.

Summerhill himself was a colorful fellow, at least by the standards he'd known before coming aboard. He looked much like a dog, a wolf-like dog that was on the small side or perhaps a coyote-like dog that was on the large side, or maybe something in between. His fur had hues of yellow and red, though in most places those colors blended to form a more appropriately canine brown, or cream, or cinnamon or deep reddish-black. The gray of his eyes matched the gray of the sky of the world from which he'd come, which he'd lately taken to thinking may not have been a coincidence.

He walked on two legs, like many of the other *Nusquam* guests (though he wouldn't have been out of place on four or six or even zero). Compared to those other guests, he felt quite underdressed wearing only a greenish-gray shirt and a pair of brownish-gray shorts instead of the formal wear everyone else had on—well, everyone who was capable of wearing clothes. Thus far, however, nobody had been gauche enough to call him out.

Escaping the awkward conversation with the Crown Prince and his companions had taken some of the edge and pressure off of Summerhill, but he was still feeling overwhelmed. Another drink like the one he'd had earlier was in order, he decided; earlier, the cyborg dinosaur had mentioned something called "alcohol" that seemed to have a very relaxing effect on Summerhill. Luckily, the ballroom's many bars made finding a refill simple enough.

The bartender looked like a seven-foot-tall wooden insect, some type of mantis or phasmid. Summerhill couldn't tell whether there was camouflage at work, or if the bartender actually was made of wood. Neither possibility seemed more probable than the other at a glance.

When the bartender spoke, it did so by clacking its mandibles together, the hollow clunking sounds suggesting that the creature was made of wood after all. The noises it made formed some kind of speech, and while the cacophony didn't equate to any form of communication Summerhill was familiar with, the dog understood it anyway.

"Yes, something fizzy," he told the bartender in reply. "I'm open to suggestions."

The bartender clacked away again, and nodded with some enthusiasm.

"I've never had that before, but it sounds lovely," Summerhill said. This was all new to him; even if he ended up with a drink he didn't like, he'd be richer for the experience. He watched as the gangly wooden insect fetched a bottle from a high shelf, undoing the cork with a satisfying pop before pouring a golden, bubbly liquid into a tall flute. It smelled like flowers and honey, the aroma striking Summerhill's nostrils with an effervescent flourish.

The bartender held it out for Summerhill to take, grasping the delicate glass with remarkable care and balance. With a polite bow, the dog took it, and sampled a quick sip before smiling his approval.

Summerhill wondered how he'd gotten on for so long without beverages, especially those with bubbles and alcohol in them. He took another, longer sip as he waded through the crowd, and soon found himself torn between wanting to savor his drink and wanting to just guzzle it all right then and there. From the look of it, the party wasn't ending anytime soon, and so he decided he could afford to take his time.

The glowing gas-creature from before floated by, electric pulses crackling in the air around its form, but if it took note of Summerhill, it showed no indication. The dog did a quick check to make sure that he had, in fact, evaded his former conversation partners, and was satisfied when he saw no sign of them waiting around.

The conversations this close to the bar were rowdier than the others, with beings needing to speak louder and louder to talk over one another. Most of the guests, Summerhill had noticed, had been outfitted with a small device tucked just inside their ear (or equivalent, depending on varying anatomy); presumably, this was what allowed them to all converse with one another despite not sharing a common language. Since he'd snuck on board, Summerhill didn't have one of his own, and so he didn't know for sure what the devices did, but that was his best guess.

Distancing himself from the throng, the excited canine tried to find a more laid back group to involve himself with. He tried to let his nose and ears be his guides, but there was so much going on in the huge ballroom that he felt himself pulled in too many different directions at once. Instead, he just wandered, and waited to see what he'd find. Anything he encountered would be new to him, after all.

What he found, with his senses overstimulated and his attention unfocused, was that walking aimlessly through a busy crowd was a bad idea. Before he'd made it even ten paces from the bar, he stumbled right into one of the other guests. He murmured an absentminded apology, quickly taking stock of the situation to make sure he hadn't spilled his fun new drink all over someone, and was relieved to see that he hadn't.

The other guest did much the same, patting himself down with one free hand while holding a glass off to the side with the other. The flustered fellow looked for all the world like a river otter in a tuxedo. He was fully bipedal, much the way Summerhill was, if shorter and with more slender proportions.

"Oh, wow, I'm so sorry," they both said at the same time.

The two of them stared back into each other's eyes. There was a moment where Summerhill could tell that they were sizing each other up for their strange similarities, and then they both laughed at the ridiculous coincidence. The otter-fellow's grin was goofy if still kind of charming.

"You all right?" Summerhill asked.

The otter nodded. "Yeah," he said, taking a quick, deep sip from his glass as if to preemptively prevent future spillage. "Just wasn't paying attention." He looked at his glass as he pulled it away from his lips, then tilted his ears back. "Maybe I've had too much to drink."

"Oh, it was probably my fault, actually," Summerhill said with a dismissive wave. "Either way, don't worry about it."

It didn't look as though the otter had heard him. "I don't suppose you've got the time, do you?" he asked instead.

Summerhill's ears shot up, and his mind raced with a sudden sense of urgency. He patted at his shirt and shorts. "I—No, I don't think so," he said, checking his pockets twice to make sure. "Seems I forgot to bring a watch."

But the otter was already slipping away, his thick tail disappearing from view as it brushed past the legs of a robotic spider. His scent lingered in the air for a moment, sharper than all the others, holding Summerhill's attention for several seconds. It made him stare dumbly into the distance before he shook it off and went back to his meandering.

He scanned the crowd while taking some more sips of his golden, fizzy drink. If he had some clearer idea of where he wanted to go, he could better avoid bumping into any more guests.

Not far from where he stood was a tall lizard-creature, talking animatedly about his planet's sun. The specifics of what he was saying were lost as Summerhill let his mind get carried away by one of his more recent memories—the moment when he realized that, despite his own world not having a sun, he still somehow carried in his mind a clear notion of what a sun *was*.

The shadows of the titanic skyscrapers of home began to loom over Summerhill's mind, and to banish them, the dog swallowed back the second half of his drink in one gulp. Dwelling on the past, on home, was the last thing he wanted to do here. Heck, by rights, the *S.S. Nusquam* was the perfect place to escape all that. He wasn't even sure where the ship was headed, but if the cruise really was the eternal party it seemed to be, he was content to stay aboard for as long as he possibly could.

That thought, too, came to a screeching halt with a tap on his shoulder. He turned around to see a young woman. She was about as tall as Summerhill, but had pale, furless skin and curly, shoulder-length blonde hair. The word '*human*' went through Summerhill's head, and though the term was unfamiliar to him, he understood its meaning all the same.

She wore the formal, black-and-white garb of the hostesses Summerhill had seen around the ship, along with small crystalline earrings that glittered with the same prismatic effect as the ballroom chandeliers. In her hands she carried a device that looked like an electronic clipboard. "Might I have a brief word over here, sir?" she asked.

Summerhill followed the hostess, who led him off of the main floor and into a corridor that was empty of other guests. Her eyes reflected a sternness that Summerhill hadn't encountered since coming on board, but then, he also hadn't gotten in trouble with any of the staff until now. At least, he assumed he was in trouble, since it was unlikely that the hostess had dragged him away from the crowd in order to strike up a casual chat.

The hostess kept glancing up at Summerhill as she manipulated her clipboard-device with her fingers. "Don't worry, sir," she murmured. "This should only take a second. I just need to confirm your identity." She then tapped a fingertip against her temple, and a hitherto invisible monocle appeared over her right eye, the lines of an optical readout faintly visible on the reverse side.

If this hostess possessed the cruise's guest list, she'd discover in no time that Summerhill wasn't supposed to be aboard. Making a run for it seemed like a terrible idea, since given the *Nusquam*'s level of technology, it was doubtful he would be able to run very far. He didn't know what punitive measures the crew might take with him, but trying to flee probably wouldn't make them more lenient.

"The scanner isn't picking up your identity, sir," the hostess said. "If you're a shapeshifter, I'll have to ask you to revert to the form you had when you were first registered, sir."

Summerhill shook his head. "Nope. I just look like this."

The woman sighed. "Let me try again, then, sir," she said, and once more she stared him down through the high-tech monocle. A moment later, she shook her head. "No, I'm sorry, but I don't have you in my database."

The dog leaned forward and pointed at the electronic clipboard. "My name ought to be on the guest list," he said. "I'm Summerhill. Try looking under 'S.'"

As if insulted that he was even trying this, the woman arched an eyebrow, then sighed again, louder. "Mr. Summerhill," she murmured, flicking her finger across the flat screen as she scrolled through a list of names. "I'm sorry, sir, but I'm still not finding you."

"Well, that's strange," Summerhill said. "I mean, if I wasn't invited, how else did I get here?"

A clever gleam appeared in the hostess' eye as the monocle disappeared from view. "Excellent question, sir," she said, her voice quieter, but also sharper. "Care to tell me?"

Telling her was absolutely out of the question. Not only would it be foolish to admit guilt, she probably wouldn't believe that he'd simply walked into the distance until ending up in the middle of nowhere, even though it was true. "You're not accusing me of being a stowaway, surely?" Maybe he could buy himself some time and some brilliant idea would come to him. Maybe.

The hostess tapped one of her earrings, and a small earpiece appeared, in the same manner that the monocle had. "Security," she said. "This is Katherine. I'm in the ballroom, and I—"

11

Summerhill felt his heart skip a beat, his eyes going wide and his fur standing on end. The name shot to the front of his mind, spelling itself out in brilliant blue letters on the inside of his eyelids when he blinked. "Wait," he blurted. "*You're* Katherine?"

Katherine rolled her eyes. "Nice try," she muttered to him before resuming her report to Security. "I'm in the ballroom," she repeated, but before she could finish that statement, Summerhill reached out and grabbed her arm.

"Hold on," he begged. "Please, I really do need to talk to you. I just need a minute to explain myself." This was Katherine. She was real.

For several seconds, Katherine was quiet as she searched Summerhill's eyes. Her businesslike demeanor and serious gaze didn't falter at all, but when she spoke again, she said, "Security, belay that. Ident scan checks out; false alarm." Her fingers brushed her earring again, and the communication device disappeared.

She set both hands on her hips. "Right, then," she said. "You've got one minute before I get back on the line to Security, Mr. Summerhill. Make it good."

Summerhill took a deep breath and paced back and forth, rubbing his hand-like paws together. "Okay. Now, fair warning, this is going to sound pretty strange."

"I'm Chief Hostess of the *Nusquam*," Katherine countered. "Try me."

The dog chuckled. "Right," he said. Oh, this was going to sound stupid. "So, the gist of it is that I was told that I needed to find you."

Katherine raised an eyebrow. "Oh? What for?"

"That's the thing," Summerhill said. "It depends on whether or not you know the person who sent me."

"Well, who sent you, then?"

Summerhill looked down at the floor. "It's a long story," he said. "Or, well, actually, I'm not sure if it's a long story or not. I'm not sure how long of a story it is."

"Mr. Summerhill," Katherine said with an exasperated growl, "I really don't have time for this. If there's something you need to tell me, give me the short version so I can figure out what the hell to do with you."

"I think *I* sent me."

ONE

Oblivion

Summerhill lived in the World of the Pale Gray Sky.

The World of the Pale Gray Sky was a quiet place, mainly because Summerhill was the only person who lived there. This didn't strike him as weird, though—not until he started coming up with questions. But the dog lived there for quite some time before he got around to that.

In the World of the Pale Gray Sky, there were no storms, and there was no rain; the sky was simply always gray, the same dull, uniform color in all directions. The gray did not come from clouds; the gray simply was. Sometimes there were clouds, or what looked like they might have been clouds, but Summerhill never paid those much heed.

There was no sun, either, and so there was no night and no day, no way to demarcate the passage of time, and so Summerhill never bothered to do so.

The backdrop of that sky was broken only by tall, angular buildings that stabbed upwards, spearing the faintly-swirled gray in all directions, as far as the eye could see. Many of the buildings were a drab green; others were steel blue or slate blue; more rarely were they hues of yellow or red. Some had windows; some did not.

Nobody lived in those innumerable buildings, though. Nobody ever went into them, and nobody ever came out. Nobody wandered the endless streets between them. Nobody except for a lone dog named Summerhill. The whole world was one unending city, all for him.

Summerhill himself was far more colorful than anything else in his world. The rich hues of his fur stood out against the backdrop wherever he went. Even the clothes he wore all had the same washed-out, drab look to them, as if the world itself refused to allow too much color into it, but try as it might, it couldn't leach the color out of *him*.

One thing the dog had noticed from time to time, when passing mirrors and windows, was that the gray of his eyes matched the gray of the sky exactly. He'd forget this on occasion, and whenever reminded of it, he would ponder the similarity only briefly before dismissing it as coincidence.

Summerhill could also make the plants grow. He would do this on occasion, in order to add a tiny splash of color to the world around him. Flowers would sprout from the grayish-green grass of the city's deserted parks or blossom on trees or grow up between the cracks in the pavement whenever he willed them to. These flowers didn't thrive in his world of no sunlight, though, and they always eventually faded and turned the same pale gray as the sky, the same pale gray as his eyes.

Plants didn't make for particularly good company, besides, and the lack of anyone to provide friendship or companionship had come to wear at him more and more as time continued to drift by. Eventually, it dawned on Summerhill that it was a little silly that he'd have a place like this all to himself. He could have all the time in the world (and near as he could tell, he did) and even then he'd still never get to see it all. So what was the point of it?

For as long as he could remember, he was the only person who had ever lived in the World of the Pale Gray Sky. It seemed obvious that other people must have lived there at some point, though, since there were all those towering buildings that struck up into the sky in all directions, and someone must have built those. Right?

The question was largely academic, but before Summerhill could spend much time pondering its ramifications, the blue light appeared.

By itself, the blue light might not have been remarkable, except for the fact that it marked, for the first time in Summerhill's memory, the one time anything had *happened* in the World of the Pale Gray Sky. That in and of itself was far more interesting than any academic or theoretical quandary.

To the unaided eye, it was a merely beam of blue light that had streaked across the sky. Summerhill had never seen a shade of blue so bright, so intense, so *different*. He would have thought it was a shooting star, except that it wasn't dark out, and moreover, neither stars nor darkness actually existed.

He contemplated the streak of light as he leaned against the wall of a tobacconist's shop that had no actual tobacconist to run it. His eyes peered out at the dull sky for what had to have been several minutes—but what were minutes? What was this concept of time he insisted on believing in?

"This world doesn't make any sense," he heard himself say. "You know that, don't you?"

With a sigh, he pushed off the wall, started walking, and tried to think of how to answer that. It was an interesting point he'd raised to himself: there were several things about the world that didn't make sense. But did everything have to make sense?

Sitting down on a bench at a bus stop where no bus ever came, Summerhill scratched his head and took some more time to think. Now that he'd been prompted to question reality, he might as well put in the effort to do a thorough job of it.

"This isn't the first time you've questioned reality, though," he said to himself again, there on the bench. "Think about when you saw the blue light. What did you think?"

"I was surprised," he admitted to himself. "Surprised that I could see the light against something other than a dark night sky."

"But there *is* no dark night sky here, and there never had been. So how do you even know what a dark night sky is?" He looked down at his own paw, patting himself encouragingly on the knee, and thought for just a moment that it looked wrong somehow. "How do you know the light reminds you of a shooting star if there are none of those in the World of the Pale Gray Sky, either?"

16

With new questions to ponder, Summerhill went to one of the many empty parks in the city. He sat down on the grass, and he made flowers grow all over, so that they could keep him silent yet colorful company as he lost himself in thought.

He came to no conclusion as to how he could possibly know these things if they weren't part of the reality he'd always been a part of. Eventually, he grew tired from his aimless theorizing, and he curled up on the flower-speckled grass to sleep for a time.

The next day (since he'd slept, he decided that he would consider it to be a new day), Summerhill explored the barren city some more, keeping an eye out for any odd-colored lights in the sky, or anything at all that might prompt him to question reality. After the events of the previous day, the true extent of Summerhill's desolation was terrifyingly apparent. No longer was it silly to think he had an entire city to himself. Now it was chilling to wonder what had happened to the previous residents, if there had indeed ever been any. Now it seemed normal to wonder why an entire city should exist only to house him.

Later that day, as he walked past the glass doors of a tall office building, he caught the eye of his reflection. In his pale gray iris, he saw the briefest glimmer of that mysterious shade of blue. "The world as you know it is a puzzle," he said. "It's like a labyrinth, one you need to escape from as soon as possible."

Just yesterday, Summerhill had been reluctant to even accept that anything was amiss about the minor inconsistencies he'd noticed about the world from time to time. "But how do I escape from the world? Isn't the world all there is? How can there *be* a place other than the world?"

But he had no answer for himself, and was instead alone with his own thoughts. If the world itself was a maze or a puzzle, then maybe there was somewhere he needed to go or something he needed to do in order to solve it. Maybe the endless city wasn't as empty as he thought.

Admittedly, it wasn't much to go on, but at least it was something to do. And now that he had something to do, Summerhill was painfully aware of how boring and oppressive the World of the Pale Gray Sky really was. Before, he'd been able to while away a lackadaisical eternity, ignorant of the idea that there might even *be* something for him to do. This new insight he'd given himself changed everything. All the flaws and inconsistencies of this drab-colored reality were becoming so obvious now. This place was boring to the point of agony.

Summerhill had no real plan of action but to wander around the empty city. With the self-assurance that it couldn't hurt to at least try, he let himself venture further afield than he normally did. The buildings in these less-familiar parts of the city were still empty and still boring, but they weren't identical, and even the slightest bit of difference removed some amount of boredom.

After plenty of pacing and wandering and napping and resting, there was still no new clue, no grand revelation or moment of inspiration. Perhaps he needed to look for inspiration more actively, he considered. He visited bookstores and read novels by writers who may or may not have ever existed; he explored open-air markets and sampled strange fruits and meats that were fresh despite the stalls never being manned; he took elevators to the tops of the tallest skyscrapers and looked out over the city, which really did stretch out in every direction as far as his eyes could see.

But it wasn't enough. It wasn't presenting him with any new hints as to why he knew things he shouldn't. Days turned into weeks, after which reading and re-reading books wasn't entertaining or informative anymore, and trying new foods failed to stir up new and different appetites. How he longed for wind or rain, for some kind of weather to break up the tedium.

Finally, one night, Summerhill dreamt about what other things must be like. He dreamt of cities teeming with people, of worlds both bright and dark, of placid pastoral vistas and of bizarre and twisted alien landscapes. He dreamt of a sweet, innocent young girl and of a sexy, alluring woman. He dreamt of lavish galas and of intimate candlelit dinners for two. He dreamt of all these things that he knew were real and yet which did not exist and had never existed in the World of the Pale Gray Sky.

When he awoke, he found himself looking into his own eyes again, and once more, the gray was tinged with that special blue. He offered a paw to himself, to help him get to his feet, and there was a smile on his face as he did so, along with a look of pride.

"You're ready to get out of here now, Summerhill. Just keep going and don't look back."

This was no mere reflection. Nor, he now realized, had it been a reflection back at the office building. He hadn't been alone at the tobacconist's or when he'd been sitting on the park bench coming to terms with the need to question his reality.

"Just keep going?" he asked himself.

"And don't look back," he replied. "You can do it. I know you can."

He hesitated, staring at himself transfixed, wanting to assault himself with questions. "What about you?" he asked first. "Are you coming with me?"

But the other Summerhill was already gone, having disappeared somewhere in the brief moment it took to blink. The scent of this other version of him, slightly different than his own, still lingered in the air, however, enough for the dog to believe that it wasn't just his imagination playing tricks on him.

A soft ticking sound tickled Summerhill's ears. The dog turned around a few times, trying to discern what direction the sound was coming from before realized that it was coming from himself. His paws patted up and down his body until he found the source of the sound in his shorts pocket—an old watch on a chain. He didn't remember ever having owned a watch before (and why would he need to tell time in a world where time didn't exist?), but he knew, on some level, that this watch was his, had always been his, and had always been there.

Emboldened with a new sense of purpose, Summerhill gazed down along the road ahead of him and began to walk it. Just keep going. That was all he needed to do. He was going to leave this place, and he was going to find the answers he was looking for.

So Summerhill walked down the street. He followed it in a straight line, making his way between the endless buildings. He walked farther than he'd ever walked before, and made his way into neighborhoods he'd never seen, but he did not stop to take any of it in. He didn't stop for anything—not to eat, not to sleep, not to rest his weary paws. He just kept going. *Just keep going and don't look back.*

And eventually, the endless city did come to an end. The paved street turned into a dirt path that cut through a field of dry grass that appeared to stretch out beyond the horizon, just like the buildings once had. Undaunted, Summerhill kept walking, and didn't even stop to bid farewell to the city that had been his home for so long. He couldn't stop as long as he was still underneath that same boring gray sky.

With the city itself long behind him, he came across a signpost jutting up from the ground next to the road. A crude wooden arrow pointed off into the distance, and then, from around the signpost itself, stepped the other Summerhill with the glimmer of bright blue in his gray eyes. He leaned against the wooden pole, his wagging tail occasionally smacking against it, and smiled before offering one final piece of advice to himself.

"Find Katherine. Make sure you stick with her and everything will be fine."

Summerhill checked his pockets, made sure that he had his watch with him, and then let out a giddy laugh. As he walked along and got more excited by the prospect of leaving forever, his joy caused flowers to spring up in the grass, lining the dirt path like landing lights demarcating a runway. He walked faster, ignoring his exhaustion, holding on to the images he'd seen in his dreams in order to spur himself on, step after step, breath after breath, until, at long last, he'd gotten so far from the World of the Pale Gray Sky that he ended up quite literally in the middle of nowhere.

THREE
Uncertainties

"You think you sent yourself?"

"I know how that sounds." Summerhill's ears were tilted back, and the pitch of his voice was rising along with his desperation. "And I know it probably doesn't make sense on the surface, but a lot of things don't make sense, right?" *Like meeting yourself, and empty, world-spanning cities inhabited by just one dog and winding up in the middle of nowhere.*

Katherine shook her head. "Mr. Summerhill, I'm very sorry. But you're a stowaway, and it is my duty to report your presence to Security."

"Look, you don't understand," Summerhill pleaded. "I'm on the run, and I was told that you could help me."

The hostess was reaching for her earpiece again, but she stopped in mid-motion. "On the run? From whom?"

"I'm not sure; like I said, it's really strange and I'm still trying to make sense of a lot of it, myself." Summerhill tried to hold himself up with as much confidence as possible. "This ship travels between realities, right? Has it ever been someplace called the World of the Pale Gray Sky?"

"Not as far as I know. At least, not in the time I've been aboard. Is that where you're trying to get to?"

"No, that's where I just came from. I'm not exactly sure where it is I'm trying to get to. I was just told to find you."

"Wait, hold on," Katherine said. "Where did you board the *Nusquam*, then?"

Summerhill pointed towards one of the view panels on the far side of the ballroom, which still showed nothing but the unbroken blackness of nothing. "Just outside there," he said. "I saw the ship sailing by and, well, snuck on board."

"Just outside there?" Katherine repeated.

"That's right."

"Mr. Summerhill, that's the middle of nowhere out there—the *actual* middle of nowhere. How could you possibly have gotten there?"

"I walked."

The young woman leveled her eyes at the dog. "You what?"

"I walked," he repeated. "I got to the very edge of the World of the Pale Gray Sky—that's where I was told by possibly-me I had to find you—and I just kept walking until I, well, until I wasn't anywhere, I guess."

Even if Katherine was struggling to believe what Summerhill was saying, she'd forgotten, at least momentarily, about calling Security. "Crossing the boundaries between dimensions takes a phenomenal amount of energy," she explained. "Something like the reality jump drive of this ship. You can't just *walk* out of the world, Mr. Summerhill."

"Look, who's telling this story, me or you?" Summerhill didn't quite snap the words, but he nearly did. Questioning his own reality was harrowing enough; having someone else do it was starting to wear him thin. "And yes, I know that I'm a stowaway and I'm crashing a shindig for a bunch of people who are more famous and important than me, but like I said, I'm kind of on the run and I think I need your help and so it would be really great if we could just both be on the same page, here."

In the wake of that sudden outburst, Katherine was just wide-eyed and silent. "I am sorry, Mr. Summerhill," she said. "But I'm afraid that I'm going to need more to go on than just 'I think I sent myself to find you' and an unbelievable story." She reached up for her earpiece, but before she touched it, she added, "And after years of working aboard this ship, I never thought I'd run into something I didn't believe again."

Summerhill stepped in closer to Katherine. "Please," he said. "I know how it sounds, I really do, but—"

He had been so fixated on the communication earpiece that he hadn't noticed Katherine's other hand move to her hip. She moved in a flash, her hand coming up before Summerhill could react. In her grip was a small device, and while the dog was still trying to figure out what the sleek, elegant piece of electronics was, it fired a pale blue-white beam that struck him square in the chest.

Summerhill braced himself for a searing pain that never came. Instead, he found himself completely immobile, though still fully aware. His eyes were stuck open, and he was treated to the sight of Katherine, flustered and anxious, speaking to Security via her earpiece, her weapon still in hand. A loud, low buzzing in Summerhill's ears prevented him from hearing exactly what she was saying, but the look on her face was one of apology as she stared back into his face the entire time.

Out of the corner of his eye, Summerhill could see his partially outstretched arm, the shape of it haloed in the same pale blue-white as the energy discharge that Katherine had fired at him. Presumably, this energy was what was rendering him motionless, and also what was causing the annoying buzzing in his ears. Some kind of stun beam or stasis field generator? Fascinating piece of technology, whatever it was. He hadn't even seen it on the hostess' hip at all before she'd reached for it. Maybe it *hadn't* been there before she'd reached for it.

It didn't take long for Security to show up, which spared Summerhill and Katherine the awkwardness of him being forced to stare at her while she fidgeted and looked guilty. The Security detail consisted of a pair of identical robotic units, half again as tall as Summerhill. They were radially symmetric, each possessing four legs that ended in sharp points, and two arms that held long, metallic pikes with tips that glowed bright white. Their unwelcoming appearance was made further unnerving by the lack of any obvious eyes or face.

One of the robots extended its pike and poked Summerhill in the ribs with the glowing tip. The strange paralysis was lifted, and the dog lashed his tail and staggered as he tried to keep from falling over now that his ability to move had been restored. Once he'd regained his sense of balance, he stretched his limbs and craned his neck from side to side to make sure that everything was working properly.

"The unidentified canine biped will follow us." The robots also lacked an obvious mouth or even a visible speaker to serve as one. Whoever built these things sure had a knack for 'unsettling,' Summerhill thought. To back up its instruction, the robot that had jabbed him now motioned down the hallway, while the other brandished its pike threateningly.

"The name's Summerhill," the dog said as he held up his hands in surrender. "Katherine could have at least told you that."

Katherine was looking away, now. She'd put away her weapon at some point, and Summerhill could see no sign of where it had gone. Giving the two robotic security guards a look, she turned around and began to walk back toward the ballroom.

"I was telling the truth, you know," Summerhill called after her, but he didn't get to see if she turned back around or not, as both of his mechanical escorts herded him into step and marched him down the hallway. Their pointed, clawlike feet made sinister metallic clacking sounds, the rhythm and cadence of eight individual limbs too much for Summerhill to keep track of.

"Find Katherine. Make sure you stick with her and everything will be fine." A whole lot of good that had done.

As he was ushered down the corridor, Summerhill tried to engage the robots in conversation, asking them things like where they were taking him and what would be done to him after they got there, but they just marched on without any response. Summerhill almost wished that they hadn't said anything when they'd come to escort him away, because then he'd just assume they couldn't speak. Instead, he felt slighted that they were ignoring him, and really, the situation was already unnerving enough without that.

They came to an elevator lobby, its décor almost as grandiose as the ballroom's. Glittering gold lined the alcoves for each elevator door, the signage above them encrusted with small jewels. Even the panels for the call buttons were adorned with fanciful inlays and had gemstones in all four corners, presumably covering the screws that bolted them to the wall. Between the doors, on either side of the hallway, were small tables topped with vases full of flowers of bright and varied colors.

Summerhill reached out to those flowers with his mind, just to feel their presence and gain whatever reassurance he could from them. They were only plants, of course, and had nothing to say back to him, but his affinity for them at least allowed him to feel that they were there. There was comfort in being able to feel something else that was alive and wasn't going to judge his grip on reality.

The different sets of elevator doors came in different sizes, the largest of which could accommodate the largest guests Summerhill had seen in the ballroom, as well as smaller elevators where beings his own size wouldn't be made to feel so small. One of the robots pressed a call button, and without any wait at all, the nearest set of doors slid open. Summerhill stepped inside without being prompted, not wanting to be reprimanded or possibly poked with one of those glowing pikes.

Inside the elevator were a staggering number of buttons, far more than enough to account for the number of decks the ship had, if Summerhill's estimate from seeing the ship from the outside was anywhere close to accurate. Rather than pressing any of those buttons, however, one of the robots emitted a low whirring sound, and then the elevator was off, shooting upwards at an uncomfortable speed, one probably reserved for security purposes.

Just when Summerhill thought the elevator had come to a stop, he heard a loud 'clunk,' and then the car jolted to the left and began to hurtle sideways at the same excessive speed as before. While the dog was still reeling from the sudden change of direction, there was another 'clunk,' and then the elevator dropped, stopped, and began to move forward.

Summerhill lost his balance, and no amount of flailing his arms or wagging his tail was going to keep him from toppling over. He reached out to catch himself on one of the walls, but instead, one of the robots reached out and grabbed him, surprisingly gently, and set him back upright. The dog gasped and panted as he stumbled up to one of the walls anyway and braced himself against it, then looked up and muttered a halfhearted "thanks" to the robot.

Once more, the elevator slowed down, and this time, much to Summerhill's relief, the doors slid open and let him out into another hallway. This one was less lavishly decorated than the ones branching off of the ballroom, but it was still clean and well-kept. The dog got a firm nudge in the back from the blunt end of one of the robot's pikes, and after a quiet bark of protest, he fell in line and let himself get herded down the corridor.

It was a blissfully short trip from the elevator to the security office. The doors opened as Summerhill stepped up to them, and the two robots flanked him and followed him inside.

The back wall was a massive array of monitors and screens, most of which currently showed different views of the ballroom. Some of the screens were overlaid with data windows that would change as the cameras focused in on different guests, but others were static, showing wide-angle views of not only the party, but other areas of the ship that Summerhill hadn't been to.

Behind a dark and solid wooden desk sat a dog-like being that looked remarkably like Summerhill. Its coat (Summerhill couldn't tell, from this distance, if it was male or female) was made of bolder colors—richer browns, starker blacks, paler whites—but its general size and shape suggested the same or at least similar species. It also wore a neatly pressed outfit of solid black with glittering silver trim.

It addressed the pair of robots with a nod, and spoke in a voice as androgynous as its appearance. "Thank you. Please wait outside." The robots both took a moment to stand at attention, then departed, their sharp legs clacking away until they disappeared between the doors.

Summerhill stood in the center of the room, trying not to stare but not doing a very good job of it. He'd never seen one of his own kind before, and to coincidentally run into one here, aboard the *Nusquam*, so far from home, made an almost alarming amount of sense under the circumstances. Maybe that's why his other self had urged him to seek out Katherine, knowing that he'd be sent along to Security and have this encounter.

"Please, sit," the other dog-creature said, motioning with a familiar hand-like paw at an appropriately sized chair on the other side of the desk. "So, you're this so-called Summerhill, then?"

"That's right." It was too much to hope that his fellow canine would know who he was. Still, it probably at least knew something helpful. Summerhill took his offered seat, then asked, "So, um, what should I call you?"

"Just 'Chief' will do for now," the other dog replied. Not the most helpful response for disambiguating gender. "I'm happy to see that we've been able to avoid an incident so far."

Summerhill folded his hands in his lap and felt his ears tilt back. "I'm not here to cause trouble, honestly. I tried explaining that to Katherine, but I guess my story's kind of a farfetched one."

The Chief smiled. "Ah, yes, Katherine," it said. "She says you're a stowaway who didn't actually stow away anywhere. Says you claim to have sneaked on board while we were already underway."

"That's exactly right. But Katherine seemed to think that was impossible."

"'Impossible' isn't a word we're big on here aboard the *Nusquam*. I'll admit that it sounds highly unlikely that you'd just be out there, but we've certainly had guests here before who didn't require things like air or sustenance to survive."

Summerhill looked back at the other dog and swallowed the lump that had formed in his throat. "Um, *do* we require air and sustenance to survive? Folks like you and me, I mean."

"Like you and me?" A look of confusion crossed the Chief's face, and then it let out a hearty chuckle. "Oh, no, no, you don't understand."

"Don't understand what?"

"I'm not actually a... well, whatever you are," the Chief said. "This is just how I'm choosing to appear right now, in the hopes of making this easier for the both of us."

Summerhill felt his heart sink. "Oh. I see." He looked down into his lap and withheld a sigh of disappointment. "Well, I guess that makes my next question kind of moot, then."

"What were you going to ask?"

"I was hoping you'd know what we are and where we come from," Summerhill said. "But I guess that since we're not really a 'we,' you probably wouldn't know."

The Chief shook its head. "I'm afraid not. Whatever you are, you aren't in our databases, which means we've never had a member of your species as a registered guest before." It then tilted its head in a curious manner, very much in the same way Summerhill himself would have. "Why don't *you* know what you are?"

Summerhill sighed. "It's a long story." That was starting to become a too-familiar refrain. "I come from a place called the World of the Pale Gray Sky, except I don't think that's actually where I come from."

"How do you mean?" the Chief asked.

Summerhill told the story of how he'd escaped his private world that made no sense. He recounted how he'd simply kept going until he'd wound up in the middle of the nowhere, found the *Nusquam*, and then crept aboard through a maintenance hatch when the ship hadn't responded to his attempts to wave it down.

The Chief folded its hands together atop the desk and smiled. "Well, we'll put you someplace safe until we reach our next port of call," it said. "Once we get there, we can figure out what to do with you."

"I see." Summerhill swallowed dryly, and just nodded. At least they'd be keeping him in a cell instead of just throwing him overboard. "I guess I'll go along quietly, then."

Pressing a button on the desk, the Chief summoned the two robot guards from before back into the room. "You're a curious one, Summerhill," the other dog said. "If you remember anything else useful during your stay, just give the sentries a holler and they'll be sure to pass it along."

Once again, Summerhill turned himself over to the pike-wielding robots, already hoping that whatever cell he got thrown in wasn't too far away. "Um, are you going to feed me?" he asked the Chief as he was led toward the door. "Because I'm pretty sure I *do* need sustenance, actually."

"You'll be made quite comfortable, I assure you," the Chief replied. "If there's one thing the *Nusquam* prides itself on, it's unparalleled comfort."

FOUR
SKY

Summerhill slept, and he dreamt.

There was a sky. A real sky, a sky with weather, with colors—*real* colors. Magnificent bright blue faded as it got near the horizon and deepened as it extended up into space, so unlike the sky Summerhill had always known. There were clouds that floated by, pure gleaming white, puffy and delicate. A yellow sun shone with the brilliant light of late afternoon.

Oh, Summerhill had had dreams before, but they had been abstract and indistinct. Never had his sleeping mind imagined colors as rich and beautiful as these.

Below, so far below as to be at the very edge of vision, was the ground. The ground didn't concern Summerhill, though. He paid it only enough attention to determine that it was not covered with the endless stretch of empty, lifeless buildings from back home, a prospect which brought with it a fleeting terror amidst the exultant jubilation he felt.

No, the ground did not concern Summerhill. What he cared about was the sky.

The blue of the sky paired well with the yellow sun. Blue struck Summerhill as the kind of color a world's sky *should* be, though he had no idea why, nor even what world it was he was seeing. He knew for sure that it wasn't the sky of the planet Rydale, which was a world that he'd never been to or even heard of before, but he knew that this was not that sky.

A quick pat to his shirt pocket let Summerhill know that he had his watch safely tucked away. Good. Come what may, he was prepared.

There was a sound, a cross between buzzing and whining. It was like the sound of an insect hovering too close to a bug zapper right before the fatal electric spark went off. Abruptly,

31

the noise crescendoed, rising in pitch and volume until it ended with a fantastic crash.

A hole tore open in the very sky itself. The rip expanded into a rift, through which Summerhill could see another sky, a separate sky, a night sky filled with stars and nebulae and galaxies that spun and swirled.

Through that hole came a sphere enveloped in fire, rocketing across the beautiful blue sky. It screeched as it tore through the empty air, the sound like the piercing wail of a banshee. In its wake, it left behind a trail of leaves, which swirled madly in the superheated updraft, creating a spiral of splendid hues of autumnal foliage. A moment later, the rift in the sky sealed itself up silently.

Far below, the ground, free of gray-green lifeless buildings, began to blossom forth with flowers of every conceivable color.

FIVE

RUNAWAYS

Bleary-eyed Summerhill was greeted not by the wide cerulean expanse of an open sky, but by the pulsing green of a buzzing, crackling energy field. The euphoria of his magnificent dream faded, and in its place rose the dismal reminder that he was in the *Nusquam*'s brig.

His hand was resting on his chest, right over his shirt pocket. He groped around out of reflex, but the pocket was empty, and he couldn't think of what he might have been looking for. Shrugging off the last vestiges of sleep, he stretched his arms out and sat up.

For a ship as nice as the *Nusquam*, the brig didn't disappoint. Summerhill was still in a prison cell, but he had enough space to pace around, and the wall-mounted bed at least had a pillow and a mattress. Of course, the actual guest cabins had to be far more spacious, with much more comfortable bedding, and without pike-wielding robot sentinels standing guard outside.

The robots felt like overkill to Summerhill. Surely a force field was enough to keep a single dog from coming and going. It wasn't as if he needed an additional deterrent to keep him from wandering off willy-nilly. Besides, since they didn't have obvious faces, it was impossible to tell whether they were or weren't looking at him, which made him feel awkward and uncomfortable, and the Chief had promised he'd be comfortable.

Summerhill sighed as he flopped back down onto the prison bed. Dogs were creatures of instincts, and after the debacle with Katherine and the disappointing meeting with the Chief, Summerhill was starting to think that he might be better off not trusting his.

Well, the *Nusquam* was going to reach its next destination eventually, wherever that was. Hopefully, the Chief would make good on the promise to figure out something to do with him. If nothing else, Summerhill had escaped from the World of the Pale Gray Sky, from an existence that didn't make any sense.

In the meantime, though, he didn't have anything to do but wait. The security robots made for poor company, and he couldn't simply will himself back to sleep in order to have more dreams (and he'd likely just disappoint himself further when he woke up again). Couldn't the Chief have at least left him a deck of cards or a newspaper or something?

Instead, Summerhill just lay on his back, staring up at the ceiling, examining the little patterns in it and making sure he didn't accidentally make actual flowers or vines sprout forth from the whirling loops and spirals he saw. Security probably wouldn't take too kindly to that, even if there wasn't really a feasible way for him to escape using flowers.

With no clock or watch to check, he tried to deliberately lose track of time; unfortunately, there was no way to tell whether or not it was working. He tried losing himself in thought, using his experiences in the *Nusquam's* ballroom as fodder for the imagination. If he'd learned anything there, it was that the spectrum of realities was so vast and imposing that he'd never run out of things to imagine that might be possible somewhere.

That line of thought naturally lead right back to Summerhill himself. Supposing that he *didn't* come from the World of the Pale Gray Sky originally, where else could he have come from? Someplace that had dogs, apparently. That didn't really narrow it down, though, as quite a few of the other guests he'd spoken to knew what dogs were, which implied that dogs were pretty common across a variety of universes.

Actually, that in itself was pretty telling with regards to the nature of different realities and their commonalities and how they worked, but it left open the question as to how or why

34

they should be like that. Being an interdimensional traveler was evidently quite headache-inducing.

Summerhill's imagination had nothing to rein it in, so he tried to focus on what shreds of information he did have in order to keep his mind from wandering too far. There were the dreams he'd been having, ones where he'd seen worlds and cities and people. Had he just invented them in his sleep? Or were there shades of memory still lurking somewhere in his mind? Try as he might, he was unable to conjure up anything from before the World of the Pale Gray Sky.

Perhaps he was going about this all wrong. Maybe it *had* all started there, and the things in his head had always just—

"Mr. Summerhill. I've brought your food."

Summerhill sat up with a jolt. Standing outside the buzzing force field, carrying a covered platter of silver and gold, was Katherine. She was still dressed in her hostess' outfit, looking as proper as ever.

"Do they usually send hostesses to bring prisoners their food?" Summerhill asked as he leaned forward and swung his legs off the edge of the bed.

Katherine huffed, the curls of hair over her forehead jostling from that puff of air. She pressed her finger against the device in her ear, and the energy field in front of the cell deactivated. "I volunteered, if you must know," she said as she stepped inside. "My shift is ending anyway, and I thought I'd see how you were doing."

"Well, I'm still in a cell," Summerhill replied. "You know, where you helped put me."

Taking a few more steps forward, Katherine set the fancy platter on Summerhill's bed. "And what would you have had me do?" she asked. "Let you wander around the ship despite the fact that you don't belong here and I have no idea who or what you are?"

"I told you all that." The dog tried to suppress the growling in his throat. "My name is Summerhill, and I was told I needed your help. Though I'm beginning to think that was all a ploy to make sure I landed in here."

Katherine paced over to the wall and leaned against it. "You seem really earnest, Mr. Summerhill, and if your story is true, then I sympathize with you, I really do." She sighed. "But I can't just take what you say at face value. Surely you must understand that."

"So why are you here, then?" Summerhill was ignoring the food that he'd been brought, perhaps a bit too pointedly. "Did you come to actually hear me out this time? Or just to gloat about getting me stuck in here?"

Katherine growled with frustration under her breath. For several seconds she eyed Summerhill in silence, then she crossed her arms in front of her chest. "You said that you were on the run. What did you mean by that?"

"What did I mean?" Summerhill thought again about his escape from the World of the Pale Gray Sky—it had been escape, hadn't it? "I don't know. I mean, like I said, I left the place I came from and I was told to find you. And yes, I know you said that's impossible."

The hostess shook her head. "But you specifically said that you're *on the run*. That's not the same thing as leaving home," she pointed out. "So, who and what are you on the run from?"

It was a fair question. Summerhill leaned back a little and looked down at his feet still dangling off the bed. "I'm not sure," he said. Then he took a deep breath. "I get the distinct impression that I was trapped there—like it was a prison I wasn't ever supposed to get out of."

"You don't really strike me as a prisoner," Katherine replied. Summerhill shot her a sharp look, and then she looked around the brig and chuckled wryly. "Sorry. That was a pretty stupid thing to say."

"It's okay." Summerhill folded his hands together in his lap. "I guess it's like you said: I can't blame you for not trusting me."

Katherine came closer again. "Look, if there's something you think you're in danger from, let me know. I can talk to the Chief, and maybe we can see about getting you out of here and keeping you safe."

Those were audacious words from the person who'd played her hand to get him thrown in the brig in the first place, but hey, maybe she *was* trying to assuage her guilt. That was her problem, though; if she really wanted to help Summerhill, he wasn't going to hold his breath. In the meantime, since he didn't have anything else to offer her in the way of proof... "Look, do you mind if I just eat? It's been ages."

With a hint of reluctance, Katherine backed off. "Yeah," she said. "Look, I'm serious about what I said. I'll be back with your breakfast tomorrow if you change your mind."

"Yeah," Summerhill murmured. He picked up the platter and turned away from her, and a few seconds later, he heard the force field turn back on, followed by the hostess' footsteps leading away down the hallway.

Find Katherine. Make sure you stick with her and everything will be fine. Things Summerhill wasn't going to trust anymore: his own instincts, and other versions of himself.

The dog lifted the cover off of the platter, and the rich, warm scent of stew filled his nostrils. The bowl was on the small side, but the stew itself looked thick and hearty, like something that would be served to an actual guest and not some weirdo who was rotting away in the brig. There were no utensils with which to eat it, probably to safeguard against any escape attempts (though Summerhill was hard-pressed to imagine how he'd be able to circumvent advanced *Nusquam* technology with a spoon).

Well, at least Summerhill had the sort of muzzle that was conducive to eating from a bowl even without a spoon. It might be demeaning, but no more so than being stuck in a cell. At least he'd been given real food.

He picked up the bowl, which was warm to the touch, but not hot. Bringing the bowl to his muzzle, he opened his mouth and extended his tongue—

—and then spotted a small note left sitting on the platter.

It had been hidden underneath the bowl of stew, the paper having curled and warped somewhat due to the heat. There was writing on it, and before he even tried to read it, Summerhill recognized the handwriting as his own.

He didn't know when he'd ever seen himself write anything, but he recognized his handwriting all the same. The words appeared to have been hastily scribbled, too. They said:

"Get ready to make a run for it."

The very instant Summerhill read the words, the lights in both the cell and the hallway shut off. For a second, the brig was plunged into complete darkness, and then emergency lighting came back on in the hallway outside.

What didn't come back on was the glowing green force field.

Summerhill was struck with three very important thoughts: that he could, in fact, make a run for it; that if he did make a run for it, the two sentry robots were still right outside his cell; and, that while he did have a possible window of escape, he was really, *really* hungry and didn't want to have to abandon his only meal in who knew how long.

He attempted to multitask, lapping offhandedly at the warm stew while looking at the two robots. The fact that they didn't have faces really did make it problematic in trying to tell whether they were looking in at him or not, but so far, they hadn't shown any obvious reaction to the power outage. Which didn't mean they wouldn't have one to Summerhill suddenly sprinting out into the corridor and making a run for it.

The sound of hurried footsteps came from somewhere down the hallway. They got closer and closer, and then Summerhill went wide-eyed as he saw Katherine run right past his cell.

A moment later, one of the sentry robots disintegrated in a bright flash. Recoiling in shock, Summerhill very nearly dropped his bowl of stew, bobbling it from one palm to the other before catching it in both hands again. Katherine let out a shriek that echoed from down the hall. The other robot sprang into action, swinging its pike up before marching down the hall in the direction the hostess had come from.

Summerhill had no idea what was going on, but he wasn't going to waste this chance. Hopping off of the bed, he pitched forward, briefly tripping over his own feet as he barreled out of the cell and into the corridor. Some of his stew sloshed out of the bowl and onto the floor, but he wasn't about to give up on dinner just because he was running for his life. He spared a brief glance to the right, saw a small group of moving figures at the far end of the poorly lit hallway, and then spun around and caught Katherine disappearing around the corner at top speed.

Yet again, Summerhill thought of the final piece of advice he'd been given before departing the World of the Pale Gray Sky. *"Find Katherine. Make sure you stick with her and everything will be fine."* Until now, he'd been fixating on the first part of that message. He hadn't given much thought to the second. "Katherine, wait!" he called as he started to run after her. "Where are you going?"

Another explosion sounded behind him, but he didn't dare stop to see what it was. He put all of his energy into running without dropping his stew, hoping that he could catch up with Katherine before he lost track of her. The combination of fear and excitement helped propel him, and while he wasn't so caught up in the moment that he was having fun, he at least had to concede that he couldn't complain about life being boring anymore.

Rounding the corner, Summerhill was relieved to see that he hadn't lost sight of Katherine completely yet. This hallway was even longer than the one he'd just run down, but it was empty except for the hostess and himself. "Katherine!" he shouted again. "What's going on?"

But Katherine didn't answer. She just kept running, swinging her arms as she tore off towards the far end of the hall. Summerhill did his best to keep up; he was just a little faster than her, and so hopefully he'd catch up to her before she got away. If it turned out that there was something they were right to be running from, then they could run from it together.

Eating while running wasn't as easy as Summerhill had hoped. Without utensils, he had to hold the bowl up high and dip his muzzle into it. He tried to keep one eye on Katherine as his tongue lapped at the stew, which was still quite hot. More of it got onto his snout and whiskers than got into his mouth, but what he did manage to get was quite tasty. His aching hunger was making him stubbornly persistent despite the minor scalding he was suffering under his short fur.

Before either Katherine or Summerhill reached the end of the hallway, a deep, gruff voice called out from behind them. "Target in sight! Open fire!"

Summerhill spun around and skidded to a stop, spilling more of his precious dinner in the process. There were three beings, all of comparable size, all wearing black, form-fitting suits and black helmets that obscured their features. One of them held up some type of rifle.

Behind Summerhill, Katherine shouted something, but he couldn't hear what it was. The rifle went off, firing a bright green bolt of energy straight down the hall. To Summerhill's surprise, it went well wide of him—but it struck the wall right next to Katherine, the impact knocking her aside.

"Stop running, Katherine," one of the three pursuers said. Due to the helmets, it was impossible to tell which one had spoken. "Come quietly, and you won't be harmed."

Though she was slightly off-balance, Katherine hadn't been knocked off her feet, nor had she lost her nerve. "Bugger that!" she snapped back, and with a quick flick of her wrist, she brought her sleek pistol into her hand and fired. Her shot struck the attacker holding the rifle, and he was instantly immobilized by blue-white energy.

The hostess wasted no time in turning and running once again. Summerhill took off after her, not waiting to see how the other two pursuers would react to one of their number being stunned. The others hadn't been carrying any visible weapons, but as Katherine had proven, that didn't mean much.

Katherine hit the door at the end of the hallway shoulder-first. It opened into a narrow, cramped stairwell. Summerhill slipped in through the open door just in time to see the hostess vault over the railing, only to have her feet come down unevenly on the steps, sending her off balance. She fell and tumbled down the stairs, crumpling onto the landing below. It hadn't looked like a particularly bad fall, but Summerhill hurried to help her all the same.

"Who are those people?" he asked as he hunched down to help her back to her feet.

Dusting herself off and wincing just a bit as she tested her feet and ankles, Katherine said, "Mr. Summerhill, you really shouldn't be here right now." She turned to keep running, then stopped to look back at the bowl of stew in the dog's hands. "Wait, are you *eating*?"

"What can I say? Walking all the way out to the middle of nowhere works up an appetite."

Katherine opened her mouth to say something, then shook her head and continued her way hurriedly down the stairs, taking them two at a time. She wasn't limping, and she kept her stun weapon at the ready the whole time.

Thrashing his tail to and fro for balance as he sprang down the stairs after her, Summerhill tipped his ears back to listen for any sign that their pursuers had entered the stairwell behind them. "And maybe I'm not supposed to be here," he called out in between heavy pants, "but under the circumstances, I don't think sitting quietly in my cell was really an option."

One deck further down, Katherine stopped at the landing to grab onto the handle of the door there. "Look, Mr. Summerhill," she said, short of breath herself. "If you want to do yourself a favor, keep heading down the stairs. They're not after you." With that, she shoved the door open and burst into the hallway beyond.

From up above came the sound of another door being violently slammed open. Either the pursuers had found out how to un-freeze their companion, or they'd left him behind in favor of the chase. In any event, they were probably better equipped for a long pursuit than either a cruise hostess or a tired dog with a bowl of stew. Summerhill appreciated Katherine's advice—and she was probably right about it, too.

Nevertheless, Summerhill went through the door after her and slammed it shut behind him. He realized this probably meant he was in for the long haul, but he couldn't really say that he'd been any good at making smart decisions up through now anyway. In the short term, though, these folks were going to keep chasing after them, and a service door that didn't lock wasn't going to slow them down.

The dog scanned the hallway. If it were like the other areas of the ship that he'd been through, then—

There, in the alcove that Katherine was about to run past, was a tiny decorative table with a small vase full of flowers atop it.

"Katherine!" Summerhill called out. "Toss me that vase!" He set the bowl of stew down on the floor and then held out his hands.

The hostess turned and looked back at him, confused and impatient. "You're not going to try to fight them off with a *vase*, are you? Because—"

"Just throw it to me. Hurry!"

With an exasperated sigh, she picked up the vase from the table and lobbed it underhand to Summerhill. He only had to lean forward a little bit to catch it, water splashing his face and chest in the process. Sputtering and shaking his head, he dumped the flowers out onto the floor at the foot of the door, then tossed the vase itself aside.

He stretched out his arms towards the flowers, focusing his mind. His pulse raced as he willed those flowers to grow,

42

to change, to sprout up impossibly fast and impossibly strong. He channeled a part of his own individual essence into the flowers, and with that effort came a form of exertion he'd never felt before, but he kept it up, knowing that if anything was going to buy him and Katherine the time they needed to get away, this was it.

And, as he willed it, the flowers did grow and transform. From their thin stems grew twisting vines, thick and strong. They climbed the frame of the door, then spread inward to cover the door itself. First they laced together in a loose mesh, and then they tightened together until the web of vines and tendrils was solid and compact.

There. It wouldn't stop a group of people armed with energy weapons forever, but it would certainly keep them occupied for a while.

"Okay," Summerhill said, dizzy and panting as he bent over to pick up his bowl of stew. "Back to running."

Katherine, momentarily dumbstruck, stood there for a second longer. She then backpedaled a few steps before managing to turn around so that she could make a run for it again. "What did you just do?" she yelled back to Summerhill.

"Hopefully just bought us enough time to get away," he replied. "Speaking of which, where are we going?"

"I was thinking one of the lifeboats." If Katherine balked at the idea of the two of them being a 'we,' she showed no indication of it. "They won't be able to follow us if we do that."

Summerhill was still woozy in the aftermath of his little stunt, and so keeping up with Katherine was even more difficult than it had been before. She did, however, stop to pull a white-and-red lever—a fire alarm, Summerhill realized after the fact—before quickly rounding yet another corner. A series of tiny sprinklers descended from concealed holes in the ceiling, and they started to spray water as the alarm blared through the hall.

A whimper rose from Summerhill's throat as the water soaked his stew. The dog hurried to get as many mouthfuls of it as he could before the more immediate need to keep running overrode his hunger, and he finally discarded the unfinished bowl with a casual toss. At least the sprinklers were helping to rinse off his fur.

He followed Katherine through another set of doors. "Why don't you just call *Nusquam* security?" he asked.

She didn't answer right away. Instead, she pressed on ahead, seemingly unperturbed by the water (which was already making Summerhill quite cold as it drenched his fur). The big metal door she stopped at next had a large lever that required both arms to lift. Doing so revealed a small wheel that she spun rapidly until an unseen lock fell open with a heavy *thunk*. She pushed the door with both hands, the water making her slip a few times until the door swung open the rest of the way on its own.

Summerhill followed her inside and closed the door behind them. If he'd had some more plant matter, he could have tried to tangle up the wheel mechanism from this side of the door, but there were no decorative elements in this part of the ship. The lighting was dim and the air was musty. This was one place where guests weren't expected to come.

A small flight of stairs led down to a short, dead-end corridor, lined with half a dozen sealed hatchways. Katherine had already made her way down to the first. As she pulled it open, she looked back up the stairs at Summerhill. "This is going to be a one-way trip, so you know," she said. "Those guys aren't after you. You can probably still slip away."

Given his options, Summerhill was still betting he had better chances sticking with Katherine than he did trying to avoid not only a group of people armed with energy weapons, but also a team of pike-wielding security robots who by now had probably discovered he'd escaped his cell. "I've come this far," he told Katherine. "No sense turning back now."

Katherine made no further attempts to dissuade him, nor did she seem upset with his decision. She held the hatch open for him, then jumped in after. The hatch then sealed itself shut behind her.

The lifeboat was a metal capsule that had enough sitting room for at least two dozen individuals of Katherine or Summerhill's size. There were footlockers stowed underneath the seats, viewing ports along the walls, and two tall cabinets in the back, labeled with wordless symbols indicating that they were stocked with medical supplies and food stores, respectively.

A large, red handle hung from the ceiling near the hatch. Katherine grabbed hold of it and pulled down on it with all her weight. Another buzzing, one-note warning alarm sounded through the lifeboat before the entire capsule shook, then shot away from the *Nusquam* at impressive speed. For a moment, the artificial gravity in the lifeboat didn't know which direction to pull them in.

Gravity soon normalized, and Katherine let out a sigh of relief before smiling apologetically at Summerhill, her curly hair still damp from the fire sprinklers. "Thank you," she said. "I don't know what you did back there, with the door and the flowers, but... thank you."

"It's the least I could do. You *did* bring me food."

The hostess sighed again. "I didn't mean for you to get caught up in this. Wherever we end up, it'll be a long, long time before those guys are able to track us. If we split up from there, you should be home free."

Home free. That was an ironic way of putting it. "I'll also be alone again. And probably lost," Summerhill said. "If we're not in any immediate danger of being found, maybe we'll be safer together."

Katherine looked back at him. "I put you in the brig," she reminded him. "Now you're suddenly willing to trust me?"

"The way I see it, we're both on the run, now."

That earned a self-deprecating laugh. "Guess so," she conceded. Then, outside the viewing port, the surrounding nothingness was washed out by a pale green light that gradually became brighter and brighter. "Well, Mr. Summerhill, it looks like we're about to see where we end up."

"What do you mean?" Summerhill asked. "This thing doesn't have a preset destination?"

Katherine shook her head. "Not exactly. The on-board computer system does a scan of all the occupants, and then it runs calculations based on their quantum and temporal signatures in order to—"

The light flared up, filling the cabin of the lifeboat, so bright that Summerhill couldn't even see. There was an unpleasant sound of metal-against-metal, and then the sensation of the artificial gravity pulling in the wrong direction as the lifeboat pitched down. The light then vanished, but the falling sensation remained, only to come to a jarring stop seconds later.

The lifeboat's hatch came open with the brief hiss of pressure equalizing. Gravity was pulling the right way down again. There wasn't a sound coming from the outside.

"Katherine," Summerhill asked. "What just happened?"

Bracing both of her hands to either side of the viewing port, Katherine looked outside. "I think we just crashed."

SIX

MAROONED

Outside the lifeboat window, the view was as bizarre as it was spectacular.

The lifeboat had crashed onto what appeared to be the surface of an enormous coral reef. Giant polyps sported a rainbow of tentacles of varying sizes. Conical sponges formed miniature forests, anchored to the reef's calcium exoskeleton at narrow points that looked like they might break off with even the slightest nudge. Blazing red tendrils fanned out like massive antlers that belonged on the head of a great hoofed animal.

None of it moved, though. The reef didn't look dead—far from it, in fact—but it was like a still snapshot of a living ecosystem. If it weren't for the fact that Summerhill could turn his head and see that the view held depth and perspective, he might have mistaken it for a photograph.

"Okay," Summerhill said, drawing a deep breath to calm himself, "if we just crashed, then *where* did we crash?"

Katherine stared out the window for a while longer, transfixed by the view outside. Her hair was still wet from the *Nusquam*'s sprinkler system. Summerhill thought at first that she'd been distracted and she hadn't heard him, but when he was about to repeat himself, she turned to look at him and said, "I think we've struck a nevereef."

Summerhill raised an eyebrow. "Should I know what that is?"

"I'm sketchy on most of the details myself," Katherine said. "I mean, some of the sailors mention them from time to time. They're some kind of navigational hazard that the ship has to avoid when sailing the gulf between realities, but I don't know much about them beyond that." She nodded towards the viewing port. "I'm actually kind of surprised that it even looks like a reef, to be honest."

"Are you sure that's what this is, then?"

"No," she admitted. "But it's my best guess. Either way, we're still stuck here."

Stuck. Trapped. Well, at the least the scenery was a change of pace from the World of the Pale Gray Sky. And Summerhill wasn't alone this time. Even so, it was hard to see the situation as a huge improvement.

Summerhill got up and walked to the food cabinet. "So, now that we're on the run together, can I ask what the deal is with those people who were chasing you?" he asked.

Katherine slumped in her seat, then undid the top button of her damp blouse and sighed. "It's kind of a long story."

"Well, we have plenty of time." The cabinet was well stocked, to Summerhill's relief, and it was larger than he'd initially surmised. "You hungry?" he asked Katherine as he rummaged through the stores for something that looked appetizing.

"Not particularly, but I should probably still eat." Katherine turned and lay on her back, hands covering her face. A droplet of water fell from one of her prism-like earrings.

Summerhill took a step back as one of the cabinet shelves automatically slid forward. He took two of the sealed meal packs from the shelf, then watched as it slid itself back into place. Assuming he and Katherine were stuck here for the long-term, he'd ask her how all this worked, but in the meantime, there were more pressing concerns.

"They said that they didn't want to hurt you," he said as he peeled one of the packs open. Inside was a small tray of processed food that automatically began to reconstitute itself upon being being removed from the packaging. "But they weren't shy about firing that energy rifle of theirs, either."

Katherine rubbed the heels of her hands against her eyes. "Which goes to show where their real priorities are," she said. "I don't know. They probably at least want to try to take me alive if they can."

48

Summerhill sat back down next to Katherine and set one of the trays of food down for her, complete with the tiny fork that accompanied it. "What do they need you alive for?" he asked as he looked at his own food. There were cubes of meat of some sort, but he couldn't tell exactly what kind. It was slathered in some type of sauce that also defied easy identification. Whatever it was at least smelled edible.

"I stole something," Katherine said as she slowly sat back up. "And they're coming to get it back."

The sauce-laden cubes of meat were quite tasty, though Summerhill was no closer to determining what he was actually eating. "So give it back to them," he said. "Whatever it is can't be worth getting shot over."

"You'd be surprised." Katherine poked her fork at her food, but didn't eat just yet. "And anyhow, I can't give them back something I don't have."

"But you just admitted you stole it."

Katherine jabbed the fork into one of the cubes of meat and let it sit there. "I stole it, yes, but that doesn't mean I still have it."

"What did you take?"

Pushing the tray away from her, Katherine shut her eyes and set her head back against the wall of the lifeboat. "Something that's worth shooting me over," she muttered. "It doesn't matter anymore. It's gone, I can't give it back, and when they find that out, they'll probably kill me as a matter of principle. So the plan stays the same: I keep running."

Summerhill took a few more bites of his food. "Can you at least tell me who you're running from?"

Katherine opened up one eye. "Now how's that for an ironic question?"

"Hey, at least now I know you can empathize with me."

"Yeah. Maybe." She closed her eye again and took a deep breath. "Honestly, I thought I'd already outrun them for good. Guess what they say is true after all: the past always has a way of catching up with you."

Summerhill looked out the viewing port at the strange reef—this nevereef, frozen in a state of pseudo-lifelessness. "And why is the past trying to catch up with a cruise hostess?" he said.

"I wasn't always a cruise hostess," Katherine replied with a faint laugh. "Really, I wasn't much of anything, aside from a girl who'd stolen something." With an expression of reluctance on her face, she reached out and dragged her tray back over to her, taking hold of the fork and finally trying a bite of the emergency rations. "You know, if all we have to survive on is this, we could be doing a lot worse."

"Who are you running from?" Summerhill asked again. "I'm guessing you at least know."

Chewing slowly, Katherine nodded, then swallowed. "They call themselves the Consortium," she said. "They're a sort of interdimensional police agency. That's my understanding, at any rate."

"You're on the run from the law?"

"I'm not going to pretend I understand how their jurisdiction works—or what the legitimacy of it is. What I do know is that, where I come from, we've certainly never heard of them and probably wouldn't recognize their authority even if we had."

Summerhill entertained the possibility that the World of the Pale Gray Sky could be some sort of dimensional prison, and that at some point in the past, he'd run afoul of this Consortium and been sentenced to that dreary oblivion. "Where are you from?" he asked Katherine, trying not to jump to any one conclusion too soon.

A wistful look overtook Katherine's face as she set her tiny fork down and leaned back again. She rested both hands in her lap as her eyes went distant. "New Zealand," she said, and then she made eye contact with Summerhill. "It's a small island country on a planet called Earth." She took a deep breath and then spaced out again. "Honestly, I'd given up hope of ever seeing it again years ago."

Tears had formed in her eyes. Small ones, nothing that required her to sob and damage her dignity. She reached in below the neckline of her blouse and drew out a thin, leather cord necklace bearing a simple rectangular pendant made of a semitransparent blue and orange material. Her fingers traced over its edges slowly as she tried to blink her eyes dry.

"Tell me about New Zealand," Summerhill asked.

The faint curl of a smile appeared at the corner of Katherine's mouth. She released the pendant and lolled her head to the side as she looked back at Summerhill. "I'm sure it's not all that impressive by your standards," she said. "Anyone who can walk between dimensions has surely seen far more amazing things."

"Actually, I'm not sure what I have or haven't seen," Summerhill replied. "And anyway, I bet your home is way more interesting than mine."

"I'll take that bet."

Summerhill smiled. "Where I come from is just a big, endless city," he explained. His smile faded as he brought more vivid memories to the fore. "But it's a city where there are no people. The sky is always gray, there's no day or night—nothing ever happens." His fur stood on end to talk about it. As far as he'd come, the shadow of that world still loomed over him, chillingly close.

Katherine hummed to herself. "You mentioned on the *Nusquam* that you thought that someone had trapped you there," she said. "So you're not from there."

"Well," Summerhill started, and then had to think about what he actually meant. "No, I don't think so, no. I mean, it's all just conjecture on my part, because I'm not really sure, but—"

"If you're not really from there, then it's not really your home." Katherine grinned as she interrupted him. "So for all you know, your real home is nothing like that."

Summerhill's muzzle broke into a big, bright smile. It was such a simple thought that it hadn't even occurred to him since he'd rediscovered his own self-awareness back in the World of the Pale Gray Sky. After the disappointment with the Chief, he'd resigned himself to maybe never finding the truth. He still might not ever find it, but Katherine had put into his head the beautiful possibility that he came from someplace amazing.

"Okay, fine," he said. "I still want to hear about New Zealand, though, so that if I ever do find my home, I'll know what to compare it to."

Katherine laughed, but she nodded, smiled, and leaned forward. She told Summerhill all about the world of New Zealand. She regaled him with descriptions of verdant, rolling countrysides, of wide-open spaces dotted with the occasional town or city, of long coasts and snow-capped mountains. From the conversations he'd had with guests aboard the *Nusquam*, Summerhill had gotten the impression that the worlds that people came from were more uniform, but this place that Katherine told him about sounded so special in its variety, in its extremes, in its wonderful non-uniformity.

And, according to Katherine, it was only a small island nation that was part of a much larger planet that was more diverse still. And that planet was just a tiny one, one of many that circled just one of hundreds of billions of stars that made up just one of hundreds of billions of galaxies.

"Wherever I come from," Summerhill said when Katherine was done, "I'll be happy if it's even just a fraction as wonderful as your New Zealand is."

"You're a strange being, Mr. Summerhill. But you're a fine change of pace from some of the guests I see on the *Nusquam*. Wouldn't you know it, lots of folks let being hand-picked for dimensional travel go to their heads."

Summerhill turned and looked out the viewing port again. The nevereef's features hadn't changed, the beautiful expanse of coral still just as wondrous and just as eerie against a backdrop of nothing. "Speaking of dimensional travel," he said, "you said you think this reef is something the lifeboat struck while it was trying to cross some kind of dimensional boundary."

Katherine peered out through the glass as well. "This kind of science really isn't my strong suit, Mr. Summerhill. Before we crashed, though, the lifeboat sure looked like it was about to make a reality jump, yes."

Summerhill scratched the end of his muzzle. "You said something earlier about quantum signatures and the lifeboat figuring out where to go."

"Yes, that," Katherine said. "The lifeboats are equipped with a very tiny reality jump drive—like a much smaller version of the one on the *Nusquam*. It's only got enough power for a single jump seeing as it's only meant to be used in emergencies.

"Since it can only make that one jump, the on-board computer does a scan of everyone on board, and based on that, it calculates the optimal reality for the lifeboat to jump to. The idea is that even if not everybody makes it back home, at least they get someplace safe."

Summerhill hummed in thought. "And how well does that usually work in practice?"

"I couldn't say," Katherine replied. "The ship's never had to launch the lifeboats in the time I've been aboard." She stretched her arms up above her head. "Anyhow, it doesn't matter what caused the crash, at this point. This thing's not making another reality jump, which means we're good and stuck here."

The whole matter of dimensional barriers and whatnot was still alien to Summerhill. He'd made it from the World of the Pale Gray Sky to the *Nusquam* just fine without any sort of reality jump drive; why couldn't he and Katherine get out of the lifeboat and keep walking until they ended up someplace else, same as he had before?

Maybe that had just been a fluke. Maybe the World of the Pale Gray Sky had an incredibly thin barrier. But Katherine was right: it didn't matter. A dog and a hostess weren't going to repair a complex piece of reality-defying technology. Not with what they had at their disposal now.

"Come on," Summerhill said, standing back up. "Let's pack some food up and get going."

Katherine stared at him in confusion. "Get going? Going where?"

"Outside, to explore the nevereef," Summerhill replied as he opened the food supply cabinet back up. Wagering that they probably shouldn't try to head to far afield on their initial trip out, he scooped up only a few of the meal packs and loaded them into one of the bags hanging from the inside of the cabinet door.

"Explore?" Katherine balked. "Are you kidding me? We should wait here, where it's safe."

"For how long?" Summerhill asked. "Until we run out of food and starve?"

A look of dread crossed Katherine's face, as if that thought had just crossed her mind for the first time. "I... Well, no, of course not," she said as she wrung her hands together. "But we *are* in a lifeboat. Maybe someone will find us."

Summerhill slung the bag of prepackaged food over his shoulder. "Someone like the Consortium?"

"Oh, bollocks," Katherine muttered under her breath. "All right, fine. We'll do it your way. I still don't know what you expect to find out there, though."

"I don't know what to expect, either. But the point is that what we have here won't help us; meanwhile, there could be any number of things out there, just waiting to be found."

Katherine chuckled as she got to her feet and slipped her pendant back underneath her blouse. She then checked her gun, and kept it in hand afterward. "All right, then, Mr. Summerhill," she said, motioning with her free hand towards the hatch of the lifeboat. "Lead the way."

SEVEN
BOUNDARY

Up close, the polyp structures and stationary tendrils that adorned the nevereef looked even more beautiful. It was just a shame that there was so little time to get a good look at them.

For the first few seconds after stepping outside the lifeboat, the coral surface supported Summerhill and Katherine just fine. Then, without warning, a series of cracks with the appearance of a giant spiderweb spread out beneath their feet.

Summerhill barely had time to register what was happening before the coral gave way. He tried to dive for the hatch of the lifeboat, but he'd already lost his footing as the surface of the reef crumbled. Katherine cried out, but her scream was cut off as she fell into the nevereef as well.

What Summerhill and Katherine fell into, however, was nothing at all like a coral reef. Below them was pure emptiness, like the space outside the *Nusquam*, but whereas Summerhill had been able to saunter through that pleasant sort of nothingness, here he and Katherine were being drawn into intimidating, unwelcoming emptiness. There wasn't even any sign of the fragments of coral that had fallen in underneath them.

They weren't pulled down by gravity, but rather *pushed* down by some other force. Summerhill didn't know what else it was, but he knew what it wasn't. It felt like being wrung through a sponge, extruded through thick, viscous emptiness by unseen hands.

The hostess' face was white with shock, her mouth wide with a scream that only barely reached Summerhill's ears despite how close she was, still the same scream she'd begun to let out when the coral had collapsed underneath her. Her legs and arms wheeled about through the emptiness at a fraction of the speed that flailing in panic ought to, the whipping of her hair and the blinking of her eyelids slowed to an equal degree. It was the look in her eyes, though, still stricken with frozen terror, that showed Summerhill that Katherine was stuck in that moment, trapped in the agonizingly slow passage of time.

The fur on the back of Summerhill's neck bristled and stood on end. Though he could not see beneath himself, he felt as if the empty skyscrapers of the World of the Pale Gray Sky were down below, were waiting for him, to catch him in their cold, lifeless grasp, like fingers of glass and metal reaching up from the coarse hand of a dead urban landscape.

With a surge of desperation, Summerhill fought against the force working on him. Moving his body as it plummeted through the emptiness was still slow going, like trying to swim through gelatin, but it was possible. The food pack slung across his back weighed him down at first, but he fought against that, as well. He dragged himself closer to Katherine and grabbed her by the hand. Her skin was cool to the touch, and felt more like the plastic of a mannequin than actual flesh, but the dog could still feel the faint twitch of life within. Gritting his teeth, Summerhill pulled her by the arm as he pitched downward and *dove*.

Now that his head was facing downward, Summerhill saw for sure that there were no buildings down below. There was nothing below, not as far as he could see, but as he kicked his legs, he was getting there faster. He kicked and kicked and kicked, dragging Katherine down along with him. Time sped up more and more by the moment, and the rushing of his pulse in his ears got stronger and harder and louder and more *real* until everything snapped back completely into place.

EIGHT
DETAILS

As soon as reality coalesced around them once more, Summerhill and Katherine fell several feet. The landing was jarring, but it didn't hurt much. The ground felt soft, spongy, negating most of the brunt of the impact. After the initial shock faded, however, and Summerhill had a chance to paw around at the surface they'd fallen onto, the ground felt hard and unyielding as solid rock.

Pitch blackness still engulfed their surroundings. The air was stale and—well, not stale, but just kind of nondescript. Neither warm nor particularly cold, not dry and yet not damp. Summerhill perked his ears and listened carefully, but he could hear no sounds other than Katherine's groaning and the drumming rush of his own pulse hammering through his skull.

Katherine groped about blindly, her hand smacking against Summerhill's arm a few times before she got purchase on his shoulder and pulled herself up into a sitting position. Summerhill helped to prop her up, and noticed that the total darkness had abated the tiniest bit, enough that he could now barely make out Katherine's shadowy silhouette. "Are you okay?" he asked her.

"I fell real hard on my shoulder," she replied, working out the stiffness with the opposite hand. "Doesn't feel like I'm banged up too badly, though." She took a deep breath and looked around. Now Summerhill could see her hair move as she turned her head. "Where are we?" she asked.

"Inside the nevereef, I would imagine," Summerhill replied. Once again, he patted his hands against the ground. It was solid, but it certainly didn't feel like coral. At the same time, it didn't feel quite like stone or rock, either. The surface of it was rough, but not as uneven as Summerhill would have expected from a natural cavern; however, it also wasn't as smooth or regular as something that had been carved out artificially.

Clutching her gun in one hand, Katherine patted at her pockets with the other. "Never should have quit smoking," she muttered. "We could use a lighter right now."

"Let me see what I can do about that," Summerhill said. If there was any sort of plant life here in this dark cavern, maybe there was something he could reach out to, connect with, control. Maybe something that—

There, something very tiny, microscopic, nestled within the miniscule grooves in the not-quite-rock. It wasn't much, and it wasn't easily identifiable, but it was plant, and that was enough for Summerhill. He took a deep breath, closed his eyes, and focused his energy into those barely detectable bits of plant life. What he was attempting might well be beyond his abilities, but it wouldn't hurt to try, so long as he was careful not to overexert himself.

He could tell it was working when he felt the fuzzy patch growing beneath his palm. That patch then spread out from his hand at an accelerating rate. A dull glow started to fill the cavern, getting brighter and brighter as bioluminescent moss blanketed the ground and then crawled up the walls and along the ceiling of the chamber.

With a gasp, Summerhill let go of his hold on the growing swath of moss. He felt a tiny hole in his being, some part of him expended in the effort. A wave of dizziness hit him as his very essence changed, albeit slightly, to smooth out the edge left by using up that part of himself.

In his mind, he could still feel that small part of him that now lived in the moss he'd called into being. It would change and become its own thing, in time, but meanwhile, there was a faint echo of self lingering that Summerhill couldn't avoid perceiving, radiating throughout the cavern.

Now that there was enough ambient light to see clearly, Summerhill and Katherine first looked around the cavernous chamber before turning back around and letting out sounds of mild shock at the sight of each other. Katherine looked different. She looked enough like Katherine that Summerhill still recognized her, but the details were off. Her hair was still blonde, but not quite the right shade of blonde; it was curly, but the curls weren't quite the right size. Her fair skin, her eyes—all of it just close enough without being quite right. She looked, Summerhill thought, like someone's idea of what Katherine might look like if they'd only been given a description of her without ever having seen her.

In place of her hostess' garb, she now wore a khaki bush jacket covered with large pockets, neatly cinched around her torso. Below that, she wore a matching khaki skirt. Atop her head was a small hat, a black band encircling the crown of it, forming a break in the pale tan. Lastly, in one hand—that hand that had been holding her futuristic stun pistol—she now carried an old-fashioned revolver.

Her wide eyes, fixed on Summerhill, were a clear indicator that he wasn't the only one surprised by what he was seeing. "Well, you look... different," she said, and then, realizing that she was being stared at in turn, took a look at herself.

Summerhill patted himself on the chest. He was dressed similarly to Katherine, though he at least had on a pair of pants instead of a skirt. Slung across his shoulder in place of the bag he'd brought from the lifeboat was a heavy leather satchel, its strap long enough to allow the bag to rest comfortably at his hip.

"You look like you're ready to head out on safari, mate," Katherine said. She chuckled, then nodded upwards. "I like the hat."

Though he hadn't felt the weight of it atop his head before, when he glanced upward, Summerhill saw the brim of said hat. He reached up and checked the fit of it. Not only was it sized perfectly for his head, but there were even holes for his ears. "You sure you don't know anything else about nevereefs?" he asked as he adjusted the hat out of some reflex.

"It sure doesn't look like we're inside a reef," Katherine replied. "Though I can't really see where else we could have possibly ended up after that fall."

"Guess we'll have to look around." Summerhill got to his feet, then helped Katherine up. She dusted herself off with her free hand, then patted at her front some more, paying specific attention to the pockets of her jacket. Wrinkling her brow in confusion, she began to sift through them.

"Oh, hey, this should come in handy," she said as she started to pull a variety of implements out from those deep pockets. Among the items kept on her person were a compass, a tinderbox, a pocket sundial, some handkerchiefs, and other such personal effects. "Not sure where any of it came from, but it's good to know that we have it."

The satchel—the one that had replaced Summerhill's food supply bag—was packed with smaller wrapped packages of jerky, dried fruit and nuts, and crusty bread. A few testing sniffs suggested that it was all still edible, if nowhere near as remarkable as the self-reconstituting meal packages from the lifeboat. If portioned properly, it could probably sustain two people for a couple of days, but not much longer than that.

Summerhill patted himself down to see if there was anything else of note in his pockets. He was outfitted with more or less the same kind of personal gear as Katherine, with one notable exception: he also carried an elaborate, gold-plated hunter-case pocket watch. On the back were engraved the words: *To One of My Favorites.*

The sight of it filled him with nostalgia without bringing any actual memories to mind. He didn't recall ever owning this watch—or any watch, for that matter—though paradoxically enough, he remembered thinking he'd owned a watch, for some reason, which was ridiculous because there was no time to keep track of back in the World of the Pale Gray Sky.

Upon opening the case to check the watch itself, Summerhill let out a quiet bark of surprise. The hands of the watch whirled around the face, their movements constantly changing speed, and sometimes even changing direction. The faint ticking from the watch's internal mechanisms didn't sound abnormal at all, and kept up the same, steady rhythm regardless of how quickly the hands were moving, impossible as that should have been.

The Chief's words came to mind again: *"'Impossible' isn't a word we're big on here."*

As a timepiece, the watch was useless, a baffling mess of hands that whirled about in nonsensical patterns. It was just as confusing as a keepsake, too, with an old, sepia tone photograph set inside the case.

Katherine leaned in and took a look. "Someone you know?" she asked.

It was the otter-creature from the *Nusquam*, the one Summerhill had bumped into after his last trip to the bar. "Sort of?" he said, staring at the photo in confusion.

Changing appearance after crossing a dimensional barrier was one thing. Finding their pockets loaded with personal effects they hadn't brought with them was another. Why would Summerhill have a photograph of one random *Nusquam* guest tucked away as a personal keepsake? And what had happened to the watch he'd brought with him from the World of the Pale Gray Sky?

Except he hadn't brought a watch with him. He remembered now. The otter in the photograph had asked him for the time. Besides, Summerhill knew full well he'd never owned a watch.

He gazed at the old picture some more. The otter's smile, the look in his eyes—there was a warm familiarity to him, and here, stuck inside the nevereef as far away from anything as he'd ever known, Summerhill found himself missing this unknown fellow, if only on some vague, hard-to-define level.

"Well, who is it?" Katherine asked.

"I'm not sure," Summerhill said. "He's not..." He'd meant to say, *"Not anyone special,"* but that wasn't true at all, was it? A painful lump formed in his throat for just a moment, but he forced it down. "I talked to him back on the ship, but only in passing. I don't even know his name."

Katherine checked her own pockets again, but came up empty-handed. "Well, we've got more important things to suss out right now. Shall we start by trying to figure out exactly what it is we've fallen into here?"

"Yeah," Summerhill said, his gaze lingering on the otter's photograph for a moment longer before he snapped the pocket watch shut and stuffed it back into his pocket. He had to focus. It was on his initiative that they'd ended up in this mess in the first place. That made it his responsibility to see them out of it. "Let's go."

There was only one obvious exit from the cavern chamber, so Summerhill led the way, with Katherine following close behind. Checking over his shoulder, he saw that she had her revolver in hand. He wanted to tell her to put it away, because it made him nervous, but he also felt that it was probably a reasonable precaution.

The glowing moss had spread a fair distance down the narrowing tunnel, and when it began to taper off, it was simple enough for Summerhill to coax it into growing further. "You're pretty good at that," Katherine said, and then her steps grew slower and more hesitant. "It is you doing that, right?"

Summerhill nodded. "Don't worry, I've got it under control."

Katherine sounded only slightly assuaged. "How?"

"I make plants grow. Never really gave the 'how' much thought."

"A dog that can make plants grow. There's something my granddad would have never come up with. Any other helpful tricks up your sleeve?"

"I don't think so," Summerhill replied. "I mean, unless you count the 'walking between dimensions' thing, but I'm not sure how I did that and it doesn't seem to be helping much in this case."

Katherine let out a sardonic chuckle. "Try to *really* want it," she suggested. "Just in case that helps any."

"I'll let you know if I start to feel any tingling in the fur on the back of my neck." Summerhill was smiling now. The atmosphere was a little less unsettling with some light banter to ease the mood.

Soon enough, the cavern tunnel began to gradually widen, and the ceiling rose higher and higher. Summerhill and Katherine kept plodding along, their one-way path set for them. There were only faint ambient sounds echoing their way, nothing distinct, nothing to suggest that anything was lurking around the nearest corner or barreling their way at breakneck speed.

There wasn't much else to do but stay alert and press on. Summerhill found himself counting his steps when his attention would wane. Keeping the glowing moss growing required some concentration, but soon he was doing it almost without thinking. Katherine's footsteps fell in line with his own, the cadence reassuring him of her presence.

The dog's ears shot up as Katherine cocked the hammer on her revolver. "Mr. Summerhill, hold it," she warned. "What's going on? When did we wind up in a forest?"

Katherine was right—they were surrounded by trees now, not the cavern walls from before. "I don't know," Summerhill replied, looking around at the dark forest. There was no sign of the cavern or any other rock formation behind them. "You've been behind me this whole time, right?"

"Yes. I mean—yes, I think so." With her gun at the ready, Katherine turned and scanned the area around them. "I don't remember losing sight of you. But I don't remember leaving the cavern either."

Summerhill shook his head. He didn't feel dizzy or groggy or like there were any gaps in his memory. "I'd been focusing on keeping the moss growing," he said, trying to backtrack his mental steps. "Maybe I just got distracted?"

Katherine stepped in closer to him. "I don't like this place, Mr. Summerhill," she said. "I don't like it here at all."

"Just stay alert," Summerhill told her. "Try to not let your mind drift."

The trees were packed close together, and their branches hung low, forming a canopy that was reminiscent of the tunnel from earlier. Very little sunlight made its way to the forest floor, and the soft, earthy ground felt mossy underfoot.

Summerhill sniffed at the air as he walked, noting that it lacked any defining character, much like back inside the cavern. He wrinkled his brow and tried to inspect the trees around him. It was difficult to say what kind of trees they were, not because Summerhill didn't know his plants, but because these trees defied identification.

As if she'd read his mind, Katherine said, "These look almost like trees from back where I come from." She gestured with her gun as she pointed them out in turn. "Those remind me of beech trees, except they're not quite right, I don't think."

Her words brought some new thoughts into Summerhill's head. Names he didn't know came to him as he reached out, trying to get to know these trees. He found Katherine's not-quite-beech, then almost-elm followed by oak-but-then-maple. The lack of distinction felt clumsy, as if reality itself had gotten sloppy.

"Are we in some kind of swamp?" Katherine asked. She used her free hand to grab hold of low-hanging branches to help keep balance with each tentative step.

Summerhill hadn't noticed anything terribly swampy about the area, at least not until a few steps later, when he realized that the ground *was* damp and squishy and muddy in places. It was still very dark, and hard to see for all the shadows cast by the tangle of weird trees. Farther in the distance, there were occasional faint signs of movement, the brief rustling of branches or the half-glimpsed form of some darting animal.

Katherine had adopted a more confident pace, hopping from tree root to rock to tree root, still using branches and the like to steady herself. "I guess this is what the inside of a nevereef is like," she said, huffing with exertion as she tugged her foot free of what was either a tangle of swamp grass or a sucking pile of mud. "I wonder if you and I are the first people ever to go inside one."

They continued to make their way through the somewhat swampy forest. Soon enough, the trees grew spaced farther enough apart that there was no longer just one obvious path to follow, but Katherine and Summerhill kept heading in roughly the same direction. One way was just as good as any other when they had no real means of knowing where they were headed or how to get there, and so long as the blandly-featured landscape offered no indication of a better way to go, continuing to follow as straight a path as possible seemed the most sensible course.

Even as he spent more time in their presence, the plants grew no more familiar to Summerhill. They retained their alien nature, never quite returning his mind's touch in the way he expected. He envied Katherine, who had no such connection to worry about; her struggles were merely physical as she trudged through the morass. Summerhill felt like he was being silently judged by this forest that would never accept him.

"Do you have forests like this back in New Zealand?" he asked.

"We have forests," Katherine replied, grunting as she hauled her weight up over a particularly tall cluster of roots. "I don't know if I'd say they're much like this, though."

Summerhill tried to force the roots to shrink, in order to make Katherine's struggle easier, but they were reluctant to comply. Probably he could force his will upon them, but that would leave him far more exhausted than Katherine would be for simply climbing over them, and so he decided to conserve his strength. The least he could do instead was offer her a hand down, which she took without complaint.

As his furred fingers slid against her smooth ones, he felt a niggling sense of loss in the back of his mind, the shadow of heartache, hints of memories that he knew immediately weren't real. His mind went to the picture of the otter in the pocket watch, and at once, his throat tightened up and a slight pressure built up behind his eyes. He had an easy enough time forcing the phantom feelings away, though, and their effects had faded completely by the time Katherine's feet were solidly back on the ground.

The two pressed on. When they reached a clearing a few minutes later, Summerhill stopped long enough to fish some jerky out of his satchel, sharing some with Katherine. It was thick, hearty, a little too chewy, but the flavor was good. Doing something mundane and personal helped to get rid of the feeling of walking through a half-remembered dream, the details of chewing and tasting and swallowing too immediate and identifiable to be anything but real. Summerhill made a point to remember that effect in case he felt his grasp on reality begin to slip later on.

"You know, when I realized I was on the run from the Consortium again," Katherine said as she wiped away some dirt or moss she'd gotten on the front of her jacket after clambering over a large rock a few minutes earlier, "I figured I'd end up someplace weird, but hiking through a swamp wasn't really what I was expecting."

Summerhill chuckled. "Yeah, I'm starting to realize that the more I get overwhelmed with expanding possibilities, the harder I get sidelined by things that happen outside of them."

"Hardly seems fair of the universe, does it?" Katherine said, grinning as she bopped him on the shoulder with a gentle fist. "That sort of one-two punch is a bit of a cheap shot, if you ask me."

"Yeah, so far, the universe hasn't asked me what I think is fair. None of the universes I've been to yet, at any rate."

Katherine turned and looked back at him, and then her smile abruptly faded. "Quiet," she hissed. "Did you hear that?"

"Hear what?"

"I thought I heard voices." She picked up her revolver and got to her feet, slowly and quietly. "You're a dog. Aren't you supposed to have good ears?"

Summerhill brought his ears up and listened. The wind picked up, and Katherine looked around in a panic as the leaves and branches above shook audibly. That sound soon died down, though, and Summerhill kept trying to hear the voices Katherine had mentioned.

"I don't hear anything," he assured her, and for good measure, he sniffed at the air again, but didn't get much in the way of scent other than a generic forest smell. "Are you sure you're not just—"

The light through the trees dimmed as some kind of flying craft zipped by overhead. Branches bowed in its wake, and the air hummed with the sound of advanced machinery. A moment later, out of the corner of his eye, Summerhill caught the movements of several humanoid shapes in the forest back the way they came.

"It's the Consortium." Katherine was already on the move, sparing only the briefest look to see if Summerhill was still with her.

Summerhill scooped up the satchel and took off after Katherine. The bag's strap caught on a nearby branch, yanking him back and causing him to trip. He spat wet dirt out of his mouth as he got back to his feet. "I thought you said they wouldn't find us out here," he coughed out.

Katherine hesitated. For a few seconds, Summerhill thought she was going to run off without him, but finally she helped tug the satchel free of the branch. "They shouldn't have," she said, wasting no further time dallying once she'd untangled the strap. "We're not even in the same reality anymore."

"That doesn't seem to have stopped them."

"Yeah, I noticed." Katherine flapped one of her hands at the roots and greenery at Summerhill's feet. "Can't you stop them with that magic plant thing you do again?"

The dog shook his head. "Not against this many at once. Besides, the plants here don't seem to like me very much."

"Guess that brings us back to Plan A." Katherine grabbed Summerhill by the hand and dragged him along with her as she ran.

The shadows of two more flying craft passed above the canopy. "And what plan is that, exactly?" Summerhill struggled with his one free hand to sling the satchel more carefully over his shoulder as he ran.

"Run and hide until we think of something better." Katherine showed little heed for her surroundings, and Summerhill struggled to match her pace. The way she dragged him put strain on his arm, and his feet came dangerously close to slipping out from under him.

The trees to either side of him became a blur. "I'm not sure I like this plan," he panted. "Are you sure surrender is really that bad an option?"

Katherine dove around a tall rock and let go of Summerhill. Using the rock as cover, she closed one eye, brought her gun up in both hands, and fired at their pursuers. The sound of the revolver roared through the forest, scaring up birds and wildlife and making Summerhill's ears ring. There was no sign as to whether the shot had hit anyone, but Katherine was already on the move again.

At least the trees had spaced out enough to make running easier. If the Consortium had gotten the drop on them back when they'd been in the more crowded, swampy part of the woods, they'd have been slowed down considerably. As it was, being outnumbered was bad enough, but if they could improve their brief head start—

A wet patch of muddy earth grabbed hold of Summerhill's foot, causing him to trip again. He yelped as his face splashed down into a shallow, stagnant pool. The water was odorless and (thankfully) flavorless, though that was of less concern than losing valuable seconds while running for his life. Now that he'd stumbled twice, there was little doubt that the better-equipped Consortium search team would be gaining on them.

Except a quick look behind him showed that they hadn't gotten any closer. The pursuers only appeared in shadowy movements far back in the cluster of trees. None of them had fired a shot or called out any demand for surrender. They didn't even appear to be moving very fast, given that their quarry was running.

"Katherine!" Summerhill shouted as he pushed himself back up and chased after her. "Katherine, hold on! I don't think we need to run!"

Katherine didn't say anything, look back, or even slow down for him to catch up. He supposed he couldn't blame her under the circumstances, even if it was her very fear that—if Summerhill was right—she was running from.

The dog sprinted after her. He imagined the ground getting flatter and smoother, easier to run on. He imagined fewer obstacles to trip over—fewer rocks, fewer roots, fewer patches of mud. He imagined fewer low-hanging branches. He imagined himself gaining on Katherine.

And this time Summerhill did not trip. His feet didn't get pulled into the mud and his satchel didn't get caught on any stray branches. The terrain changed exactly as he hoped it would, the forest opening up, the path leveling out. A forceful gust of wind blew at his back as he willed it to.

He grabbed Katherine's shoulder from behind. She spun and tried to shake him off, but the dog instead grabbed her by both arms and dragged her to a stop. "Katherine, it's okay," he said, trying to exude calm at her. "They're not real. The Consortium's not really out there."

"Of course they are," Katherine shot back. "They're right—"

"They're always just at the edge of where you can see and hear them, because that's where you're expecting them," Summerhill said. "That's where your subconscious is putting them."

Katherine struggled against the dog's grip. "Mr. Summerhill, please, we don't have time for this," she pleaded. "They're going to be—"

"They're going to be on us any second. Yeah, I know." Summerhill let her go and spread his arms wide. "Except they're not here, are they?"

The sky above the canopy was silent. Further back in the trees, the shadows of secretive movements became more infrequent. The sounds of footsteps through the underbrush grew quieter and quieter. Katherine stared back at Summerhill. "I don't understand. What's going on?"

Summerhill tapped a claw against his temple. "I think what's in our heads is filling in the details here," he said. "Haven't you noticed how bland and generic everything is until you stop and try to observe it?"

Katherine shook her head and shifted her grip on her gun. "But the Consortium," she insisted. "They were out there. We both saw them, didn't we?"

"Yes," Summerhill said. "Right after you'd started talking about being on the run from them again, and we both started thinking that they might be out there."

And now that Katherine had been distracted by the new flow of conversation, the signs of pursuit had disappeared completely. "The trees. When I started trying to remember what kinds of trees I remembered from back home, I started noticing them out here in the forest," Katherine said. "But it's not like I'm an expert."

"And so the trees only look and feel half-real," Summerhill pointed out. "Half-detailed. I think the world itself is trying to adapt to our expectations of it."

"Well how the hell is it doing that?"

"How should I know?" Summerhill flashed Katherine a reassuring smile. "I'm just pointing out what I'm noticing."

The air grew warmer as Katherine paced around the clearing. "Fine," she said, holstering her revolver and rubbing her hands together as she walked. "If the world is taking what's

70

in our head and making it real, then where's the spaceship I'm imagining to fly us out of here?"

Summerhill shook his head. "It doesn't seem to work like that," he said. "Like I said, it feels like our minds are filling in the details. That's why our imagination can put the shadows of Consortium agents amongst the trees, but can't actually create real people who are chasing after us."

Now the branches up above shook despite the lack of wind, sprinkling the clearing below with spiraling leaves. Katherine clutched the sides of her head and grunted in frustration before she finally ceased pacing and looked back at Summerhill. "Fine. Let's say your theory's right. What do we do with that? Where does that get us?"

"For starters, I say let's imagine that the forest comes to an end just past the point where we can see now," Summerhill said. "Think about the rolling hills and open plains of New Zealand that you told me about, and I'll try to do the same."

"You don't seriously think that we're going to wind up in New Zealand just by wishing it and clicking our heels together three times, do you?"

The last part of that remark made Summerhill furrow his brow in confusion. "I—no, I mean, I don't think it's going to take us anywhere. I think it'll just be nicer to walk through an open field than a dark and spooky forest, don't you?"

Katherine drew her gun again, but left her hand hanging at her side. "You're crazy," she said. "But fine. I'll humor you." She eyed Summerhill with open suspicion, but said nothing further.

Within a minute, the leaves and branches above were spaced far enough apart that Summerhill could see the sky, the pale expanse tinged with the barest amount of blue. His steps quickened, and Katherine let out a sound of exasperation as she followed suit. Focusing their thoughts was working, Summerhill could tell, and he broke into a jog, eager to show Katherine that he was right.

At long last, they made it to the treeline. Spread out before them were gently rolling hills of pale green and a soft blue sky dotted with fluffy clouds. Despite it being wholly unremarkable in how plain and idyllic it was, the sight was the most welcome in the world.

Summerhill came to a stop and took slow, heavy breaths as he looked straight up. This was the first real sky he'd seen since leaving home—no, since leaving the World of the Pale Gray Sky. That wasn't his home, he told himself. His real home was some other amazing place that was out there amongst countless somewheres, like Katherine had said.

High up above was the sun—or at least what passed for the sun. Instead of a bright yellow ball of light shining down on them, it was just a fuzzy, yellow-white blur without a defined shape and without the satisfying heat of a real sun. It was still more of a sun than Summerhill had ever known.

"Okay," Katherine said, letting out a deep breath of her own. "How did you do this?"

"Not me," Summerhill said with a smile. "Us."

Katherine crouched down and ran her fingers through the grass. She plucked a few blades from the dirt, then patted the ground with her palm. "This is impossible," she muttered.

"I thought 'impossible' was something the *Nusquam* crew didn't believe in."

One of the puffy clouds drifted in front of the not-quite-sun for a moment, and Katherine looked back up at Summerhill. "'Impossible' has to exist out there somewhere," she said. "But if we haven't found it yet, then maybe we'll get out of this place after all."

Summerhill extended a hand to help Katherine back up, but before she took it, a jolt ran up his spine and his ears perked. He thought he'd heard something, something faint, subtle and quick, too hard to catch.

A steady twitching vibrated inside his pocket. He set his hand over it, then realized that what he'd just heard was something inside his watch—the mainspring or the gear train or something—had broken or popped out of alignment or—

His train of thought was cut short as he felt his vision growing hazier. The ground under his feet started to feel less solid, less real; the color of the soft blue sky began to leach out into white; Katherine's presence grew more distant.

His senses flailed in an attempt to find some anchor back to where he was, but when he finally found himself again, he wasn't where he was supposed to be.

NINE
DISPLACEMENT

Night was encroaching, the sky a deep, velvety purple that had yet to fade into true dark. The last rays of sunset were fading, marking the horizon with a band of bright orange, like a strip of distant fire.

Higher up in the sky, stars came into being against the darkness. First they appeared one by one, but as the moments ticked by, they began to emerge in greater number. They were so simple, mere pinpoints of light, and yet they were so beautiful, the first and only stars Summerhill could ever recall seeing. He was filled with the urge to make constellations out of the unfamiliar patterns they made.

A shape shifted next to him, and then nestled in against his left side, warm and solid, comforting. Then came a voice, sweet and almost-familiar, its tone teasingly playful. "You never asked."

Summerhill heard himself reply, "Would you tell me?"

His reply came unbidden from his own lips, as if he had already been part of this conversation and knew what to say. But who was he talking to? When he tried to turn his head to look, his body refused to respond.

What was this? *When* was this? The person talking to him sounded familiar, but how? Was this someone or something from before the World of the Pale Gray Sky?

Was this even real?

Summerhill felt the individual at his side tuck in more cozily against him before letting out a hum of contentment. "It's kind of a long story," murmured whoever-it-was.

With that, Summerhill's eyes turned back up toward the starlit sky, the last traces of sunlight having now disappeared completely. From beside him came a louder, happier hum, followed by a soft sigh, audible only due to the sheer idyllic quiet of the scene.

The dog felt himself drawn breath—

—and then he caught the scent of smoke—

TEN
WILLPOWER

—and then he saw Katherine, wide-eyed and panicked against a backdrop of pure, pale blue.

"Summerhill!" she cried out, her hands grabbing him by the shoulders to shake him. "Mr. Summerhill, come on, snap out of it! I can't—"

The dog's sudden and total loss of balance made him topple to one side, which in turn made Katherine lose her grip on him. He lashed his tail to help regain his sense of equilibrium, but it wasn't quite enough. Just before he fell over, Katherine grabbed hold of his arm with both hands and hauled him back upright.

He panted for breath and got his bearings. He was inside the nevereef, in the field just beyond the swampy forest, the sun-blur glowing overhead, cold air tickling the insides of his nose and ears. The afterimages of the nighttime stars had disappeared, but the tingle of smoke still lingered in his nostrils.

"Are you all right?" Katherine asked as she took a few more moments to make sure Summerhill wasn't going to suddenly pitch over again. "You just started staring off into space." A sheepish look crossed her face. "And then your shirt caught on fire."

For a second, Summerhill froze in alarm before seeing that he clearly wasn't on fire anymore. He patted his front and looked down at himself, and spotted his breast pocket, the fabric scorched black, barely still attached to the rest of the shirt.

Katherine swallowed a lump in her throat. "I tried to put it out as fast as I could, but in the process, I think I may have broken your watch." She coughed quietly. "Sorry."

Summerhill pulled the pocket watch out and inspected it. He wiped soot and ash from the outside, then opened it up. The face was smashed, and one of the hands jiggled loose inside. The picture of the otter had burned up, leaving only charred bits of paper around the edges.

"It's not your fault," Summerhill said. "I think it was the watch that started the fire in the first place." He used his thumb to rub away more of the black tarnish and read the engraving again: *To One of My Favorites*.

"And anyway," he added, "I'm not sure what good a watch is when it doesn't even tell the right time." Filled with sudden revulsion for the thing, the dog pulled his arm back and hurled the watch away into the trees. He heard it hitting some branches, and then, silence.

Katherine scuffed her feet against the ground anxiously. Summerhill gave her a reassuring pat on the shoulder. "Come on," he said. "What we need now is to find a way out of this place." He turned away from the forest and faced the open expanse of rolling hills and gently blowing grass.

He began to march in that direction, with Katherine close behind him. As he walked, he tore the ruined pocket from his shirt, and was relieved to see that the fire hadn't burned through the fabric underneath to his fur and skin. The distraction caused by his disjointed daydream had ruined his ability to appreciate the beautiful landscape for the time being. He hoped that would pass.

"So," Katherine said, breaking the awkward silence after a few moments, "the fire notwithstanding, what happened to you back there?"

"What do you mean?"

"You just... stopped," Katherine said. "Your eyes were wide open, but you couldn't seem to see me or hear me, not even after your pocket burst into flames."

Briefly reliving what he'd experienced in those few moments made Summerhill feel the pangs of heartbreak. "I'm not sure," he said. "I must have just spaced out."

"Well, I'm glad you're not hurt. Or mad." Katherine quickened her pace so that she overtook Summerhill and could turn to look him in the eye. "Are you sure you're feeling all right, though? Do you want to stop and rest? Maybe eat something?"

Summerhill shook his head. "No. I want to focus on getting out of here. That needs to stay our top priority."

Katherine started to lag behind again. "Mr. Summerhill, I don't mean to sound negative, but what if there isn't a way out of this place? What if it comes down to the two of us needing to survive down here?"

"There's a way out," Summerhill insisted. He'd come close to snapping at her, but caught himself at the last moment. None of this was her fault. "There's got to be. I just know it."

"Oh, hey, something else you just know. There's a surprise. And just what makes you say that this time?"

Summerhill whirled around and leveled his narrow snout at Katherine's face with a snarl. "Because I'm meant for something important!" His fur bristled, his ears went fully erect, and his lips peeled back to reveal his sharp canine teeth.

Katherine's mouth dropped as she staggered half a step back, and Summerhill immediately clapped both of his hands over his muzzle and laid his ears back. He saw her hand twitch a fraction of an inch closer to her holstered revolver, but either the motion was subconscious or she thought better of herself, because she didn't reach for it.

"Oh my god, I am so sorry," Summerhill said. "I don't know where that came from." And he really didn't. He wasn't even sure who or what he was, so what would give him any cause to think he was important? Other than his running theory that he'd been imprisoned, and that certainly didn't bode well.

The shock faded from Katherine's face, and she sighed as she breathed into her cupped hands. "No, it's all right," she said as she straightened back up. "I shouldn't have provoked you like that. I—"

Katherine kept talking, but Summerhill tuned her out. He set one hand on his stomach, feeling nauseous and lightheaded. His eyes scrunched shut, and his fur stood on end again, a shivering sensation running over his body. His stomach gnawed at itself and his torso grew cold and stiff.

"Mr. Summerhill?" Katherine's voice cut through the haze surrounding Summerhill's head. "Is it happening again?" She snapped her fingers in front of his eyes. He was so disoriented that the only way he could show her that he was still responsive was to hold up one of his hands.

The nausea and chills were joined by a growing sense of dread. Summerhill's ears popped upright and he snapped his head to one side and looked across the field, back towards the forest. "The watch," he said. "Oh, god, I need to get the watch back." Without waiting for Katherine to acknowledge him, he ran for the trees.

Running was difficult; he was dizzy and his legs came close to giving out. Katherine called after him, but he didn't process her words. Momentum carried him forward even as he lost balance, but he turned it into a controlled fall until he finally landed on his hands and knees a few yards into the forest.

His fingers scrabbled madly at the dirty, leaf-covered forest floor. "It's got to be somewhere. We have to find it."

Katherine had come to a stop next to him. "Mr. Summerhill, slow down," she begged. "What do you need a broken pocket watch for?"

"I need it back," Summerhill whimpered. "I don't think I was supposed to lose it."

"Is this even where you threw it?"

The dog lifted his head up and looked around at the trees. None of them seemed familiar. "I don't know. But I threw it somewhere." Placing his nose against the ground, he started to crawl forward, sniffing as he went, hoping to catch some trace of metal or fire.

Katherine padded after him, her feet crunching through the dry, nondescript leaves. "Mr. Summerhill, I'm not even sure this is the same forest we came out of. I mean, it is, but it isn't. I—you know what I mean."

With a sigh, Summerhill took another look around. The infuriating half-defined nature of the scenery made it nearly impossible to tell if there was any permanence to the landscape they'd come through earlier. The nonsense trees and made-up foliage felt different than the plants Summerhill had sensed before. "But I need to find it," the dog whined.

"Mr. Summerhill." Katherine said, crouched down alongside him. "Please, it's like you said yourself: we need to find a way out of here, and I don't think a busted watch is going to help us."

The truth of Katherine's words sank in as Summerhill stared out hopelessly over the dark underbrush. His throat clenched up, and his dizziness returned. Part of him was sure that the pocket watch was still out there, somewhere. When he closed his eyes, he could see fur-lined ears and a smile of sympathy and encouragement.

"Can we... Can we just look for a little bit?" he asked. "You and me together?"

Katherine sighed and took another look around the forest floor. "Fine. But only ten minutes. It's starting to get dark."

The sun had been high in the sky only a few minutes ago. Of course it would get dark now, when it was was least convenient.

The two spread out and searched. It was uncomfortable, dirty work, with no obvious signs of progress. Summerhill considered the amusing irony of not having any way of telling when ten minutes had passed since they didn't even have a broken timepiece.

Finally, a combination of darkness and frustration made Summerhill concede before Katherine had to nag him any further to give up. Defeated, he got back to his feet, wiped away the dirt and dead leaves that clung to him, and followed Katherine out of the forest.

Back amidst the open fields with the gently rolling hills, some form of pseudo-night had fallen. Instead of a sun-blur, there was a moon-blur, which gave off enough light to see by. It lacked the eerie quality of real moonlight, and was more like a dimmer version of sunlight. There were no stars, which Summerhill felt was just as well, because thinking about stars right now made him feel worse about having thrown away the pocket watch.

"I think someone used to love me," he told Katherine.

Katherine didn't answer right away. "The otter-person in the photograph?" she eventually wagered after a few quiet seconds.

"That's my best guess," Summerhill said. "The watch was engraved with '*To One of My Favorites*,' which... okay, now that I think about it, that seems like a weird thing to say to someone you're in love with."

"Maybe it's not that weird," Katherine said. "There are cultures back on Earth where having multiple lovers is accepted and encouraged." She let out a chuckle. "I mean, mine's not one of them, but I've heard of way weirder things in my time aboard the *Nusquam*."

Summerhill sighed. "Maybe that's why I feel so bad for throwing it away? Because he gave it to me."

"But you didn't have it with you before we fell down here, did you?"

"No, I didn't," Summerhill said. "At least, I don't think I did." He pressed his palms against the sides of his head as he kept walking. Did he or didn't he have a watch with him when he left the World of the Pale Gray Sky? "I just wish I knew who I was."

Katherine set a hand on Summerhill's shoulder. The two stopped walking for a little while, both of them standing there in the open field, neither saying a word.

"Come on," Summerhill said after shaking off another attack of guilt before it could take root. "Let's keep going."

"Right," Katherine said. "I hope it gets light again soon, though."

Night had fallen while Summerhill had been desperately searching the dark forest floor. Maybe that was because his fear and anxiety had colored in that part of the world's details, or maybe it had all been a coincidence. It was worth trying to fix, though.

Summerhill looked around the dimly lit field as he walked, trying to imagine them as they'd looked in the faux sunlight. He called up his mental imagery of what he imagined New Zealand looked like. He tried to forget his guilt and sadness at losing his pocket watch.

The guilt and sadness stayed; however, slowly but surely, the light of the blobby moon grew brighter, as if it were hooked up to a dimmer switch that Summerhill could turn very slowly with his mind. The dog wrinkled his brow in concentration. "Katherine," he mumbled. "Help me out with this?"

"Help you with what?" Katherine then saw the look on Summerhill's face and looked up. "Oh. Right, then."

Night gave way to day more quickly. Katherine shook her head and laughed despite herself. "Depending on what this place can and can't do with what thoughts are in our heads," she said, "this could get very dangerous or very surreal in short order."

"Possibly both," Summerhill agreed. "All the more reason to find our way out as soon as we can."

Katherine hummed, and now she swung her arms as she walked at a new, brisk pace. "I don't know. It might not be that bad, living somewhere where you can change the view and scenery at will. Where the sun doesn't rise before you're ready and where the best nights of your life can last as long as you want them to."

Summerhill smiled. "We probably can't control that much," he pointed out. "Details. Specifics. I mean, there's clearly a world here that exists outside of what we're thinking of."

"So let's see what our limits are," Katherine offered. "Apparently I can't just conjure a spaceship out of thin air, but do you want to see if there's a seashore beyond the next hill?"

The hostess had a gleam in her eyes that made Summerhill smile. "A seashore, huh?" he asked. "Just like that?"

"Race you for it."

Summerhill twitched his whiskers. The hazy sun grew brighter. "Seriously?" he asked.

A broad grin appeared on Katherine's face. "On three?"

"All right, fine," Summerhill agreed. "Ready? One—"

But Katherine didn't wait. The moment Summerhill started counting, she was off in a full sprint. One of her hands came up to catch her hat before it blew off in the wind.

Summerhill called after her, then broke into a run as well. He could hear her laughing, which made him smile even more in turn. She wasn't as fast as him, but he wasn't sure he'd overtake her before she made it to the top of the hill. He swung his arms and worked his legs as hard as he could, but she was too far ahead.

Sure enough, Katherine made it there first, coming to a dead stop at the very top, her arms falling to her side, hat still in hand. Summerhill slowed to a trot and came to a stop alongside her. "No fair," he panted, tongue lolling out of his muzzle for a few more breaths. "You said on three."

Katherine didn't reply right away, though. A moment later, Summerhill realized why.

Stretching out far below was a winding coastline, presumably ripped right from Katherine's imagination. A wide strip of white sand separated the dry green grass from the bright blue sea. Quite unlike the poorly detailed landscapes Summerhill and Katherine had come through, the ocean was a crisp and brilliant blue, the ripples of gentle waves visible even from far away. In the sky above danced the tiny forms of mewling seabirds, their cries echoing over the sounds of the tide crashing against the beach.

After several long moments of being caught up in the beauty of the view, Katherine brought her hand up to her forehead, shielding her eyes as she gazed out into the distance. Summerhill tried to follow her line of sight, squinting.

"Is that what I think it is?" she asked.

Summerhill tried to resolve the speck in the far distance. From so far away, it was little more than a featureless silhouette at the water line, but every so often, a bit of white would flutter into view before disappearing again. "Is that a ship?" he asked.

"I think it is." Katherine was beaming again. "And if it is, then that means we're not alone down here!"

This time, Summerhill didn't wait for Katherine to get the jump on him. He hopped down from the crest of the rise and started to run downhill. It was a little steep, but with his tail he was able to keep balance well enough that he didn't trip. Soon, thanks to gravity and momentum, he was racing down towards the beach at breakneck speed.

Katherine trailed close behind. The air echoed with her exultant laughter, and Summerhill joined in. Sometimes she would overtake him, and he would overtake her in turn, the two of them trading places, switching back and forth as they hurtled down the embankment in their ecstatic race for the seashore. Wind whipped through Summerhill's fur, and sunlight glinted off of the waves into his eyes. At some point he clasped Katherine's hand in his own, and then they ran together.

When they reached the beach, it felt like they'd arrived in the first "real" place since falling into the nevereef. The white sand underfoot was fine and soft. Bits of driftwood and pieces of seashell jutted into view here and there. Clumps of reedy grass grew, and patches of dried kelp were strewn about far from the water's edge. Tiny crabs skittered about, darting out from behind rocks or piles of sand before scurrying out of sight.

Katherine and Summerhill walked along the beach together. The slope they'd run down turned out to be part of a much larger and steeper escarpment that ran parallel to the shoreline. The heat was strong but pleasant, not at all oppressive, adding to the very welcome realism of the beach scenery.

"So, what are we looking for, Mr. Summerhill? Anything in particular?"

"Any sort of sign that we really aren't alone, I suppose. I'm guessing you didn't imagine that ship into being out there?"

Katherine shook her head. "I was just thinking about the seashore. Exactly like this. Reminds me of back home."

Summerhill smiled, and felt a mix of comfort and anxiety at the thought. He'd find his way home someday, he resolved. Just as soon as he had a way of finding out where home was.

A few hundred yards farther down the beach, tucked into an alcove in the cliff face, Katherine spotted a small wooden dinghy. She and Summerhill gave it a thorough check, and the little wooden boat appeared to be of sturdy make, with no visible holes or leaks. There was some wear and tear, but nothing that suggested the craft wasn't seaworthy. It even came complete with a pair of oars.

"We should try to make for the ship out there," Katherine said. "No sense ignoring our one obvious lead."

"It's our only real landmark to shoot for," Summerhill agreed. He shared some of the food in his satchel with her, then they went about getting the boat ready, dragging it along the soft sand toward the water. Soon enough, they'd both know if this was a dumb idea or not.

Their assessment of the dinghy's structural integrity proved accurate enough. The waves weren't as gentle as Summerhill had been expecting, but the boat held up, rocking up and down as the ocean steadily tossed them about.

Katherine took charge of the rowing. "You're pretty good at that," Summerhill noted after they were a ways out.

"I'm pretty good at a lot of things," she replied with a chuckle. "Besides," she added with a grunt as she rowed harder to overcome the current trying to push them back toward the shore, "it's not exactly rocket science."

Summerhill leaned back in the dinghy and draped one arm over the edge. His fingers dipped into the water, which was cold enough that he didn't want to fall in. If Katherine knew how to row a boat, he was fine letting her be the one to do it. Perhaps he could conjure up some sort buoyant seaweed to act as a flotation device if things got worse.

After several minutes, the ship's form was easier to make out. It was a large one, with a long prow and four tall masts, its sails currently furled. At this distance, there was still no sign of any activity on deck.

"Do you think they have cannons?" Summerhill asked. "Any likelihood of them hitting us at this distance?"

Katherine snorted. "If I were them, I'd be more curious to see who we were first before just blowing us out of the water." She looked back over her shoulder at the waiting vessel, then turned back to Summerhill. "I hope they think like I do."

The dinghy drew closer and closer to the ship. Summerhill continued to hope that the crew would be friendly and helpful, even as the ship itself grew more imposing. There were definitely cannons, too.

The ship appeared to lurch and loom higher above them, and it wasn't until too late that Summerhill realized the ship actually had risen up. An enormous wave, much larger than anything before it, came rolling towards the small dinghy at terrifying speed.

"Oh, bugger. Grab onto something, Mr. Summerhill," Katherine said as she worked the oars frantically, but the dog was already clutching the sides of the small boat as hard as he could. The wave cast its shadow over the dinghy, and then the sea rose from underneath.

Summerhill lost his grip on the sides of the boat and fell into Katherine as they shot upward. With what little concentration he could muster, he tried to impose his will upon the huge wave, to shrink it with the force of his mind, but fear overcame his imagination.

The dinghy crested the wave, momentum carrying it airborne, and rather than gently sliding down the other side, it dropped through the air several feet, hitting the water below with a crash. The oars were ripped free of Katherine's hands, and then the wind took her hat.

Water filled the bottom of the dinghy now. Summerhill tried to use his own hat to bail the water out, but the ear-holes made his attempts futile. He felt the next wave coming before he saw it.

The dinghy pitched upward faster and higher than before. Katherine shouted something, but her words were lost under the roar of the sea. Looking back over his shoulder, Summerhill was almost able to read the name of the sailing vessel on the prow, but then the dinghy dropped again and was pulled underwater.

As freezing cold overtook his body, and as Katherine was pulled away from him by the undertow, all Summerhill could think about was whether or not he'd ever see his antique pocket watch again.

ELEVEN
TAUTOLOGIES

The roar of the ocean echoed in Summerhill's ears one last time before fading away. There was no sign of the dinghy, no huge waves casting shadows, no seawater and no cold and no desperate need for air. The dog found his feet on solid ground, his heart pounding, his stomach still queasy.

With his eyes still screwed shut, he heard the low, constant drumming of machinery. In the air hung the scents of oils and coolants and strange gases. The sturdy floor beneath his feet pulsed and shook in time with the sounds that ran up through his bones.

Summerhill opened his eyes slowly, daring a look at his new surroundings. He was in a drab industrial complex of some sort. Tubes and pipes ran along the ceiling, and assorted valves and seals jutted out from the walls. Next to him was Katherine, her features looking as they did when he'd first met her, khaki bush gear replaced by her hostess' uniform. A brief look of panic crossed her face, then she brought her hand to her chest and breathed a sigh of relief as her fingers found the outline of the small pendant beneath her blouse.

"I'm not dreaming, am I?" Summerhill asked aloud. "That wave didn't drown me, I hope."

Katherine pinched herself and winced. "If you're dreaming, then you're dreaming of a part of the *Nusquam* that you never saw."

"The *Nusquam*?" Summerhill took another look around, but nothing about this place appeared familiar. "Are you sure?"

"I'll be damned if I know how we got here," Katherine said. "But this is one of the service passageways that leads back to the engineering section and the reality jump drive. Which means that if we go that way—" She pointed down the narrow hallway to her right. "—we'll come back out somewhere down in the lower decks."

Summerhill hopped up onto his toes and clasped his hands together. "That's great!" he chirped. "That means we can sail on to some other world, right?"

Katherine shook her head as she began making her way down the corridor. "I don't know if it's that great. We have no idea whether the agents the Consortium sent are still on board. This might be the worst possible place for us to be."

"Okay, that's not what I was hoping to hear," Summerhill said. He stayed close to her as they both hunched down to make their way underneath a low-hanging bundle of exposed wiring. "What do we do, then?" he asked, cautiously sneaking looks behind them as they went.

"The plan," Katherine said as she gripped a hatch with both hands and pulled it open, "is that I figure out ASAP whether the Security Chief will offer me asylum or extradite me. Hell, I don't even know if the ship recognizes Consortium jurisdiction. Either way, it looks like my career as a cruise ship hostess is over."

Summerhill scratched his head. "Wait, there's a question," he said, holding the hatchway open after Katherine stepped through. "You were on the run from the Consortium before all this started, right? So how did you end up working on the *Nusquam* in the first place if you were a fugitive back then, too?"

"You know, I almost didn't think you were going to piece that together." Katherine shot him a proud grin and tapped him on the nose. "It's a little trick I call 'act like you're supposed to be there and nobody will call you out on it.'"

The dog's eyes widened. "Wait. Meaning that you were—"

"A stowaway, yes," Katherine finished for him. "At least initially. After I sold off the modu—the, ah, object I stole, I brokered passage to a drydock in the Orion Nebula, snuck aboard the ship, then just acted like I worked here."

"And that actually worked? Nobody caught on?"

"Not right away, at least. There are so many people running the *Nusquam* that it's a logistical nightmare to keep track of them all. Frankly, I suspect the Security Chief figured it out eventually, but by then I'd become so ingrained with the working of the ship that it probably made more sense to keep me than to kick me off." Katherine sighed, then kept moving. "Which I hope means the Chief has a soft spot for me."

After closing the hatch as silently as possible, Summerhill scampered after Katherine, who had already stood back up and was striding purposefully down the corridor that followed. They were in a more typical hallway now, leading away from the guts of the ship. "What if the Chief isn't on your side?" Summerhill asked, remembering his awkward conversation with the genderless, shapeshifting dog-creature. "What then?"

"Then I guess I'm off to steal another lifeboat," Katherine said. She stopped and looked back at Summerhill with a frown on her face. "And no offense, Mr. Summerhill, but on the chance that it *was* your presence that caused the on-board computer to freak out when scanning for a destination, I'm going to have to go alone."

"Alone?" Summerhill felt his heart sink, and thought about his other self, bright blue eyes shimmering with earnestness. "But I'm... I'm supposed to stay with you."

Katherine cracked a tiny smile, though there was a distinct look of pity on her face. "It's sweet that you want to try to protect me. But I don't think you can protect me. Not from this."

She started to walk off again. "It's not that," Summerhill insisted as he trotted after her. "We make a great team, you and me. And I think you... well..."

A noticeable sag showed in Katherine's shoulders as she tried to press on unfazed. She let out a sigh, then slowed to a stop again. "You think what?" she asked quietly without turning around.

Summerhill wrung his hands together. "I think maybe you're the one who's supposed to help me find home. Or something."

Katherine let out a one-note laugh and shook her head in self-reproach. "I don't know the first thing about your people or where you come from. To say nothing of how to get there."

"No, but you know way more about this sort of thing than I do," Summerhill pointed out. "Things like reality jumps and interdimensional law enforcement and—heck, you know how to shoot a gun."

Silence hung between them. Katherine took out her stun pistol, looked at it for a few seconds, and holstered it again. "Look," she said finally. "Let's figure out what's happening on the ship with the Consortium first. I've got my own problems that I kind of can't ignore right now."

Summerhill swallowed and nodded. "That's fair." He tried to brace himself for the reality that, in a matter of minutes, he might be out on his own again. "You lead, I'll follow."

As they got farther from the aft section of the ship, the sounds of machinery grew quieter, allowing Summerhill to make out other noises. Sometimes, he heard heavy footsteps on the deck above them. At least once he heard the unsettling rhythm of a small group of four-legged security robots pass by, heading in the opposite direction. He wondered if Katherine's human ears let her hear the same things he did, but she was very visibly not in the mood for needless chatter.

What she did notice, not long after, was the hustle and bustle coming from beyond the next set of doors. She held up one hand to motion for Summerhill to stop, and she held her breath, listening intently for a few seconds. "This is the galley beyond here," she explained. "I'm not afraid of cooks trying to jump me, but I want to make sure nothing weird is going on, first."

Summerhill nodded, and stayed crouched behind Katherine just in case, his ears perked to listen for anything suspicious. Most of what he heard was the frenzied clattering of pots and pans, the clamor of kitchen staff milling about, shouting orders and acknowledgments. The *Nusquam* was host to the ultimate party, and so it made sense for the kitchen to be as crazy as the rest of the ship. Still, it sounded like a busy kitchen should, not like the cooks and bussers were under duress from a team of interdimensional agents armed with energy weapons.

Katherine apparently came to the same conclusion. "Let's go," she said, walking up to the doors. "Act casual. If anyone asks, you're with me." She adjusted the hem of her blouse to make sure her gun remained out of view, then pushed her way into the galley.

Countless rows of cooking and prep stations cut long parallel lines through the enormous galley. Summerhill tried to take in all he could as he fell in step behind Katherine, wondering how any one kitchen could prepare food for so many people of so many different species. There had to be some trick to it; the diversity among the cooks was no less impressive than the diversity of guests in the ballroom upstairs. Also, there were what looked to be specialized side-galleys branching off from the main one, though Summerhill never got close enough to see what was going on in any of them.

The way Katherine slipped through the overcrowded kitchen was akin to some migratory animal that somehow innately knew how to get to where it was going. Of course, she knew where she was going, but *how* she was doing it was something Summerhill had a hard time figuring out. He kept bumping into galley staff and tripping over people's feet or pseudopods or whatnot, while Katherine moved completely unfettered. Perhaps there was some mystical art that hostesses picked up somewhere along the way, or maybe the staff all knew who she was and knew to stay out of her way; in any event, Summerhill was stuck mumbling hurried apologies and awkwardly sticking his arms out to wedge his way between packed rows of people while Katherine drifted farther away.

Summerhill's nose was overwhelmed by the myriad dishes being cooked. With each step, new scents entered his nose, and his sense of smell alone made him even dizzier than the constant darting back and forth he needed to do in order to keep up with Katherine. Luckily, the black of her hostess' uniform made her stand out from the galley chefs all decked in white, but the small sea of people wasn't easy to navigate, and if Summerhill lost sight of her entirely, he might not easily find her again.

Thankfully, despite her hurried sense of purpose, Katherine finally came to a stop when she reached a branching corridor that led into one of the side-galleys. Only then did she turn to make sure that Summerhill was still with her. She did seem relieved, however belatedly, that she hadn't lost him.

"Through here, there's a stairway that'll take us up," she explained. "If we can make it up to one of the guest decks, I can check one of the computer terminals for any active security alerts."

Summerhill scratched his chin. "Haven't you still got your electronic clipboard and your earpiece?"

"Yes, but as soon as I tap into the shipboard network with either of those, they'll know exactly where I am. And if they are out to get me, then I'm pretty well buggered, aren't I?"

"Ah." Summerhill was glad that Katherine knew as much as she did about what to do in this sort of situation. Even with all of his inexplicable knowledge from a lifetime before he could remember, he wasn't equipped to deal with things like this. "So all we need to do is get through here, make it upstairs, and find a computer terminal?" And then find out whether Katherine was going to ditch him or not.

Katherine set one hand against the swinging door. "All while making sure we don't get spotted by Security," she confirmed. "The likelihood of which depends entirely on how much trouble I'm already in."

She pushed the door open, started to step in through it, then stopped with a quick gasp before jerking back and slipping back around the corner. Summerhill tried to sneak a peek in through the door as it swung closed, but he didn't see anything special. "What's wrong?" he asked. "Security?"

Katherine's face was almost white, and she had a distant, hollow look in her eyes. "No," she said, her voice dry. "*I'm* in there."

Summerhill stared back and forth between Katherine and the now shut door. "Well that doesn't make any sense," he said, but even so, he was feeling nervous on account of her being so plainly aghast. "How can you possibly be out here and in there at the same time?"

How could he have met himself back in the World of the Pale Gray Sky?

"I know what I saw, Summerhill," Katherine said. She'd regained a modicum of composure, and was now looking back at the door again. For several moments longer she stayed still, though her eyes flicked and twitched in thought and concentration. "I actually think I might know what this is all about."

She cautiously edged the door open again, enough for both her and Summerhill to peek an eye into the galley area beyond without exposing themselves to view. At first, Summerhill didn't see anything, but sure enough, not long after, an exact double of Katherine walked by.

"My shift is winding down in ten," she said in Katherine's voice. "I don't suppose there's anything else being sent up to the grand ballroom?"

An arm draped with red and blue feathers waved into view and then disappeared. "Not from here," a cawing, vaguely male voice replied. "I won't tell anyone if you want to ditch early." He ended with a brief cackle of a laugh.

Next to Summerhill, Katherine brought her hand up to her mouth, muffling her quick gasp. "I was right, Mr. Summerhill," she whispered. "This is last night, before I came to visit you in the brig."

The fur along the back of Summerhill's neck stood on end, and for an instant, his mind was overcome by the array of possibilities unlocked by having come back in time several hours. This was quickly supplanted by the more immediate questions and problems that arose from them being here now. "So what does this do to our plan?" he asked.

Katherine shushed up and leaned her ear closer to the door. The other her—the past her—was talking again. "Is that the meal for the prisoner?"

"Yup, yup," squawked the birdlike voice. "Chief sent down some dietary guidelines. Showed me a picture, included some bio readings. Figured this'll be the sort of thing he'd eat."

Summerhill wondered how the Security Chief had gotten dietary specifications for what he would and wouldn't eat. Did the *Nusquam*'s database have information on his species after all? Or had they simply made an educated guess? Presumably Katherine didn't know one way or the other, but maybe, after they found this computer terminal—

"I can take that up for you, if you want," the past-Katherine said.

"Security said they'll send someone to make the delivery," the chef replied. "Don't worry."

"It's on my way up anyway," past-Katherine said. "Tell Security I'll handle it."

Present-Katherine, meanwhile, looked uncomfortable, but she kept the door open, and kept her eye on the galley beyond. Summerhill watched her for a while, letting one ear pick up the conversation from beyond the door.

The chef sounded hesitant and concerned. "He's a prisoner. Why not just let Security handle it?"

"Because," past-Katherine said, "I'm not sure that he'll eat something that a security officer brings him, but I think I can get him to trust me."

Summerhill tried to catch the present Katherine's eye, but she avoided his gaze.

"Trust you?" The birdlike chef cawed and chuckled again. "What's that got to do with anything?"

"Because I don't trust *him*," the past-Katherine insisted. "I think he might be dangerous, even. But if I can get him to open up to me, maybe... I don't know, maybe we can figure out what he is and what he's doing here."

Summerhill folded his ears back as present-Katherine bit her lip hard. "You think I'm dangerous?" he asked.

"That was before. Back then, I didn't know you were—"

"And so all that stuff about telling me I could confide in you? What was that all about, huh?"

Katherine made eye contact with him again. "I wasn't sure I could trust you back then," she said, clenching one hand up into a small fist. "But like I said, that was—"

"Hey, you're the admitted thief who's on the run from the space police. If anyone should have trust issues here, I think it's me."

"Look, can we please argue about this later? We've got to—"

"Is someone there?" the other Katherine called out from the galley.

Present-Katherine quickly grabbed Summerhill around the muzzle, wrapped her other arm around his chest, and pulled him away from the door. The dog squirmed and kicked on reflex for a moment, but settled down as the hostess pulled him back up against the wall with her.

Dangerous. Get him to open up to me. Figure out what he is. And now she might just abandon him after everything else. But then, she was a criminal on the run from the law. Why should any of this surprise him all of a sudden?

She held onto him for a little while longer, until the moment had passed with no further attention from within the galley. "Okay," she told him, her mouth close to one of his big ears. "Now, if I remember things correctly, the chef tells me that the stew isn't going to be done for a few more minutes, so I head back out into the main galley, do one last check of things, and then come back and grab the food. We just have to make sure we don't run into, uh, me, and then we can cut through to the stairwell as originally planned."

Summerhill nodded, and then to his surprise once more found Katherine's hand coming in around his muzzle to hold it shut. He whimpered briefly until she whispered for him to shush again, and she kept her arms around him as she leaned flat back against the wall. Close to a minute later, the door behind them swung open, and out walked the past-Katherine, striding into the main galley, eyes fixed forward the whole time.

Katherine held Summerhill for another solid ten-count, then released him. "Okay, here's the plan: I'll head in there and distract the chef. You stay down and try to crawl on through to the other side, and whatever you do, don't let him see you."

"Got it," Summerhill said, cracking his knuckles in an attempt to look serious. If Katherine was impressed at all, she didn't show it.

After pushing the door open with one hand, Katherine motioned for Summerhill to get down on all fours before she entered the side-galley ahead of him. She approached the counter and set both her hands on it, leaning forward to address the chef.

Summerhill quickly crawled forward as the chef asked Katherine what she was doing back so soon. Katherine prevaricated with some follow-up questions about the food delivery and what the chef had heard about the prisoner, what sort of food preparation details had been sent down by Security, and so forth. It would be enough to distract the chef for a little while, but if anyone else happened to swing by while Summerhill was trying to crawl along the galley floor, there wasn't any good excuse for him to fall back on.

Stealing a look around the corner of the center prep station, Summerhill saw that, contrary to the avian creature like he'd been expecting, the chef was actually some type of feathered lizard, brilliantly colored in bold reds, blues, and golds. His attention was on Katherine, with no sign that he was suspicious of anything. The lack of any obvious ears hopefully meant that he'd have a harder time hearing the dog scampering on his knees and elbows across the kitchen floor. The door to the stairwell that Katherine had mentioned was only a couple yards away.

The smell of the hot stew made Summerhill's stomach growl, but he wasn't afraid of anyone actually hearing that. Mainly, it was just a painful reminder that he hadn't gotten to finish it during the escape attempt after the sprinklers had—

The note! Summerhill had left himself a note telling himself to run, and he'd hidden it under the bowl of stew. This had to have been when he'd done it, right here and now. But how was he supposed to do that with Katherine barely keeping the chef distracted? She was only buying him enough time to make it from one end of the galley to the other, not to rummage around the kitchen trying to find writing utensils.

But this had to have been the time that he'd done it, and clearly, somehow, he'd succeeded, since he'd gotten the note to himself successfully the first time. How? He didn't have anything to write with. But surely the galley staff had need to write things down. There had to be a pen and some paper in the kitchen somewhere, regardless of whatever advanced technology was prevalent.

Summerhill looked around from his low vantage. There were plenty of drawers and storage cabinets all around the small galley, but looking through any of them would make noise, and he couldn't afford to do that—not without a better distraction, at any rate. Even finding the right drawer was a shot in the dark, but he reminded himself that, hey, apparently he'd succeeded at this once before. Maybe if he just went with his gut, it'd all turn out fine.

That still left the need for a convenient, untraceable distraction. What could he do from down on the floor behind the prep station? Something that wasn't obvious, something that wouldn't make the chef look right at him, something that—

Aha! In one of the bowls atop the prep bench was a heavy pile of some kind of alien root vegetable, something that had been used in the stew. These hadn't been cooked, and were still fresh and alive. Summerhill reached out with his mind, found and isolated one of the vegetables, and willed it to grow.

He felt the root take on a longer shape, growing quickly but silently. It rode up the edge of the bowl, higher and higher until it became top-heavy enough to make the bowl spill onto the floor on the opposite side of the prep bench. Summerhill heard the chef call out in a squawk of alarm. Hopping up onto his knees, the dog pulled one of the drawers open, his head briefly popping up above the prep bench so that he could look inside.

The reptilian chef had hopped back and was scurrying about trying to pick over the spilled vegetables. Katherine, however, was looking right at Summerhill, shooting him a sharp look that told him that she knew exactly what he'd just done.

We can argue about it later, Summerhill thought to himself in Katherine's own words, and he quickly sifted through the contents of the drawer. Sure enough, tucked neatly to one side were a small pad of paper and a few pens. He grabbed one of the pens, tore a sheet of paper from the top of the pad, and jotted down the words: *"Get ready to make a run for it."*

He'd gotten the note written, but there was no way he was going to be able to get around the other side of the prep station and slip the note underneath the bowl of stew. Trying to magically knock another bowl over would make the chef suspicious, too, and might get Katherine in trouble at the same time.

Well, that just meant that Katherine had a vested interest in not getting caught, either. Summerhill slapped the piece of paper onto the counter, looked at Katherine, and did his best to mime putting the note underneath the bowl with his hand-like paws before he ducked out of view of both her and the chef.

He wasted no time in scurrying for the exit on all fours. Hopefully, Katherine would take the hint. "Here, let me help you with that," he heard her say to the chef, her voice helping to cover the sound of the back door opening .

Summerhill was still getting back to his feet when Katherine came through the door a few seconds later. "What the hell was *that* about, mate?" she asked, motioning with her hand for him to keep walking down the short hall, toward the next door.

"What did you do with the note?" Summerhill asked, taking point. The next door opened directly into the stairway.

"I slipped it underneath the bowl like I think you told me to. Now would you mind telling me why you just risked both our asses by causing a scene like that?"

The stairwell was quiet, but Summerhill still kept his voice down. "When you brought me that stew earlier—well, earlier for us—I found a note from myself, to myself."

Katherine stopped and leaned against the guardrail. "Why is nothing ever simple with you?"

"Hey, you're one to talk. Besides, things are very simple with me; you just keep telling me that they can't possibly be true." Summerhill kept climbing upwards, trusting that Katherine would say when they'd reached the right deck. "But anyway, this brings up three very important things."

"Oh? And what might those be?"

Summerhill held up his fingers as he counted. "First, if you haven't brought me my dinner yet, that means the Consortium hasn't gotten here yet. Second, if the Consortium isn't here yet, then that means Security isn't looking for you yet, either." He smiled as he got to his last point. "Third, if Security isn't on to you yet, then that means maybe you can make your case to the Chief and explain yourself before the Consortium gets here."

It took Katherine a few moments to take that all in, but Summerhill could see her going over the ramifications in her head. She tapped her fingers together and she muttered under her breath, her voice too quiet for Summerhill to hear. "That doesn't leave us a lot of time," she said, having apparently done the mental math. "And there's no guarantee the Consortium wasn't here ahead of time. Still, I suppose it's worth a shot."

"I'll go with you," Summerhill said, stepping out of the way to let Katherine go on ahead and lead the way. "You know, in case you need a character witness or something."

Katherine chuckled. "I'm sure the word of an eccentric stowaway will carry a lot of weight," she said, but Summerhill could tell that she was merely teasing him, her voice lacking the faint nasal edge it had when she was really being snide.

"Fine. Maybe you can be the one vouching for me, instead," Summerhill offered. "I'm not exactly supposed to be out of my cell, myself."

As soon as he said that, Summerhill came to a stop in the middle of the stairwell. Katherine made it up to the next landing before she noticed, whereupon she turned to look back at him. "What's wrong?"

Summerhill looked back at her, his brain spinning in a dizzy panic. "It's about how I got out of my cell in the first place," he said. "Right before the Consortium agents came chasing after you, the power to the brig shorted out—that's how I was able to escape and come after you."

"I remember the lights going out," Katherine said. "I guess I just assumed that was some side-effect of the Consortium reality-jumping onto the ship."

"So you didn't see them do anything to override the power systems or anything?"

Katherine shook her head. "I just saw them round the corner before they started to come after me."

Summerhill paced back and forth on the narrow step. He reached up and tugged at one of his ears while his other hand clenched and relaxed repeatedly. "Okay, how soon from 'now' do you come and bring me my dinner?"

"I'm not exactly sure. In around ten to fifteen minutes, I think? That's just me going by memory."

"All right. That still gives me some time." The dog stopped his pacing. "How does the ship's power system work?"

Katherine raised an eyebrow. "I'm not an engineer; I'm just a hostess."

"Right, but you seem to know a lot about how the technology aboard the ship works," Summerhill pointed out. "Where would someone go if they wanted to shut down power to the brig?"

"I don't know. There are probably power distribution nodes all over the ship, but I haven't the faintest idea where they'd be." The hostess looked at him with confused impatience. "Mr. Summerhill, what does this even have to do with anything?"

Summerhill went back to fidgeting, his feet padding in a tight, constant circle. "All right, so," he said, thinking aloud, "if the power is being redistributed, where does it all come from?"

"Well, the main power generators are located aft, with the reality jump drive, but—"

"How would I get there?"

"Please, we have to get to the Chief and figure out whether he's already been in touch with the Consortium or not," Katherine insisted, brushing off the interruption. "We can figure out the specifics of how they shut down the power later."

Summerhill shook his head. "I don't think it was them. I think it was us." Planting one hand on the guardrail, he hopped down onto the stairway landing below. "And if I'm right, we might only have ten minutes."

Katherine leaned over the railing and shouted down at him. "Mr. Summerhill, we don't have time for this!"

For a brief instant, Summerhill felt like he could see the exact way that time had looped back on itself, bringing him and Katherine back to this point before their own escape.

"You're right," he called back to her. "You head on to the Chief's office. We'll make this work."

As Summerhill opened the door to the hallway one deck below, he heard Katherine's voice booming through the stairwell. "Wait! I'm not sure this is such—"

The door slammed shut behind him, and Summerhill broke into a run. This was going to work, he told himself, because it had already worked once before. It was just like with the note and the bowl of stew—the fact that he was here now was evidence that he'd already succeeded.

It didn't matter if he didn't know how just yet. Somehow, he'd find the right power conduit or circuit breaker or whatever. He was filled with elation for having figured this out, and he found himself grinning like an idiot as he ran through the ship as fast as he could, arms swinging, tail lashing back and forth. His heart raced for reasons beyond mere physical exertion.

He skidded and turned and changed direction at L-shaped intersections, always opting to take the first turn that would point him back in the right direction. Katherine had told him 'aft,' and so that's where he did his best to head. Doors and branching corridors whipped by as he ran along, but if time really was of the essence, then he had to just barrel on ahead in a straight line wherever he could. He'd reach the aft section eventually. Then it was just the simple matter of finding his way to the power generators and figuring out how to cut power to one very specific area of the ship, all while avoiding security robots, ship staff, and possibly the Consortium.

None of that was anywhere near as impossible as walking between realities or traveling back in time. Hell, considering the things he and Katherine had done together already, this would barely be a footnote in their—

Summerhill didn't have time to react as someone came walking around the corner, right into his path. The dog collided at full speed, yelping as he lost balance. He heard the other's cry of alarm, along with the thump of a body hitting the floor just before his own feet slipped out from underneath him and he pitched over as well.

"Sorry," Summerhill babbled quickly. "Really, really sorry. I'm just kind of in a hurry because of some life-or-death plan to..."

His words trailed off as he picked himself up and saw the other form sprawled out on the floor next to him. There, flat on his back on the soft carpeting, looking dazed but otherwise unhurt, was the tuxedoed otter from the ballroom.

The otter from inside the pocket watch.

The otter who was so achingly and agonizingly familiar.

"Well," the short little otter said with a chuckle as he pushed himself up into a sitting position. "That makes twice in one day. I hope this isn't some weird new trend we're setting."

Summerhill swallowed a few times, working up enough saliva inside of his mouth to be able to speak. "You," he said, pointing with a single shaky finger at the otter. "I know you."

"Yes. We bumped into each other earlier, too. Though not quite this spectacularly." The otter grunted softly as he braced a webbed paw on the wall and got to his feet. "I promise you, though, if you want me to notice you, you don't need to hit any harder than that." He let out a partial giggle through his lopsided smile as he rubbed his backside.

Something about that smile made Summerhill's heart melt. He struggled to suppress a momentary flash of giddiness as he took a step closer to the otter. "No, I remember that. I just..." He tried to think of better words, more eloquent words, but none came to him. "Look, this might sound weird, but did we used to know each other, you and I?"

"You mean other than my nearly spilling your drink on you earlier?"

"Yeah. Before that." Summerhill wrung his hands together. "And I apologize if that's a stupid question, but I... I'm not sure I fully remember who I am." He stared into the otter's eyes. "But you—I feel like I know you."

The otter smoothed out his tux, then smiled again. "It's nice to think I could leave that sort of lasting impression on someone. But no, I don't think we know each other." A glimmer appeared in one of his eyes. "Well, not yet, at any rate. My name's Tekutan." He held out one of his webbed paws for the shaking.

"It's wonderful to meet you, Tekutan." Summerhill took the offered paw and shook it, and his already racing pulse started to pound even harder and faster. "My name's Summerhill."

"My friends call me Tek." The otter took his paw away, and for a moment, Summerhill was reluctant to let go. "Anyhow, I was going to head back to the ballroom, but it sounds like you had someplace else to be." He intoned his words almost like a question and nodded down the hallway leading aft.

But now that he was here with this otter, Summerhill could scarcely remember what he'd been in such a rush to do. "Oh, it wasn't that important," he said, scooting closer still to Tek.

Tek smiled and let out an awkward laugh. "I believe you said something about it being life-or-death?"

"An exaggeration." Now Summerhill was practically standing on the otter's toes, and he reached down to take both of those little webbed paws in his own hands. "I can definitely make the time for someone like you." *Time.* What *had* he been on his way to do?

There was some visible embarrassment on Tek's face, and the otter shifted and squirmed a little, but he didn't pull away. "I don't want to keep you," he said.

"And what if I want you to keep me?" Summerhill dipped his muzzle closer to the otter's face and took a deep breath in through his nose. The insides of his nostrils tingled at the pleasant scent.

Now Tek's pulse was running almost as fast as Summerhill's, the dog could tell. "Well, if you want to come to the ballroom with me..."

"I was thinking someplace less public." Summerhill closed his eyes and bent down to give Tek a kiss on the cheek.

Memories that felt so distant flitted into mind. The ship. The hostess and thief. What about them? What about any of it?

"I..." Tek swallowed and squeaked. "Well, I mean, my cabin's right back down the hall, here, but—"

Summerhill started walking, clasping one of Tek's paws firmly in his own hand as he pulled the otter along. "Your cabin sounds just fine," he said with a wink.

Tek's hesitation wavered and wavered until it disappeared completely. "I guess that works," he said, his attempts to hold in his excitement quite transparent. He worked his short legs faster until he was the one leading Summerhill.

Summerhill's own steps were filled with a jaunty exuberance such as the dog had never felt before. As he followed Tek down the hallway, his vision narrowed, making the walls and floor and ceiling disappear outside of his vision until the otter was the sum total of his world.

TWELVE
INCENSING

The door to Tekutan's cabin slid open silently at the simple touch of a finger. Summerhill had part of a moment where he made the assumption that a vessel with the *Nusquam's* level of technology probably had advanced biometric sensors and the like. The rest of that moment, however, was given over to the more immediate concern of the following the otter inside.

Given his time spent wallowing in the brig, gallivanting through service passageways, and crawling through the crowded galley, Summerhill had forgotten, on some level, that the *Nusquam* was a luxury liner. The inside of Tek's cabin recalled all the charm, wealth, and splendor of the grand ballroom, with animated sculptures, interactive three-dimensional vidscreens, a polished minibar, and—very importantly—a large, lavish bed.

As far as Summerhill was concerned, this room contained everything he could possibly need. He'd found this mysterious little otter, the one that had left such an unusual hole in his heart, and now they were together (together again?), and they could patch together whatever was missing.

"So, who is this fellow I remind you of?" Tek asked, grinning up at Summerhill as the cabin door slid shut, sealing the two of them off in their own world.

"Just you. You remind me of you." Summerhill's words were barely more audible than a mutter. His hands caressed Tek's sides, the fabric of the neatly pressed tuxedo nowhere near as nice as the otter's fur would be. That would come in due time, though.

Tek reached up and set a webbed paw on Summerhill's chest. "Ever been to Rydale before, then?" he asked with a bright and curious smile.

Rydale. The name flashed through Summerhill's mind, almost taking root as something familiar before getting pulled into the emptiness that was his memory from before the World of the Pale Gray Sky. "Don't think so. Is everyone there as cute as you?"

The insides of the otter's ears went bright red. "Wow, you don't waste any time with your flattery, do you?"

"Why waste time?" Summerhill asked before cupping Tek's cheek in his palm. Time, of no consequence now, not ticking by with each second, but whirling around meaninglessly like the nonsensical arms of a broken pocket watch. He steered the otter's hesitant gaze back to meet his own before leaning forward to kiss him square on the lips.

The instant their lips touched, Summerhill felt as well as saw a brilliant burst of color behind his eyes. His head swam and spun, and he let out a throaty whimper as he heard words echo inside his head.

"Would you tell me?"

"It's kind of a long story."

Then, his own words: *"Why waste time?"* They urged him to deepen that simple kiss into something more, his lips and tongue tingling and twitching, as if being burned and simultaneously cooled by some freezing flame.

If Tek was still feeling shy, he didn't show it. The way he kissed back was soft and delicate, like he was relishing something new. Summerhill was torn between matching that innocent, careful pace and giving in to his urges to turn the kiss more fierce and passionate. In a compromise, he kept the kiss soft for the time being while also allowing his hands to grope and knead more intimately at the otter's hips and flanks.

Bit by bit, Summerhill nudged and pushed Tek back towards the bed, and bit by bit, Tek acceded. The otter kicked off his dress shoes as he backpedaled, losing even more height to Summerhill as the dog pressed in more heavily against him. Now it was Tek's turn to let out some impassioned whimpers, and the sound of those simple noises was like music to Summerhill's ears, so much so that the dog could hear an actual tune forming in the back of his mind.

Tek's legs bumped up against the edge of the bed. The otter broke the kiss with a wet gasp and looked dumbly up at Summerhill. "I, uh, I'm r-really not completely sure I'm ready for this," he stammered, "but, I mean, I guess..." Prevaricating wasn't his strong suit; Summerhill could see and smell just how much he wanted it.

The cabin now spun with a rainbow of colors. Perhaps, at some point in the shuffling trip across the room, Tek had turned on some mood lighting or whatnot, but Summerhill couldn't recall when the otter would have had the time to speak any commands or push any buttons. For now, he was too caught up in that swirl of colors to care, especially in how they reflected off of Tek's eyes, and the way they appeared to spin and whirl from *within* those eyes, impossibly. Summerhill brushed his thumb over one of the otter's stubby ears and smiled. Here they were, together at last, and everything was okay. "I want to if you want to," he said. "And I know you want to."

Tek's soft laugh was again accompanied by a tinkling scale of notes. "Well, you *are* the sort of fellow I'd like to get to know better," he said, his voice adding to the music wafting through the air. "I guess this counts as getting to know someone."

"I want to know you, too," Summerhill said, and once more he pressed his muzzle to the otter's. His eyes screwed shut, and instead of blackness he saw explosions of color like fireworks as he and Tek kissed, soft warm tongues pressed together, fingers and paws groping and searching.

All it took was Summerhill leaning his weight forward some more, and Tek fell backward onto the bed, his knees buckling at last. Summerhill fell with him, landing atop the otter, grunting into his muzzle as he made sure not to let their kiss break. Yes, now they were here, together, at long last, for the first time since—since whenever it had been.

Maybe their future was behind them and their past was ahead of them. Time didn't matter anymore. Summerhill knew indisputably that he wanted to know Tek, that this was without a doubt the one who'd been missing from his life, that this was the key to what had been bothering him for so long. They could be together now, the two of them, like they were meant to be.

THIRTEEN

APHROLUCINOGEN

The bed was gone. So were the moving sculptures, the vidscreens, the minibar, and the rest of the cabin. There was only Summerhill and Tek. One moment, there was an icy chill and a sensation of all-consuming cold, and in the next, there was an equally overwhelming surge of warmth and contentment.

Then that passed, as well, and Summerhill felt the open air on his fur. Tek was still beneath him, the dog and otter still holding that passionate kiss, but beneath Tek, Summerhill could feel grass, dirt, stones and flowers. The scent of nature flooded the dog's nose, enough that it made him break the kiss and throw his head back with a deep, sharp gasp of delightful fresh air.

His eyes opened, and the scene before him was just as invigorating as the feeling of the warm body beneath him. He and Tek were in a field of flowers that stretched out as far as the eye could see. The flowers themselves comprised a mind-boggling spectrum of colors, like an insane rainbow where the colors were the pure indigo of passion, the shimmering crimson of delicious hatred and the blinding white of an exploding star destroying everything in its path. Each of those beautiful and heart-rending colors rippled and whirled and changed within the petals of each individual flower. The sight of it held Summerhill entranced, and when he tried to reach out with his mind to touch those ever-changing flowers, the sense of vibrant life and unblemished purity burned through his very being, making it hard to see, to hear, to breathe or to think.

Up above was the open sky, strewn with wispy clouds that pulsated and changed shape, their shadows glowing with an array of colors, just like the meadow far below. The wind

111

picked up, ruffling the fur on the back of Summerhill's neck, between his ears and atop his head. The dog enjoyed the chill that traveled up his spine, and then he looked down at Tek with a big smile.

The otter wasn't wearing his tuxedo anymore. Somehow, his attire had been reduced to a simple black shirt and a pair of iridescent blue shorts—a far cry from the immaculate formal wear that had been de rigueur aboard the *Nusquam*.

Wherever Tek's new clothes had come from, Summerhill made sure the otter didn't have them on for much longer. Soon enough, his own clothes were out of the way, too, and it was just the two of them, down to nothing but the fur, their bodies pressed together, pressed against the grass and the flowers, twisting this way and that.

Summerhill couldn't bring himself to stop kissing Tek. He kissed him on the lips, on the side of the mouth, at the hollow of his throat. He licked and lapped at the otter's fur, dragging his tongue over that whiskery snout, those bushy cheeks, his warm neck and sleek chest. With each soft kiss, each firm press of his lips, each swipe of his tongue, Summerhill felt a surge of life and color explode inside his mind, accompanied by the ever-increasing grip that adrenaline had on his entire body. He surrendered to it, and Tek's musical cries begged him not to stop.

Somewhere in the middle of their ardent lovemaking, Summerhill and Tek managed to lock eyes again. The otter's irises swirled with all the same colors as the sky, all the same colors as the wildflowers, whirling around inside his beautiful eyes. It was an effect that would have been hypnotic if Summerhill weren't already fully mesmerized by the otter. He knew that he was fully under his lover's control, and he was happy to be so.

It was the sweet and reassuring fragrance of wildflowers that overpowered Summerhill's sense of smell as he allowed himself to be subsumed in a rush of ecstasy unlike any he'd ever felt. The dancing colors on the backs of his eyelids grew fainter and blurred together more hazily as his pulse slowed down, his breathing grew raspy, and his body grew tired. He felt Tek's furry arms slipping around his body as he stopped trying to fight the exhaustion that was claiming him, and it was the rhythmic pattering of the otter's contented heartbeat that kept Summerhill lulled into complacency as he drifted off.

FOURTEEN

AFTERGLOW

The smell of wildflowers was also the first thing that Summerhill became aware of as he woke up. His eyes were still closed and his body was still overcome with a sense of tiredness, but with each slow breath, he was treated to the scent of fresh flowers, sweet and reassuring. It was almost enough to make him fall right back asleep.

Instead, he woke fully with a jolt as he shot upright. His eyes flew open, then immediately snapped shut again as he got an eyeful of bright sunlight that he was unprepared for. With a hiss of discomfort, he brought a hand up to shield his eyes, and then groaned as he once more tried to figure out where he was.

The meadow of flowers was familiar. No longer did the landscape swirl with colors. The flowers themselves were still a bright assortment of purples, yellows, red and blues, but their colors stayed constant. Likewise, the sky was a steady light purple, and the clouds that drifted by did not glow or pulsate.

Summerhill's head throbbed. His fur felt matted and unkempt. He realized that he was naked, and when he looked down at the wide patch of flattened grass and crushed flowers that he was sitting in, he remembered Tek and what had transpired before.

Well, he remembered the gist of it, the fervent passion and the fact that they'd been together. The details were awash with a haze of hallucinatory memories and the emotional aftermath of what he'd felt, stamped somewhere in the back of his mind like photographic negatives that might be turned into real images with the right techniques and processes. He still felt a mild echo of happiness, but that joy was mixed with more than a little bit of apprehension and worry.

114

Then, as the fog of sleep finished lifting from his mind, Summerhill remembered where he'd been before all this had happened.

What had ever possessed him to follow the otter back to his cabin? He clutched his head and groaned as his headache flared up, and he fought to make sense of where he was and why. Katherine was still back there, on the ship with the Consortium and—

"Summerhill? Are you okay?"

The dog turned his head, despite the ensuing dizziness, and looked back to see Tek several yards behind him. The otter was just standing there, clad in the black shirt and blue shorts that had replaced his tuxedo. He looked afraid to approach closer.

"I'm fine," Summerhill responded. "I think." Seeing the otter again was stirring up some of the residual romantic feelings from before, but the severity of the current situation enabled him to keep them suppressed to some degree.

Tek came a few steps closer. "You're awake now, at least," he said, his muzzle splitting into one of his crooked smiles as he let out a halfhearted laugh. "I almost wasn't sure if you were going to wake up."

Summerhill wanted to scoot a little farther away, but he stayed put. He did feel silly, sitting there buck naked, but the way he was huddled up at least kept him mostly modest. "I didn't mean to worry you," he said, and he at least meant that much. "Are you okay? Where did you go?"

The otter gestured behind himself. "Since you were still fast asleep, I thought I'd scout around a bit and see if I could figure out where we are, exactly." He laughed again, and this time it was less forced. "I'm still not even sure how we got here."

There went Summerhill's hope that Tek might have a better idea of what was going on. "Did you find anything out?" the dog asked. Out of the corner of his eye, a few feet away from him, he finally noticed his own clothes, folded in a neat pile.

"Well," Tek said, looking skyward, "we're definitely on Rydale. Someplace pretty unpopulated, too, from the look of it. I went up over the next hill and still couldn't see any towns or cities nearby."

Rydale. "This is your home planet?" Summerhill asked.

"Yeah." Tek took a deep breath and gazed around the open meadow. "Isn't it beautiful?"

It was certainly that, Summerhill had to admit. He reached out to all the flowers surrounding him, and now that his mind wasn't in the grip of—well, whatever had been affecting him earlier, he didn't experience any sensory overload this time. The vivacity of the life force here was pretty amazing, though, and drawing on just a small amount of that was enough for Summerhill to force away his headache.

"So, how did we get from the ship to here?" Summerhill asked.

"Like I said, I'm not sure." Tek reached up and rubbed at one of his ears. "One minute, we were in my cabin, and then you fell on top of me, and then... well, then we were here."

Summerhill crawled over to the small pile of clothes. This wasn't his grayish clothing from back home. Instead there were a pair of neat tan cargo shorts and simple brown leather vest, both in his size. His clothing must have changed the same way that Tek's had, and he simply hadn't noticed because—well, because he'd been distracted on multiple levels at the time.

He got dressed, noticing that Tek made no effort to turn away or avert his eyes. "So, if we're on Rydale, is there a way to get back onto the *Nusquam*?" he asked the otter, trying to sound casual about it.

Tek didn't answer right away. He looked down at his feet, his bare, webbed toes curling through the grass. "Are you in a big rush to get back?" His voice was quieter now.

Summerhill took a few steps closer to him, and as the otter's scent hit his nose, he felt pangs of sympathy for Tek's dejected state. "I didn't mean that I'd leave you here by yourself. But I

116

left a friend of mine back there, and it's really important that I find her."

"Oh. Okay." Tek chewed his lip as he looked up at Summerhill. "I'm sorry, though. I'm not sure there's much we can do."

"What do you mean?"

The otter shuffled his feet through the grass. "My civilization hasn't developed reality jump drive technology," he explained. "So unless the *Nusquam* were to come here, I'm not sure there *is* a way to get there." Folding his stubby ears back, he then asked, "Are you sure you didn't—"

Summerhill reached out and touched Tek on the cheek. "Hey," he said with a smile. "If we can't get there, we can't get there. It's not a big deal."

No. No, that was wrong. That was all wrong.

"I've still got you here," he continued. "That's all that really matters, right?"

Wait, what? This wasn't right at all. This shouldn't be his immediate concern. What about the *Nusquam* and the quest to find home and Katherine and—

What about Katherine? Bah, what *about* Katherine?

Summerhill learned in and nuzzled the crook of Tek's shoulder, eliciting a delicate moan from the otter. Webbed paws settled at the small of the canine's back. Summerhill licked at the pulse point in Tek's neck before kissing and sucking at that tender, throbbing spot, and his lips and tongue tingled as the oils in the otter's fur seeped into them.

Colors once more started to frame the edge of Summerhill's vision. They swirled and pulsed even as the dog closed his eyes, as his pulse quickened, as his breathing got ragged and his desire to be with Tek overrode any and all rational thought. No longer did he have any spare thoughts for his missing past, for his friend who was in danger, for—

Summerhill abruptly brought up both arms and planted his palms against Tek's chest. He shoved the otter away from him with all his might, breaking their tender embrace. Tek's eyes went wide with shock as he tumbled backwards and tripped, falling flat on his back in the field of flowers.

The clouds in the sky bent and twisted as Summerhill looked up while he backpedaled away from the fallen otter. His pulse pounded in his ears, forming the beginnings of a bass line for a tune his brain wanted to stitch together. "Stay there!" he called out, his voice tinkling musically as he pointed an accusing finger that left a color-shifted motion blur behind as it moved. "Stay right where you are."

It was Tek. Somehow, it was Tek—beautiful, wonderful Tek, who was still so close, and if Summerhill wanted, he could just walk back up to him, help him to his feet, tell him he was sorry and—

No, no, no, Summerhill had to focus. His breathing was still rushed and labored, and when he shut his eyes he still saw bizarre patterns playing through his vision, but he could fight it off. If he could get far enough away, let his mind dissociate from where it had been stuck, he'd be fine.

"Summerhill?" Tek squeaked. He hadn't gotten up. "Summerhill, what's the matter? Did I do something wrong?"

Summerhill risked opening his eyes and looking back at him. He looked so scared and sad and confused. Did he really not know what was happening, what he was doing? Or was this all part of the act, part of a clever deception that had lured Summerhill here to Rydale in the first place? "You're fine. Just... Just don't get up." Just for a little while longer. Just until Summerhill's mind cleared up.

The sky was reverting to its normal lavender. The extraneous colors that muddled Summerhill's vision were fading away. The flow of time was shedding its awkward lag.

"Please, Summerhill, you're acting really weird." The insecurity in Tek's voice *sounded* sincere. "Are you okay?"

"I'm fine," Summerhill insisted. "I'll be fine." He took a few more steps backward. His head was clearer, now His breathing had returned to normal. His pulse had slowed back down. His vision regained its focus. "I just need to stay away from you while I sort this all out."

Tek's eyes wavered and watered; even from several feet away, Summerhill could see it. "Stay away from me?" the otter asked. "But you said you'd stay with me forever."

Summerhill balked, his muzzle hanging open afterward. "I said no such thing."

"Maybe not in those exact words." Tek sat up and brushed his shirt off. "But you consented to essentially the same thing."

"Was this when you were doing that thing where you were controlling my brain?" Summerhill asked. "Because if it was, then that doesn't count." He was struck with the thought that this might have been the otter's plan all along.

Tek still had that wounded look on his face, though. "I'm not controlling your brain, Summerhill." His voice carried a sort of pouty insistence. "Are you sure this isn't your excuse to weasel out of a commitment?"

Summerhill rubbed the side of his head. Whether it was Tek's claim that the two of them were now permanently partnered or if it was just a result of standing far enough away, the dog's mental state had sobered up completely. He took a deep breath, hoping to calm himself down and rid himself of any snide, knee-jerk reactions. "Look, I don't have any memory of saying I'd stay with you forever."

"Well, that makes this really awkward, then."

The two of them stared back at each other, the distance between them exacerbating the cold accusation that Summerhill felt. He'd felt so sure that Tek was this piece of his old life that he'd been missing. "I'm trying to sort things out," he said, locking eyes with Tek in an attempt to look as sincere as possible. "It's been a very weird few days, and a lot of what's been happening to me hasn't been making a whole lot of sense."

Tek snorted. "I think that 'We can't do this unless you promise to stay with me' makes perfect sense."

"But I don't remember you saying that!" Summerhill hadn't meant for that response to be so loud or forceful, and so he made sure to tone himself back down. "And I don't remember my saying yes or..." His fingers clutched at the empty air in frustration. "Look, when I get close to you, it's like I can't control myself."

"Gee, thanks. That's real romantic."

Summerhill growled under his breath, but this far away, Tek probably couldn't hear it. "I... That's not what I mean. I mean I *actually* lose control of what I'm doing. I see things, hear things, get my senses mixed up." Again he looked into the otter's eyes. "You're saying you're not responsible for that?"

Wind whipped through the meadow again, carrying some flower petals aloft. "Hey, you're the one who bumped into me and started going on about how I reminded you of someone you used to know," Tek said. "I could say that you're the one who seduced me."

Except you're not the one who's getting his head scrambled, Summerhill thought to himself. "You don't mean that."

Tek sighed. "No, I don't. This is just—This is a big deal for my people, for me, and I'm not sure what to do now."

Summerhill looked off into the distance. The orange Rydale sun glowed bright in the purple sky. "Want to talk about it while we try to figure out where we are?" he offered.

"I guess that works," Tek said, and then he got to his feet, smacking clumps of dirt and grass away from his legs. "Can we at least walk together?"

"We can walk in the same direction. Until we can sort out what happens when I get close to you, though, I think we should keep our distance."

Tek didn't look at all happy about it, but he nodded all the same. "Okay," he said, and then he started walking in the direction of a nearby hill. "Let's see if we can get a better vantage point from over there."

The field was quiet except for the occasional gust of wind. Neither Summerhill nor Tek spoke for a while as they marched toward the small hill. Every so often, Summerhill would turn to look at Tek, and once in a while the otter would turn to look at him, but they remained silent.

The hill was steeper than Summerhill had guessed from a distance. The dog was still exhausted from—well, from the night before, and he had a hard time masking his tired grunts and raspy panting as he fought to make his way uphill.

"And here I thought you had more stamina than that," Tek murmured. Maybe he hadn't meant for Summerhill to hear it, but the canine's keen ears picked it up anyway.

Now that Tek had broken the silence, staying quiet was more awkward than continuing the discussion. "You don't regret what we did, do you?" Summerhill asked.

Tek came to a stop and looked back at Summerhill. "I didn't at the time, no," he said. "But I thought we both knew what we were getting into, and it looks like I was wrong about that."

Summerhill laid his ears back. "Just so I know, what were we getting into? I mean, from your perspective."

The otter blinked a few times. "You really don't remember, do you?"

"If my plan were to go back on my word, I'd like to think I'd come up with something more clever and convincing than 'I don't remember.'"

Tek was silent for a while, but he never took his eyes off Summerhill. "You're right," he said at last. "I respect you more than that." Summerhill winced, feeling the words as a barb against him. "And to be fair, it's not like I had the time or the presence of mind to fully explain the situation to you in the heat of the moment."

It was everything that Summerhill did remember that made him feel even worse about the situation he was in. He still remembered all the passion and devotion he'd felt at the time, far stronger than the strange echoes of the scattered memories that didn't make sense. "I'm listening now," he said to Tek. "If you still want to explain it to me."

"Sure." There was a heavy sigh in the otter's voice. He started to climb the hill again, leaving Summerhill with no real choice but to follow. At least their brief stop had let him catch his breath. "Just give me a minute to find the right words."

They made it to the top of the hill, finally, getting a look at the area beyond. There was still no sign of civilization, but the sight was still one that made Summerhill pause to collect himself. Wide swaths of rainbow-colored Rydale wildflowers covered the gently sloping valley down below, a soft breeze making the tall grasses ripple elegantly. Large trees dotted the open landscape, their tops flat, the expanse of their branches wider than their trunks were tall. Orange sunlight glinted off of the surface of a small creek that wound its way through a rockier section of the valley.

There were probably worse fates than having to stay here forever, Summerhill had to admit. Still, though this would make a lovely home, it wasn't *his* home. He still had to find his way out of here. He still had to find Katherine.

"Basically," Tek said, his voice pulling Summerhill out of his reverie, "you and I made a commitment to each other. A very serious commitment."

Summerhill kept his eyes on his feet as he started walking down the hill. "Because of what I said?" Try as he might, he didn't remember swearing any oaths or making any elaborate promises.

"Well, no." There was awkwardness in Tek's body language that didn't show in his voice. "It was more what we did."

"Oh." Summerhill made even more sure not to look up as he kept walking. "Did we do something special?"

Tek started walking faster. "You mean other than sleep with each other?" Out of the corner of his eye, Summerhill could see that the otter had both of his paws stuffed into his pockets. "I'd say that's pretty special."

"I'm not saying it wasn't." Summerhill's steps started to get slower as Tek's got faster, and eventually the dog came to a halt as he put all the pieces together. "Wait, you're saying that, because we slept together, we have to stay together?"

It looked like Tek almost tripped over his own feet as he stopped and turned around. "That's a strange concept to you?"

In truth, Summerhill couldn't say whether it should have been strange or not, since he wasn't sure what his own people's views on that sort of thing were. "Not necessarily strange. It just seems kind of... final."

"Look, I realize that you're an otherworlder, but this is how my people do things. And I did explain that much ahead of time."

Summerhill overtook Tek again, letting gravity help propel his steps downhill. "I don't suppose that otherworlders are excluded from these traditions of yours."

Tek took off after him. "Summerhill, come on, I'm being serious," he said. "I get that all this is unfamiliar to you, but we do have a good reason for doing things this way."

"I never said you didn't. I'm just trying to figure out what the best solution for both of us is."

"The best solution is for you to stay here with me." Tek had gotten closer now, close enough that Summerhill was just barely able to smell him over the aroma of flowers. "I know that you left your friend behind on the *Nusquam*, but there's not really a whole lot we can do about that right now."

Summerhill strode faster, trying to put more distance between them, but Tek kept up, his shorter legs allowing him to trundle downhill with less risk of stumbling. Now the scent of otter was once again full and strong in the canine's nose. It was enough to make him stop and let his companion catch up. "I'd appreciate it," he said as Tek drew up closer to him, "if you'd be willing to help me find something to do about it."

Tek looked a little nervous. "I guess we're not completely out of options," he admitted. "We could always see about petitioning to be colonists on one of our off-world colonies."

"Wait. Off-world colonies?" Summerhill asked. Part of him was struggling to even hold up this line of questioning, the rest of him just wanting to hold the otter close. "Your civilization has space travel?"

Tek nodded. "Of course. I mean, it's still not faster-than-light, but I was thinking maybe, by the time we emerged from cryo-sleep at our destination, enough time might have conceivably passed that we'd have developed it, and—"

"You want to put us into suspended animation?"

"Well, if you're that intent on finding a way to contact the *Nusquam*, probably our best bet is to jump ahead in time until we have the technology to reach a civilization that has a means of doing exactly that."

Summerhill backed away several steps, inhaling deeply of the wildflowers to clear the otter's scent out of his mind. "Tek, my friend is there *now*," he explained. "Jumping forward in time several decades doesn't really do me a whole lot of good."

Tek just laughed. "It's a ship that breaks the rules of reality and flies between different universes. You think it can't travel in time, too?"

Katherine's spiel about things that ought to be impossible came to mind, and Summerhill wondered whether he should even bother thinking that Tek's supposition might be ridiculous. "Okay, fine," he conceded. "Assuming you're right, we just... what, we settle down for a few years and hope that we get picked as a couple to help colonize some new planet?"

A proud smile crossed Tek's blunt, whiskery muzzle. "I've got some pretty good connections. We could probably pull it off."

Summerhill rubbed his fingers against the bridge of his muzzle. "So, because we slept with each other one time, we're actually an official, legal thing, now?"

Tek nodded. "With good reason. Our species typically gives birth to litters of anywhere from two to six pups at a time, and so our social contract naturally evolved to support the tradition that, if you mate with someone, you're committed to not just abandoning them."

A hard lump formed in Summerhill's throat. He looked deep into the otter's eyes, unable to mask his freshly reemerged anxiety. "Wait. Are you saying I got you pregnant?"

There was a long, long moment where Tek stared back at him, and then, without warning, the otter doubled over with raucous laughter. His giggles were like chirping barks that rang through the valley, and his thick tail pressed against the ground to keep him stable as his body shook. He waved a webbed paw in Summerhill's general direction, as if to imply reassurance as he gasped and caught his breath, his wriggly body still off balance for a few moments longer.

"Sorry," he said once he could speak again. "Sorry. I know I shouldn't laugh. That's just really funny."

Summerhill could feel the tiny hairs that lined the insides of his ears stand on end as he fought back a blush. "So then I didn't get you—"

"I'm not a girl, Summerhill. I'd have hoped you noticed that." Tek was still grinning like an idiot.

"You just said that this whole 'staying together' thing was all because of raising children!"

"I said that's where it started," the otter said. "I didn't mean to imply that tradition superseded basic biology."

"I was just on a cruise ship where balls of gas can talk and where giant insects made of wood can take bar orders. How am I suppose to know what 'basic biology' is on your planet?"

Tek smiled. "Fine, I'll grant you that."

Summerhill paced around on the grass. "Okay, so I'm male, you're male, and there's no risk of us having a family together," he said, thinking aloud. "But by sleeping together, we're still committing to each other?"

"The gesture is still effectively the same," Tek explained. "Truth be told, I kind of always assumed that I'd wind up with another guy. Winding up with an otherworlder... well, that's another story."

Now that the laughter was behind them, Summerhill took it upon himself to get them moving again. "How are you supposed to know if you even want to be with someone for the long term if you haven't ever been intimate with them?" he asked.

"There are more important things to a relationship than sex," Tek said. "But moreover, since this has been the way we've always done things, we've developed instincts that lead us to figure out who we're compatible with." He gestured with his webbed fingers as he walked and talked. "And I mean, it's not like people don't date or go through courtship rituals first."

"What about me?" Summerhill asked.

"What about you?"

"You knew me for how long before we had sex? Like, a few minutes?"

Tek lowered his head sheepishly. "Like I said, we've developed instincts, too," he murmured. "You struck me as a good fit for what I was looking for."

Summerhill sighed. As much as he liked Tek, he didn't want his whole life derailed just because of Rydale custom when he had important things to do. "And so the part about the two of us being an official couple. That's your 'in' for this colonization project that can get us off the planet?"

"Pretty much," the otter affirmed. "I don't have a very big place to live right now, but I guess it's not like you have a lot in the way of material possessions, so we should be okay until we can afford—"

"Tek, I think you're missing the fact that it might not be *safe* for me to live with you," Summerhill interrupted. "I know you're not doing it on purpose—" (He was willing to give him the benefit of the doubt, at least.) "—but that doesn't mean these problems won't still happen."

The otter was silent for a while. Summerhill couldn't really blame him for feeling bad about the situation; it was clear that he was really attracted to the mysterious canine from another world, and societal awkwardness notwithstanding, there was still a rather large wrench in the works. "You seem to be okay if you stay away from me, though," he pointed out. "Does that still seem to be part of it?"

Summerhill nodded. "Once I get close enough to you that I can smell you, I—" The obvious answer finally hit him. "That's it. It's being able to smell you that does it."

The sudden pause caused Tek to pick up on Summerhill's train of thought, too. "My scent makes me irresistible?" He laughed tepidly. "Coming from one of my own people, in ordinary circumstances, I'd take that as a really nice compliment."

"And it's not just that," Summerhill continued, his mind putting together the other pieces of the puzzle. "I also seem to hallucinate when I, er, taste you."

Now Tek's wide little eyes went even wider. "Tell me you're joking."

"I'm not sure what it is. Maybe the oils in your fur. But whatever it is, it's a very... unique sort of mind-altering experience." Summerhill ran his tongue along the back of his teeth, recalling the sensations he'd felt when kissing and licking the otter.

Tek plodded along glumly. "So you can't smell me, touch me, or kiss me." When he spelled it out in those terms, he sounded even sadder.

"Now imagine what might happen if I go into an entire city full of you guys," Summerhill said. "Probably nothing good."

They were closer to the creek now, near enough that Summerhill could clearly hear the water burbling over the gentle breeze. Tek walked up to it, taking an exaggerated circle around Summerhill as he kept his distance. He knelt down and ran his fingertips through the water. "So then I guess we really can't stay together."

"Well, look at it this way," Summerhill offered. "We're out in the middle of nowhere, right? So it's not like anyone else knows what we did."

Tek sighed and knelt closer to the water's edge. His tail lay flat and still against the grass. "I'd know," he said, almost too quiet for Summerhill to hear.

SIXTEEN
INSIGHT

Walls went up around Summerhill's mind as he struggled with the prospect that he might be trapped here on Rydale with this otter named Tekutan. The empty skyscrapers of the World of the Pale Gray Sky cast their long, unending shadows across his thoughts, instilling in him a sense of utter dread and panic. He felt his pulse race and his breath quicken, all while Tek kept still, staring blankly into the limpid water that flowed gracefully by.

Trapped. As beautiful a world as this was, as much as something about Tek healed that hard-to-define hole in Summerhill's heart, he couldn't let himself be stuck here. From within the emptiness of his memories, he could almost feel a desperate scrabbling, some vain attempt to break free from the very concept of confinement.

He tried to reach into that empty hole, into his own amnesia, but there were no secret notes to himself to guide him, no hostesses to chase after, no otter pheromones to pull him along. There was only the endless horizon of empty skyscrapers against a dull backdrop of gray, and the icy feeling of hopelessness that came with it.

Then, somewhere in there, lost amidst the terrified confusion and the memories of imprisonment, was the briefest flicker and fragment of something lost, something from the past, something from before Rydale and Katherine and the *Nusquam* and even the World of the Pale Gray Sky. This was something from *before*, something that proved that there was and had been a before at all, that there had been a Summerhill before the life he remembered.

He seized onto that moment, on that flicker and fragment, and held it still in his mind so that he could examine it in detail. What he found was a simple, tiny seed. From within that seed, Summerhill could hear the ticking of a watch and the beating of his own heart. The seed didn't exist anymore, not like this—that seed had since become him, had grown into the individual Summerhill now was.

The lost dog hadn't found a way home, but in its place he had found some minute, imperfect understanding of what he was, who he was and who he used to be. Inside that tiny kernel of self was something that, if he were crazy enough, might be of use in helping to escape imprisonment once again.

 # SEVENTEEN
APOMIXIS

Summerhill could only see Tek's face in the reflection in the water, the rippling flow of the creek masking the otter's expression. Even so, he could read the otter's body language with all the familiarity of a long-time lover, though he knew now that he hadn't been, like he'd once assumed.

"I really do like you," Tek said, pulling his fingers out of the water, letting his claws hang above the surface, dripping. "I know this is weird to you, and that we just met, but I really do feel like you'd grow to like me back." He sighed, his small ears folding back.

A small fish jumped out from the water, snatching up a low-flying insect before disappearing back under the surface. "I already like you," Summerhill assured the otter. "You know that, right?"

"You like me because you don't have the choice not to." Tek flicked his paw, shaking off the excess water from his slick fur. "It's just some fluke of otherworlder biology, not because you actually want to be with me."

Summerhill stepped closer. He thought about the seed in his memory, the one that had grown into who he was now. "That's not true." He smiled just in case the otter happened to look up, which he didn't. "I think we'd be really good together." Again, he allowed himself to be awash with those feelings of longing and adoration he'd felt for Tek back in the nevereef.

Finally, Tek did look up, his face a mix of incredulity and sadness. "Yeah. Except for the fact that you can't get near me and don't even want to be on this planet anyway."

"I think there's a way I can fix that. Do you trust me?" Summerhill asked, taking another step closer. Hints of the otter's scent tickled the inside of his nose.

132

Tek's throat tightened visibly. "If I didn't trust you, I'd never have done what I did with you."

The flowers around Summerhill's feet started to get larger and more vibrant as his mind washed over them. The otter's scent fueled the dog's dedication to his mad plan. "Stand up for me," he said. *This is for him. This is for you. This is for both of you.*

With some amount of hesitation, Tek got to his feet. He wrung his webbed paws together, then tried his best to relax, though his posture indicated plenty of nervousness. "What are you going to do to me?" he asked.

Flowers that had been wilting regained their health. Grass that had been trampled underfoot sprang back up. "Just this," Summerhill said, and he closed the gap between Tek and himself. He set his paws on the otter's shoulders, leaned forward, and kissed him atop the head, between the ears. After the oily fur tingled against his lips, Summerhill then licked between the otter's eyes, his tongue moving swiftly.

He welcomed the colors and the music, and then he reached under Tek's chin, tilted it up, and kissed the otter full and deep on the mouth, their muzzles locking as they both let out matching, passionate whimpers. The hallucinogens quickly shot into Summerhill's mind, loosening his grip on reality enough for him to do what he wanted to do next.

It took effort to push Tek away from him, but the very yearning he felt was what enabled him to break away. He took several plodding steps backward, then bit down on his own lip, hard. The sensation as he drew blood was too warped from normal to quite be pain, and instead of letting out a squeak of discomfort he let his eyes roll back exultantly. He touched the cut on his lip, held his arm out, and flicked his wrist, sending a single drop of blood down to the ground.

His mind searched the flowers, and in short order he found which one the drop of blood had landed on. The energy from inside him wrapped around that flower, singled it out, and then poured into it. With a twisted sense of concentration that would have been impossible while in a sober state of mind, he kept focus on that flower while also reaching out to the rest of the Rydale flora around him, studying it, learning it, memorizing how it felt, how it resonated, how it formed its own brand of life and beauty.

The flower grew with unnatural swiftness, and then it started to change. Summerhill watched intently, aware that Tek was also staring as the flower folded in upon itself, around that droplet of blood. It grew even larger, transformed into something resembling an orange and purple cocoon, then grew bigger still, half as tall as Tek, as tall as Tek, slightly taller than Tek.

Summerhill called to mind all that his brain and body alike had known of Tek. He pulled together those hazy memories, the impassioned lovemaking, and all the affection, devotion, and inspiration he felt about the otter. He took these thoughts, memories, and emotions and allowed them to combine and coalesce into something more tangible. When they'd been fully gathered, Summerhill then constructed a mirror inside his mind, so that he could look back at himself and direction his attentions.

He took that bundle of thoughts and emotions and separated them from himself. Envisioning his mind and soul as if they were a tree, he made those feelings and memories into a lush cluster of fruit growing out from an outlying branch. With careful thought and precise imagination, he made the fruit inviting, tantalizing and irresistible, much the same way that Tek was.

In the mirror, Summerhill watched himself reach up to pick the fruit that had been placed within reach.

Summerhill and his reflection reached out and brought their fingertips to the mirror, touching that smooth surface, feeling a sense of warmth radiating through to the other side. It was like a different person was looking back into Summerhill's eyes now, a person into whom he'd placed all his thoughts of Tek—a new individual, a seedling, a scion, a framework into which something else could grow, blossom, flourish.

With a touch of one of Summerhill's fingers, the orange and purple cocoon split open on multiple axes like a flower blossoming. Closing his eyes, he stepped into it, and then willed it to close back around him. As the cocoon sealed itself back up, Tek cried out, but Summerhill had too much occupying his mind to let himself hear the otter's words.

On the opposite side of the mirror, behind the other Summerhill, appeared a young girl. Her fur-lined ears flicked and then disappeared, and she offered a smile of sympathy and encouragement to the first Summerhill before the second turned around. The girl reached out to him, then spread her arms, pulling the dog into a reassuring hug.

And then Summerhill's mind split in half along the border marked by the mirror. Imaginary glass shattered, and the girl and other dog disappeared, leaving only darkness and an urge to scream in agony.

A rush of endorphins and hallucinogenic chemicals flooded Summerhill's brain anew, giving him a moment's respite from the pain. It was something tragic and wonderful, at once both painful and necessary, like a parent sending a grown child off into the world. The finality of it had been shocking and brutal; the split was complete, and the other part of him was gone.

The floral construct split open again, this time with violent force. Summerhill was sent tumbling to the ground. Dizziness and nausea gripped his head and his gut. His vision spun with residual colors from having kissed someone he couldn't quite recall. Unable to either see straight or think straight, he staggered backward and fell to the ground.

Falling onto the ground on the other side of the cocoon was an exact duplicate of Summerhill. He was strewn amidst the wildflowers, his eyes closed, his body covered in nothing but a familiar pattern of reddish, brownish, whitish fur. For several moments, he didn't move at all, but after several tense seconds, his chest started to rise and fall with slow, quiet breathing.

Summerhill—the first Summerhill—was panting. Exhaustion was like a miasma around him. After watching the cocoon dissolve back into ground, he lifted his head to look up at the short otter-person. "There. I think that's the solution to our problem," he huffed, though he couldn't remember, exactly, what the problem was, or who he was talking to.

The otter-person's eyes were wide with awe and disbelief. "Summerhill, I..." he said, voice drying out before he could get a whole thought out. "What did you do?"

To Summerhill's surprise and dismay, the nausea he felt wasn't going away. The hallucinogenic and aphrodisiac effects had passed, but he was still lightheaded and starting to feel sick to his stomach. "It's like... with plants," he stammered. "I split a part of myself off. Part of me that's full of..." Full of what? Now that he tried to think of it, he couldn't even remember.

"Did you just clone yourself?" The otter was staring at the naked, unresponsive Summerhill copy crumpled in the grass before him. He reached out as if to touch the unmoving dog, but wouldn't let his fingertips get closer than a few inches away. "How did you do that?"

"Plants." Summerhill's heart was pounding. He felt a painful tightness in his chest. "I control plants." Thoughts and words came only with great difficulty. "Rydale biota. Biochemistry. Shouldn't be a problem anymore." What was Rydale? This was Rydale, yes? Tiny bits of disjointed information tried their best to reassociate themselves within his mind.

The otter—Tek? Wasn't his name Tek or something like that?—looked back and forth between the two Summerhills before stepping closer to the original. "Are you okay?" The worry in the otter's voice made Summerhill feel strange, like he should have been feeling concern that he wasn't. "Do you need help?"

"No, no." Summerhill scrambled to his feet and backed away, vaguely aware that being close enough to smell the otter was a bad thing. "I—He—The other me," he said, waving towards the unconscious copy of himself. "That's for you. For me. For us."

He fell over onto his hands and knees at the edge of the creek. He caught his reflection in the water and immediately yanked his head back to look away. His stomach churned.

The other Summerhill stirred and groaned. His tail thumped the ground, sending up blades of grass and flower petals. The plants surrounding him grew more healthy and vibrant by the second.

"Summerhill, please, tell me what's wrong!" Tek was frantic, pacing back and forth in his tiny spot, unwilling to approach either of the two dogs. "Should I run and get help? What do I—"

"No, it's okay," Summerhill blurted, and he smiled as he looked back into the otter's face. Yes, there was still something inside him that remembered, still some pieces that he hadn't pulled away. "This way I can stay with you."

Tek didn't understand, Summerhill could tell. Summerhill didn't understand, either. The otter kept looking between the two Summerhills, opening and closing his mouth as he tried and failed to form coherent questions. Eventually, he mustered up the capacity to say, "So, now you're in two places at once?"

"He's me. The part of me that gets to stay with you."

Tek wasn't crying, but tears—whether they were tears of sorrow or panic or something else—were forming in his eyes. "But what about the rest of you? What about *you* you?"

Once again, Summerhill looked at his reflection in the water, and this time forced himself not to look away. "He is me. He's me, so I can stay here. Because I can't stay here. Can't stay behind. Can't be trapped." *Trapped.* "Have to escape." Skyscrapers. Gray sky.

"Summerhill, I don't think you're in the condition to go anywhere. I think you need a doctor." Tek looked around the empty field and the open valley, as if desperate to know which direction to go. "Just wait here. I'll—"

"No!" Summerhill snarled, his lips drawn back as a low growl rumbled in his throat for a second afterwards. "I can't. I *won't*." Skyscrapers. Gray sky. Cruise ship past future Katherine time reality pocket watch.

"I promised not to abandon you," Tek said, and now he'd found some forceful conviction within himself, and hearing it made Summerhill look up as a part of himself registered, however faintly, how proud he was of the otter.

The other Summerhill lifted one hand up. It hovered above his face, and then his fingers wiggled and splayed, their movement tested for the very first time. His tail thumped the ground some more, pace quickening and force increasing.

Tears started to form in Summerhill's own eyes. "Take care of him," he said, nodding to the other Summerhill stirring from its catatonia. The inside of his mouth started to dry up, and with some difficulty, he added, "I feel like I'm going to miss you."

Tek stood there, mouth hanging open, the words not coming. He was still just standing there when Summerhill lifted up one arm, balled his hand into a fist, and slammed it down hard against the ground, causing the flower-strewn world to disappear around him.

 # EIGHTEEN
GRIEF

Everything went dark, as if Summerhill had flipped a light switch.

Skyscrapers. Pale gray sky. Prison. Nusquam. *Katherine. Pocket watch. Time. Back and forth. Find Katherine.*

Find Katherine. Find Katherine. Stick with her and everything will be fine. Find Katherine.

One eyeblink later, he was someplace else.

He didn't bother to ascertain where he'd ended up. He'd escaped, and that was all that mattered, but he felt neither joy nor relief at that. How he'd managed to do it was a mystery even to him, but he didn't care about that, either.

All he cared about now was the terrible thing he'd done. Still down on his hands and knees, his whole body shook with heavy breaths and dry sobs. His stomach churned, his chest grew tight, and then he threw up.

The entirety of his being—what was left of it, at any rate—was overcome with guilt. He could feel the hole in his mind where the missing part of him had been. A very real part of him was gone, and he wasn't ever going to get it back. He might as well have hacked off a limb.

This was worse than just losing a limb, though. A leg or an arm was a part of the body. What he'd torn away had been part of who he'd been as a person. Experience and memories, feelings and emotions, thoughts and quirks and little bits of personality—ripped away, gone forever, discarded as if they'd been nothing.

His fingers clawed at the ground. Beneath him was hard earth, cold and dark and dry. Lifeless. There was light, very faint, but Summerhill didn't lift his head to see its source. Instead, he stayed on all fours, crawled away from the puddle of his vomit, and then fell onto his side on the ground and curled up on himself.

He started to cry. Where his tears hit the ground, tiny leaves and petals sprouted, coming into existence for just a moment before dissolving back into the barren soil. His sobs were heavy, and they echoed clearly back to him, as if he were in some earthen chamber of some sort. Still he refused to open his eyes or lift his head.

Oh, he thought he'd been so clever! He'd thought he could solve both of his problems in one fell swoop, appeasing a clingy, would-be lover while leaving himself free to continue on his mad journey unfettered. Only now, now that it was said and done, did he see and appreciate the true extent to which he'd mutilated himself, and all in the name of trying to take the easy way out of a no-win situation.

Well, now he was out, and he was alone, and he didn't even have his entire self to keep him company. His was a journey to search the cosmos for who he really was, and when confronted with a stumbling block on that path, he'd taken a part of who he was and thrown it away. He'd even had the chance to see the sort of person he'd be if given the chance to settle down and live a normal life, and he'd thrown that away, too, because it had been mildly inconvenient.

Beyond merely feeling shame and regret at what he'd done to himself, he also felt—at least on some level—jealousy that the other part of him would get to know life with someone who cared about him. The rest of him might never find home, or find Katherine, and he was filled with sorrow at realizing that the part of his self he'd seen fit to get rid of might have a life worth living while the rest of him suffered.

He wailed, and the sound of his cry rang back in his ears three times. He wanted so badly to beg forgiveness, and yet he had no idea from whom to beg it. Here he was, weeping alone in the cold darkness, in a place that might not even have a name. Perhaps this was his punishment.

He deserved the World of the Pale Gray Sky. He deserved nothing more than the confinement it represented, a prison of solitude, a prison of ennui. There he could be kept isolated, safely hidden away, unable to bring further harm to others or to himself, and he could let his mind get overtaken by the death of inspiration and the death of imagination.

As he thought about how he might return there and relinquish his freedom in favor of self-imposed exile, his blunt claws scraped at the tightly packed dirt. Anxiety surged within him as he made random, desperate scrapes. The very thought of going back made his heart race with panic, and he tried so, so hard to think of a reason how and why another version of himself had helped him out of there in the first place. He scoured his mind for any hint of distinct memory and dug harder at the top layer of dirt, trying to reproduce something that even vaguely resembled words.

There had been... there had been *something*. If he'd been trapped in the World of the Pale Gray Sky, it was because someone wanted him stuck there. Why confine someone? To keep them from doing something. Something that needed his attention. Something bigger than himself.

Choking back his final sobs, Summerhill forced himself back to his feet, the damp ground left swarming with microbial plant matter that would die off all too soon. Yes, he'd lost sight of what was important. He's lost Katherine, and he'd even lost part of himself, but that wasn't going to deter him. There was something out there waiting for him, and he'd find it. He wouldn't go back. There was no going back.

And if there was no going back, then that meant he could only press onward. And the first step to doing that was figuring out where he was and how he was going to get out of here.

For a few seconds, the sound of a ticking watch echoed faintly somewhere in the distance, its mainspring in working order, its gears in alignment, its ability to track the passage of time smooth and flawless.

Summerhill at last took stock of where he was. He was in fact in a cavern of some sort, as the previous echoing of his cries had indicated. Before him, embedded into the natural rock, was a set of large doors, fully twice as tall as he was, with massive handles and metal knockers to match. Torches burned in sconces set into the rock wall on either side.

The doors themselves were rather ornate, each side carved with matching symmetrical patterns, and in the flickering torchlight, Summerhill could see the different colors as well as the metallic gold and silver trim used throughout. With all the painting and ornamentation, it was impossible to tell by looking whether the doors were made of wood or stone or something else altogether.

Behind Summerhill was nothing but darkness that stretched on forever. He recognized it as the darkness of the nothingness between worlds, the same nothingness through which the *Nusquam* sailed. Without any temporal context, though, Summerhill had no idea if the *Nusquam* was out there right now, or if it had yet to be built, or if it had long ago ceased to be. Even if it did currently exist, there was a lot of nothing out there, and Summerhill wouldn't be lucky enough to run into it by chance twice.

That left the doors as his only way out. He rolled up his sleeves, noticing that they were the sleeves of the dull, greenish-gray shirt he'd worn back home. Dismissing the change in fashion as being of no real importance, he approached the door with refreshed purpose and determination. He wasn't going to stay here and wallow any longer.

First, Summerhill rapped on the door with its knocker to see if anyone would answer. He doubted that anyone would, but it was the polite thing to do. After a minute passed, he knocked harder. The doors were definitely made out of some sort of heavy wood, and the sound of Summerhill's knocking echoed ominously off of the curved cavern walls, back into the emptiness.

"Hello?" he called. "Is anyone in there?" The echo magnified the uncertainty and lingering despair in his voice, despite his attempts to quash it. He couldn't be discouraged, though—not now. "My name is Summerhill." Now he shouted louder, still doubting that his voice would even carry through the thick doors. "Please, if there's anyone there, can you let me in?"

Silence. He banged on the door harder, with the knocker and with his fists. He shouted and he kicked and he made the loudest ruckus he could, but to no avail. The doors remained shut. Still no sound came from the other side.

Kicking the dirt in frustration, Summerhill growled and paced around the empty cavern. He took a few moments to catch his breath and recompose himself lest he slip back into helpless dejection. Very well. If nobody was willing to let him in, then he would just have to barge in. He took hold of one of the doors' oversized handles and pulled. The door did not budge, though.

The dog grabbed hold with both his hands and tried again, and again the door stayed firmly put. Was it locked or barred from the inside, or was it just too heavy to pull? Summerhill dug his heels into the dry ground and pulled harder still, but still the door did not yield. He strained his ears as well as his arms, hoping to catch some sound that might indicate that a bar or a locking mechanism was under stress, but there was no such sound. Panting, he released the handle and took a step back, dizzy from exertion.

He had no fire, nor anything to cut or chop with. Wood this heavy wouldn't readily buckle just from pounding or kicking at it, either, nor would it—

Wait. Wood came from trees. It was dead, sure, but trees were still a kind of plant. Summerhill could do something about plants.

With one arm fully outstretched, Summerhill placed his palm and spread fingers against the door. He fixed his gaze at that spot, and then concentrated, calling out to the dead wood. Faintly, very faintly, the dry fibers within began to stir. Summerhill narrowed his focus even further, and started to exert his will upon the wood.

Just as he began to feel progress, the door itself began to fight back. Some kind of force was resisting him, and he knew right away that it was far stronger than him. He tried to redouble his efforts, but the barrier redoubled its power in kind, and Summerhill was forced to pull his hand away from the door, the wood warping back into its proper shape. It was as if the door itself had a will of its own and didn't want to be opened.

"Oh, come on," Summerhill growled. He tried the handle again, once more wrapping both hands around it, and yanked with his full body weight behind him.

Still nothing. The doors may as well have been a permanent fixture of the cavern wall for all the opening they weren't doing. Summerhill was sure these doors led somewhere. If someone wanted to keep people out, they built a wall; they only built a door if they wanted to let people in or out.

While trying to think of some new plan to either break the door down or get the attention of whoever was on the other side, Summerhill let his gaze wander unfocused. As he did so, his eyes naturally followed the pattern in the wood grain, and he found it naggingly familiar.

He couldn't place where he'd seen it before. It was something from after the World of the Pale Gray Sky, though. That much he knew for sure. The exact significance of it escaped him, but recognizing it at all gave him at least something to work with.

Once more, he reached out to the door with his power. This time, though, instead of trying to warp the wood or break it, he let the energy from his body flow through the grain. There were several paths to trace, but Summerhill let his hazy memory fill in the blanks for him, finding that there was no resistance from the door so long as he stayed within the confines of the proper pattern.

When he'd suffused the full pattern with his spiritual energy, the wood grain briefly glowed a bright, familiar blue. A moment later, the double doors blew open with violent speed. Light blinded Summerhill as the force of the doors opening knocked him backward, sending him clear off his feet and making him tumble ears over tail. He landed on his back in the dead dirt, limbs splayed in all directions, his weary body now bathed by the bright light pouring in through the open portal.

NINETEEN
DESOLATION

The sudden surge of light into the empty darkness was so overwhelming that it blinded Summerhill for several seconds. He rubbed at his sore, stinging eyes, and in his exhausted state, it took a good while for him to recover and be able to see clearly again. As his vision returned, he got to his feet, shielding his eyes with one hand as he stepped up to the edge of the open door.

The first thing he could make out was a dull gray sky. He started to panic, but before that panic could build, he saw amidst the gray the darker curves and billows of clouds—actual clouds, moving clouds, real weather. This was not the sky he'd feared. This was someplace else.

Beneath the cloudy sky stretched a snow-covered landscape. He was looking downhill, into a tiny valley, bounded by mountains whose height he could not gauge without frame of reference. Trees were few, or else they were difficult to make out through the uniform white of snow. If there was any real sun behind the thick clouds, there was no sign of it.

It was cold, too, but it felt to Summerhill that his fur should suffice in keeping him warm. This world might not be the most inviting of places, but it was still an actual world, and that was better than the empty darkness behind him. At least this was somewhere.

Summerhill stepped over the threshold, and only then did the full shock of the cold hit him. He was now clad in a small jacket, but it was nowhere near heavy enough to suit the current weather. His ears flicked back as the wind bit the insides of them, and his tail curled up protectively against the back of one leg. It wasn't snowing; the air was dry, which made it a little worse in some ways. He spun around and saw that the door he'd come through was gone. Wherever he was now, there was no going back.

Though the sun wasn't visible through the thick clouds, the amount of light suggested that it was late afternoon. Summerhill surveyed the horizon in all directions, finding that the valley appeared to be in the foothills and not surrounded by unscalable mountains. Downhill from his current position, he spied what looked to be a tiny cottage, its roof covered in snow, its chimney spouting smoke into the cold air.

The cottage was the only sign of civilization he could spot, and so he began to trudge in that direction. The snow was several inches deep, so the going was slow, but since the path led downhill, it wasn't as tiring as it might have been otherwise. His new ensemble included a pair of boots and some full-length pants, sparing his fur any more immediate discomfort. The jacket had no hood, though, leaving face, ears, and whiskers fully vulnerable to the biting wind.

He did his best to keep his head down as he approached the cottage. If there was smoke coming from the chimney, then hopefully that meant someone was home and could offer him shelter from the cold. The thought of being inside made him trudge faster. Getting closer still, he saw that there were small patches of farmland around the cottage, the fields blanketed neatly with snow.

Summerhill stopped atop a small rise a few dozen yards from the house. A lone tree also overlooked the tiny stretch of farmland. Its branches were frostbitten, and just from the look of it, Summerhill could tell that it would not bloom again when the season changed. It had once been a fruit-bearing tree of some sort, and it was sad that, despite being so close to a farm, it had been allowed to die.

A short jog later, Summerhill was standing at the door to the cottage. It was barely taller than he was, the building itself just a simple, one-story stone structure built in a square shape. There were tiny windows, but they were so frosted over with ice and snow that Summerhill couldn't see in through them.

Still, given the choice between wandering the snow-filled valley aimlessly and trying to make nice with the locals, Summerhill didn't have a difficult time deciding. He huddled in close to the door and knocked hard. The wood felt very old, the surface of it rough and dry.

Snow fell from the eaves of the cottage as the door swung open. Standing in the entryway, backlit by the fireplace set within the far wall, was a robed figure about four feet tall. Its cowled head was impossible to see, and the robes were so thick and heavy that it was difficult to discern any physical details of its body other than the fact that it had two arms and two legs. The robes likewise made demeanor tough to discern, and for several long seconds, the figure just stood there in silence, as if staring at Summerhill with eyes that the dog couldn't see.

Without breaking that silence, the figure gestured hurriedly with one hand for Summerhill to enter. No sooner had Summerhill complied than the figure slammed the door shut behind him, and through the blurry windows, the dog saw more snow fall from the roof.

The interior of the cottage was nice and warm, and Summerhill took a few moments to relish the heat of the fire and the absence of wind. While the dog basked in that relief, the robed figure shuffled up behind him and jabbed him in the flank with a poking finger. "Foolish," it hissed at him in a dark and raspy voice. "Too cold for one such as you. Foolish."

Turning around to face his chastising host, Summerhill finally noticed that the two of them were not alone. Huddled on a low couch off to one side were two more beings, both likewise robed and cowled. One of them was only about half the size of the other. A child, perhaps?

The cottage itself was cramped and simple. There was only one room, filled with all the necessities of a basic kitchen, common area, and bedroom, all piled in different corners. The smell of dust and mold was strong in the air, though not overpowering.

The figure who had invited Summerhill inside gestured sharply to a patch of hide on the floor near the fireplace. "Sit," it instructed. Summerhill eyed the creature's outstretched hand; for a moment, he felt a twinge of excitement at the sight of furred fingers much like his own, but upon closer inspection, it was clear that the creature was wearing gloves of some sort, leaving its true form a mystery still.

Summerhill was happy to sit by the fire, but very soon, the accusing stares of three beings whose faces he couldn't see grew quite awkward and oppressive. He kept his tail curled against himself, and waited to see if his hosts were as accommodating to his presence as he hoped they might be. "I am sorry to intrude," he offered when none of them said anything right away. "It's just very, very cold outside, and I've gotten lost."

"Foolish," the first of the creatures repeated. Its voice sounded masculine enough to Summerhill, but he couldn't say for sure. "You travel almost naked. You will freeze to death."

Sparks from the fire crackled and landed harmlessly on Summerhill's jacket. "I'm hoping to avoid that," he replied, trying to inject some humor into his voice, hoping these creatures even had a concept of what humor was. "Any help you could provide would be greatly appreciated."

"One meal," the raspy-voiced host said, already picking up a small metal pot. He hung it by its handle over the fire. "Directions, maybe, if you need them," the creature added as he sat on the floor opposite Summerhill, his back to his family.

"I'll take what I can get," Summerhill said. He was in no position to be ungrateful, here. "Do you mind if I ask where this is?"

The creatures did seem to be unfortunately humorless, betraying nothing in their body language as they sat and just kept their hidden faces pointed at Summerhill. "We are in the mountains," the host explained. "To be lost here is ill fortune."

Summerhill tried to smell what was in the metal pot, but whatever it was didn't give off much of an aroma. "This place does seem pretty inhospitable," he said. "How do I get out of the mountains, then?"

Now the family on the couch *did* react physically, both forms shrinking in upon themselves. The host, from his position on the floor, reached out to stir the contents of the pot, and he started to laugh. At least, Summerhill assumed it was a laugh; the sound of that raspy voice undulating wordlessly was eerie and unfriendly. "You do not leave the mountains."

The adult figure on the couch stood up and silently walked across the small cottage. It fetched a small bowl from a crowded shelf and carried it over to the host, who merely set it in his lap. For a brief moment, from within the darkness of its cowl, Summerhill thought he saw the flash of eyeshine from the creature who had fetched the bowl, but he couldn't be sure it hadn't been his imagination.

"Is there nothing but the mountains, then?" Summerhill asked. "Surely, it must be possible to get somewhere."

"Adjoining valleys, perhaps," the host said. "Other farms. Other homes. But you do not leave the mountains."

The child-figure leaned forward. "There is the Plain of Ice," it said, its voice chirping while retaining the same raspy darkness as the host.

"If the traveler wanders the mountains like a fool," the host snapped, "then he will find the Plain of Ice all on his own." He sounded offended by the child's sudden intrusion into the conversation, though he vented his ire towards Summerhill instead. Again, he stirred the pot, this time with angry motions.

"I really don't mean to be an imposition," Summerhill insisted. "You've already been more than generous by letting me in to sit by your fire."

"Yes," the host agreed too quickly. "We have. One meal I promised, however, and so one meal you will get." He then started to scoop the contents of the pot into the bowl in his lap. It appeared to be some kind of porridge or gruel.

Given the creatures' diminutive size, the bowl was likewise very tiny by Summerhill's standards, and so the amount of food within could scarcely be called a full meal. Still, he could hardly beg for more, and he was still grateful that these strangers would give him anything. It smelled bland, tasted blander, and filled Summerhill with a sense of pity for these creatures that this was probably the bulk of what they had to eat.

Before he finished completely, he stopped to ask, "If this sounds like a stupid question, then I apologize, but what is this Plain of Ice you spoke of?"

The adult on the couch lowered its head and tugged the child closer to its side. The host snorted, shook his head in resignation, and then explained, "The Plain of Ice is the last thing you see before you die. That is the only escape from the mountains."

Summerhill left the last few bits of food inside the bowl and set it down on the floor. "Do you have anything warmer that I could wear before I set back out again?" he asked. "It's very—"

"No," the host interrupted. He was already getting to his feet. "You only take, and give nothing in return. You have taken enough, and now you must go." He strode over to the door and gripped the handle.

"Please," Summerhill said, wishing that this creature had visible eyes that he could look into. "If you have anything else that could help me, I'd—"

"Hope that the inhabitants of the next valley have more to spare than we, foolish one," the host said, and he pulled open the door. "Go, and hurry; you waste precious heat."

For Summerhill to dig his heels in at this point would only be petulant, and also unfair to this family who had already taken him in, however briefly. "Thank you again for your hospitality," he said with as much sincerity as he could put into his voice. He then scooted out through the open door, and when he turned to say a parting farewell, the host had already slammed the door behind him.

Already, the icy cold of the outside was robbing Summerhill of all benefit he'd gotten from staying in by the fire for a short time. He hugged his arms close to himself as he looked around the snow-covered farm and the mountains surrounding it. These people hadn't just come from nowhere; there had to be somewhere else in this world where he could go for help.

As he trudged his way out of the farm, Summerhill stopped once more at the dead fruit tree. He thought again about the family in their tiny cottage with their bland food and cramped living area. How long before the crops of this snowy farm could be harvested? How long before it was possible to hunt for meat or trade for goods or have contact with anyone who didn't already live here?

Summerhill pressed his hand against the dead, frosted-over bark. In its current state, the tree was good for little more than firewood, but Summerhill could change that. He took a deep breath, the air chilling his lungs, and then he exhaled as he willed the tree back to life. He put the spark of his own vital essence into it, and changed the nature of the tree itself, changed it into something this world had never seen. Before his eyes, the bare branches twisted, grew, and reshaped themselves before bursting forth with flowers, a spray of vibrant color against the cloudy gray sky.

The wind picked up, and a small flurry of petals blew away as various blossoms turned into fruit. Summerhill filled the branches with several different kinds, each a different color and shape. He imagined different flavors into them, too, and when that was set, he insured that the tree would bear such fruit year-round, that it would resist the cold and remain strong.

He was still cold and hungry and tired, but he was now filled with a sense of rightness. A smile spread across his muzzle, and he looked up to see that some more flower petals had been caught up in a swirling eddy of wind. One by one, those petals broke away and drifted off in the same direction, and the dog followed them, even if the snow made it impossible to keep up.

There was a way out of this world. He'd found his way out of the World of the Pale Gray Sky, out of the nevereef, and out of the darkness. He'd find his way out of here, and then he'd find his way back to Katherine, wherever or whenever she might be. Yes, his host at the cottage had been correct in that he was foolishly unprepared for his journey, but he'd just have to press on and hope he found better ways to prepare himself along the way.

The mountains turned out to be taller than they had looked at first. While not insurmountable crags that scraped at the sky, they were still steep, and though Summerhill didn't need any climbing gear to make his way up, the patches of knee-deep snow and the constant wind in his face made it slow, arduous going. The gray clouds whirled overhead, still yielding no sign of any sun.

After what he was sure had been hours of trekking uphill, Summerhill noted that it hadn't gotten appreciably darker than it had been when he had first arrived. Was this place like the World of the Pale Gray Sky, with no sun to rise and set? Or were the days just interminably long, the sky forever hidden by swirls of gray? The dog scoffed as he thought about how desperate he had been to escape his old life, only to now be stuck trapped in a desolate place that was far too much like the prison he'd once called home.

At last he reached the top of the mountain, after far more time and effort than he'd expected. Far below was another valley, longer and narrower than the one he'd just left, and beyond that were mountains taller than the ones he'd just scaled. From this height, he could see no signs of any cottages, any smoke from chimneys, or any paths that travelers or traders might use to make their way through.

Summerhill made his way down into the valley, trying to spot anything in the way of landmarks or hints of civilization along the way. He walked for hours and hours, until he was exhausted. He dug into the hollow space below a dead tree and slept there for as long as he could before waking to find the sky just as dull and half-lit as before. Resuming his trek, he made it nearly to the top of the next mountain before making camp in a rocky alcove that could barely be called a cave, resting through a night that did not come.

In the morning, he told himself, he'd make his way into the next valley, and he would keep searching until he found someone else. Someone else was out there, he was sure, and if they couldn't or wouldn't help him, he'd find someone else again.

TWENTY
WINTERTIME

For weeks, Summerhill had wandered the mountains, but he refused to accept the conventional wisdom of the local inhabitants that mountains were all that existed. During those weeks, the sky never darkened nor got brighter, and the cold never lifted, but the world wasn't empty. There were still the natives, and their ways and culture, from what little Summerhill could glean of them, suggested that at some point, perhaps long ago, there had been more than what there was now.

It was in that third valley that Summerhill finally had his second run-in with the natives. They, too, were robed and cowled and kept their forms hidden, but instead of a single hovel, they lived in a hamlet of three small cottages with a tiny farm of their own. Like Summerhill's first host, they told him that the only way out of the mountains was via the Plain of Ice that appeared on the brink of death, but he refused to believe that. They told him how the winter never ended, how they lived off of what little they could make grow in the ice and cold, along with meat from what few beasts survived in the wild.

Even these people, miserable though their conditions were, hadn't lost their will to live and surrendered to the winter. They hadn't lost all hope that there was something better, and neither would Summerhill.

In fact, if it hadn't been for the natives, Summerhill likely would have frozen to death several times over. Though none ever let him stay for very long, none of the homes he came across ever turned him away completely, even if it was just to sit for a spell in front of the fire. Twice he'd needed to trade for new clothing after the ice and snow had reduced his old garments to tatters, using his talents with plants to give the people food in exchange. He'd even been able to learn some tips and tricks on how to navigate the land, and places to go when in search of other snowbound villages hidden in the winding network of valleys.

After a month of travel, Summerhill found the largest single settlement he'd seen since his arrival: a group of five cabins built on a flat stretch of land high in the mountains, surrounding the pathetic remnants of a hot spring. A recent landslide had taken out a crop of nut-bearing trees and a patch of land where root vegetables could grow. Summerhill used some of his own life's energy to bring the trees back and to allow the vegetables to thrive in the soil once more.

In exchange, the small band of natives heralded him as a sorcerer, and told tales around the fire of the hero who was to have banished the eternal winter.

Long ago, they told him, sometime after this winter had fallen, a champion of the people had set off to find some way to return the world to its former glory. He traveled the valleys and got help from all he could, and then, seeing no other course to take, resigned himself to making his way across the Plain of Ice in the hope of finding a way to bring some life back into this dying place.

Before Summerhill could balk and dismiss the message of the story, the storyteller continued, speaking of the Plain of Ice as if it were a real place. This got Summerhill's attention, but unfortunately for the story and the hero and the rest of the world, this hero never did return.

"Is there really a Plain of Ice?" he asked the storyteller. "An actual place, and not just a gateway to death?"

The storyteller chuckled with the eerie, raspy laugh that the hooded natives had. "There is a Plain of Ice," he assured Summerhill, "though that is not to say that it is anything more than a gateway to death all the same."

"How does one get there?" Summerhill asked, unable to mask his excitement at this revelation, strange though it was. "Nobody else seems to think it exists."

156

"It exists," the storyteller said. "But you must travel far."

Summerhill smiled in understanding. "I have already traveled far. I am willing to travel father still."

"Then travel farther still you must, sorcerer," the storyteller said, his dark voice taking on an even more serious edge. "First, you must travel farther than anyone has ever traveled. Travel until you find the mountains that are higher than anyone has climbed. Climb those mountains, and you will be able to see where the world stops."

The storyteller paused to take a long sip from his small, hot bowl of vegetable stew. "Far above, up in the sky, will be the Sun That Gives No Heat, shining upon the Plain of Ice. From there... Well, one way or the other, it leads to the world beyond this one."

Summerhill lay awake when he should have been sleeping and resting for the next leg of his journey, unable to stop thinking of the storyteller's words. In place of a stubborn insistence that there was nothing beyond the mountains, he now had fantastical directions to a place that was impossible to reach.

But impossible, as Summerhill had learned during his time with Katherine, was something he had a leg up on.

And so Summerhill set out once again, traveling the mountains as before. This time, however, the trek grew more arduous. The paths through the mountain peaks grew more treacherous, and the homes and farms grew fewer and farther between. Each time he stopped to sleep, he felt himself grow mildly delirious from exhaustion.

The isolation was maddening. Having run out of people to talk to, he sometimes took to talking to himself, just to have something to do. He yearned for the sharp-edged company of Katherine, vowing every time he set out anew that soon, he would find her, wherever she might be. Sometimes, he felt lonesome for the otter Tekutan, though even after long hours with nothing but his own thoughts to occupy him, he could not remember who that was, or why his absence would inspire such feelings.

In one ice-filled mountain pass, he found a solemn marker of carved stone, noting the passage of the hero who never returned. Hours after coming across it, however, he became convinced that it had been nothing more than his mind playing tricks on him after days spent alone trudging through the snow and the cold.

But then, a day later, after cresting the tallest mountain he could remember climbing, he brought his hand to his head to shield his eyes from the bright, burning light that struck them.

High in the sky, burning from behind a wispy haze of clouds, was a brilliant white sun, which shone bright but which indeed did nothing to stave off the biting cold. Far below was an unbroken expanse of flat white that stretched out towards the horizon as far as the eye could see, reflecting the sun's light to give the illusion of a sunset that was mere minutes away but would never come.

After being first captivated by the beauty and enormity of this Plain of Ice, Summerhill was filled with dismay at the thought of having to cross it. From here up in the mountains, it looked like it went on forever. It really was like gazing at the very end of the world.

Then, Summerhill realized what he was really seeing: an ocean, frozen solid. At the near edge of the plain, he could make out the snow-covered beach, and from there out to the horizon was nothing but a smooth sheet of motionless white.

He turned around to face the way he'd come, back at the likewise endless series of mountains and valleys he'd crossed. If there ever had actually been a hero, and he'd made it this far, Summerhill might not have blamed him for deciding to abandon any crazy plan to try to cross the Plain of Ice.

But Summerhill only had crazy plans. It was either this or nothing. Either this, or go back. Search a whole frozen world of mountains in the hope that maybe there were other legends, other ways to escape. Do that, and hope he didn't freeze to death in the process.

He pulled his coat more snugly against himself, looked at what little food he had left after his journey here, and gritted his teeth before setting out to cross the Plain of Ice.

Two days of constant walking later, there was still nothing but gray clouds, a cold sun, the horizon, and the flat, unending sea. There was no telling how far he'd come. There was no telling how far there was to go. There was nothing else.

Summerhill's old life seemed so far away. His memories of his adventures aboard the *Nusquam* and his too-brief journey with Katherine seemed to belong to another person. On occasion, he saw glimpses of the otter he didn't remember, creeping in as delusional traces of movement against the frozen sea, glimpsed out of the corners of his dried-out eyes.

The unreachable horizon taunted him with blinding whiteness that kept interrupting the pleasant visions he tried to distract himself with. His body shivered with cold that his coat could not protect against. His stomach begged for food, but he had run out of his meager stores, and he could make no plants grow from within the lifeless ice even if he'd still had the strength to do so.

With his delirium-ridden loneliness and a grip on reality that kept slipping, Summerhill's body and spirit both grew weaker. He soon lacked even the energy to wonder why he'd ever come out here. He lacked the energy to walk. He lacked the energy to stand.

With that, Summerhill went limp, and it felt so good to collapse, to not have to walk anymore, to not have to stand anymore. He lay there, his breathing slowing, his eyes freezing over before they could shut, and he welcomed the blissful emptiness as he let himself drift off to die alone in the snow.

ZERO
(RE)STARTING

White. Why did the afterlife have to be white? After his fruitless trek across the frozen ocean, Summerhill would have preferred any other color.

The dog's bones and muscles ached, which made him wonder why things like pain and discomfort would linger after death. Sitting up was a chore, and he felt self-conscious when he whimpered because of it. It took him a few seconds to realize that he still had circulation in his hands, feet, and ears, because they now stung with warmth.

The afterlife was at least not merely a plane of empty, featureless white. Summerhill was sitting up on some kind of small dais, and there were shadowy angles that gave the impression of walls and possibly also corridors that led away from his chamber. The only sounds he heard were those of his own body and the thoughts ringing about within his mind. There was no weightlessness, and he was decidedly still corporeal, as his aching body was keen to remind him.

Standing took more effort. He managed to get only partway up before he collapsed, falling a short way, his backside landing back on the dais.

"Don't strain yourself. Your strength should return, in time."

Summerhill turned his head quickly, and saw behind him a young woman—no, still barely just a girl, borderline prepubescent. Her features changed every time he blinked; she would be a canine creature like himself, a human girl like Katherine, and all sorts of things in between while still somehow remaining undeniably the same being.

She smiled at him. "It's nice to see you again, Summerhill," she said. "Unorthodox, but nice."

Months of being snow-blind and isolated began to melt away from the edges of Summerhill's mind, and in the thaw

160

he recalled the foolish details of his journey through the land of mountains. His preceding memories fell into position like a mosaic, and he remembered the World of the Pale Gray Sky, his escape, and everything after.

What he didn't quite remember, however, was this girl. "Who are you?" he asked, remaining calm and still.

"I am Shoön, the Beginning," she said, her voice cheerful, genial. "And don't worry about not remembering me. That's normal."

Summerhill looked her over again, but it was hard to place her because she kept looking different, subtly and not-so-subtly. "We've met before, haven't we?"

Shoön chuckled. "I meet everybody once. It's only very rarely that I see anyone again after that."

There was still no sound that didn't come from either Shoön or from Summerhill himself. Near as Summerhill could tell, there was nothing going on here other than their conversation. "How did I get here?" he asked. "Did I... am I dead?"

Finally, Shoön seemed to have settled on a single appearance, at least to Summerhill's perceptions of her: the form of a young girl, slightly human with more otherworldly features, her hair dark black and braided into twin ponytails that ran down along her back. The laugh she let out at Summerhill's question, however, was more that of a young woman than that of a girl.

"Dead?" she repeated. "Oh, no, Summerhill, you're very much alive. Actually, if you don't mind my saying, you look rather a mess, and I'm guessing you feel like one, too."

"That explains why I feel like I've been run over by an ocean liner," Summerhill muttered. "So, this isn't the afterlife, then?"

"Nothing of the sort," Shoön assured him. "If you wanted to call this place anything, you could call it the beforelife."

The white stung Summerhill's eyes less, now. He could also now see (and appreciate) the more subtle hues of gray and off-white in his surroundings. "It's warm here. I like that."

Shoön smiled and sat down next to him. "I'm afraid you won't be able to stay long. I tried to be as subtle as possible about pulling you back here and nursing you back to health. Hopefully you'll feel well enough to be up and about soon."

"Do you have any blankets or something?" Summerhill asked. "Can I lie down and take a nap?"

There was a blossoming sensation of warmth that spread all through Summerhill's back and torso as Shoön set her hand upon his shoulder. "No, Summerhill," she said, and now she sounded a little sad. "As I said, you're going to have to leave soon. I'm very sorry."

Summerhill turned to look deep into Shoön's eyes. Something about her filled him with a heartening feeling; he might not recognize her, but he *knew* her, somehow, from somewhere. "I feel safe here," he said. "I feel safe with you."

She drew him into a hug, and sighed warmly as she held him. Despite being smaller than him, she didn't feel it, and being in her arms soothed the aching he felt in his limbs. "Everyone has to move on from here," she murmured into one of his big ears. "Everyone has to go out into the world."

"You make it sound like I've already done that, though," Summerhill said. It was with reluctance that he drew away from Shoön and her embrace.

She nodded. "And so you have," she replied. "So very, very long ago."

Summerhill wrinkled his brow, sniffed at the air, and stuck out the tip of his tongue. "Except time has no meaning here," he said.

A new grin—an approving and impressed grin—appeared on Shoön's face. "That's exactly right. Still, I know that, to your perceptions, it was a long time ago, and you've come so, so far since then."

"Why did you bring me back here? You make it sound like I'm not supposed to be here."

"You're not, no," Shoön said. "By that same token, you're not supposed to die cold and alone out in the snow."

A chill made its way up through Summerhill's warmed spine. "Is this some kind of destiny thing?" he asked. "Do you know how I'm fated to end up?"

"Mine is the dominion of how things begin," Shoön said. "That being said, knowing how something begins can tell you a lot about how it's bound to end, and your end wasn't supposed to be back there."

"And so you brought me back to life so that I can start over?"

Shoön flashed him a smirk. "Strictly speaking, I pulled you back here before you had a chance to die. Which, strictly speaking, I'm not supposed to do, but I couldn't bear the thought of leaving you there for my sister to find."

"Your sister? Who's your sister?"

"Now, now," Shoön said, patting Summerhill on the cheek. "You're a smart dog. If I'm the Beginning, who would my sister be?"

Summerhill just nodded. "I see. And the reason you're in such a hurry to get me on my way is because—"

"—if she found out I stole you from her, she'd be quite cross with me, yes." Shoön stood up and pulled her hair back in her hands, then let it fall back down straight. "Now, what we can do, here, is just say that this is the beginning of the next chapter of your journey, so technically, that'd fall under my jurisdiction."

"Willful misinterpretation of the rules?" Summerhill asked with a grin.

"Not *mis*interpretation," Shoön protested. "*Selective* interpretation. Technically, it's not cheating." She touched Summerhill on the forehead, stroked the fur there a bit, and then asked, "Could you lie down?"

Summerhill leaned only partway back. "I thought you said I wasn't supposed to."

"Well, now I need to send you on your way, and I want you to be comfortable. Close your eyes and think about where you want to be."

"I want to be back with Katherine. I feel like that's where I'm supposed to be."

"Then that's just fine," Shoön said as she gently pushed Summerhill down flat atop the dais. "You can be wherever you want to be."

"But is that where I'm *supposed* to be? I think I met a future version of myself telling me that I needed to—"

"Close your eyes and relax," Shoön repeated. "Don't try to interpret fate before it happens. That never ends well for anybody."

Summerhill started to close his eyes, but then he quickly opened them again. "Wait," he said. "Before I go, I... You said you knew me, from the beginning." He reached out to take her hand, squeezing it. "Can you tell me what my beginning really was?"

Shoön stroked the top of his muzzle and smiled sadly. "It's not that simple, Summerhill," she said, and then she leaned down and kissed him on his furry forehead.

"But, I mean, surely you can just *tell* me, right? If you were there?"

This time, Shoön cupped Summerhill's cheek and touched her nose to his. "I already cheated once by bringing you back here," she said with an impish grin. "I can't just—"

"You said it wasn't cheating!"

"Shush," Shoön said, tapping him on the nose. "The point is that I can't just give you the answers you're looking for; you need to find those yourself, if they're to mean anything."

Summerhill swallowed, nodded, and then shut his eyes. "So I just...think about where I want to be?"

"And then let your mind go blank." Shoön was caressing his ears and forehead, and the feeling was so relaxing and soothing. She then stopped abruptly and perked up. "Oh, how silly of me. I almost forgot to give this back to you."

Out of thin air, she produced a small object in her palm. With a smile, she pressed it into Summerhill's hand. "You've earned this."

It was cool and smooth and round. With some trepidation, Summerhill held it up and looked at it. It was the engraved pocket watch he'd had inside the nevereef. "Where did you get this?" he asked.

Shoön took the watch from his hand and stuffed it into his shirt pocket for him. "Try not to lose it this time, okay?" She then resumed petting and stroking Summerhill on the head, and his desire to argue began to ebb and abate.

Summerhill took a few deep, quiet breaths. "Hey, Shoön?"

"Yes?"

"Thanks for saving me." He opened his eyes back up to look at her one more time. "It means a lot to me."

Shoön smiled, and then rested her palm flat against his forehead. "Close your eyes," she said again. "Relax, and let the next part of your journey begin."

TWENTY-ONE
STREAM

Summerhill slept, and again he dreamt.

The dream was clear and lucid, as clear and lucid as the stream that Summerhill saw. The sun reflected off the water's surface, tracing the lines of the gentle current. The air was crisp, echoing only with the sound of the babbling stream.

Fallen leaves, still fresh and verdant, flowed downstream. Different parts of the current carried them at different speeds; at times, some leaves would be clumped together, only to separate for a while before the flow brought them all together again. There was a measurable semblance of tranquility to those steady movements.

Here and there, tiny silver fish would show themselves near the surface, and sometimes they would hop out into the air for a split second, as if trying to catch something. The spots where they emerged and where they landed would ripple and radiate out, temporarily disrupting the current, changing the flow of the tiny leaves for just a few seconds before the stream returned to normal.

From upstream, there came the wind, and borne on that wind was a soft, melodious humming. It wasn't the hum of nature or the hum of the breeze through the branches, but the hum of a person, actively musical and always changing, the tune going wherever it would with no sign of building in one direction or another.

Farther downstream, there was the burbling sound of the stream going over a short drop, the water roiling gently before the stream continued, well out of sight and out of earshot.

Summerhill gazed at one of the rippling spots in the water where a fish had jumped. He felt himself growing more tired, a sign that he was waking up and pulling away from the relaxing dream.

166

TWENTY-TWO
REORIENTATION

Summerhill's last conscious thoughts from before the dream came rushing back to him. *Katherine is on the ship. She needs my help. The Consortium is coming for her.*

He snapped awake and snapped into existence all at once, the sensation making his whiskers tingle. The rest of his body followed suit as his pulse picked back up, his breathing restarted, and he regained his sense of place.

Wherever he was, though, it wasn't anyplace familiar, and that bothered him. He'd been expecting to show up somewhere aboard the *Nusquam*, either in the Security Chief's office, or in one of the hallways, or even in an access stairwell with Katherine right after he'd run off to try to shut the power down, only to be sidelined by... well, he couldn't remember what had cut his attempt short, only that he hadn't succeeded.

But Summerhill was none of those places. He was in a small, sparsely decorated bedroom. The lights were all off, and his eyes were still adjusting to the darkness, so it was difficult to make out details. There was definitely a bed, neatly made, along with a nightstand free of clutter. What little light there was came from a digital chronometer set into the wall and an electronic panel next to one of the doors. A faint ambient humming sound resonated in the dog's ears.

He then took stock of himself. Already he could tell that he didn't feel nearly as weak or weary as he had when he'd woken up with Shoön. Patting himself down, he found that he was at least fully clothed, and not in the ragged, shabby garb he'd picked up back in the mountains, either. It felt nice, in a simple pleasure way, to be wearing normal pants and a nice shirt again.

A quick flash of memory hit him, his ears going up as he grew instantly more alert. He patted at his shirt and pants, trying to find where the pocket watch was. His pockets were all empty, though. Even so, he double-checked. He distinctly remembered Shoön giving the watch back to him. Had he already been dreaming at that point?

Unlike how he'd felt back inside the nevereef, however, he wasn't filled with a sense of overwhelming anxiety at it not being there. Something told him that it was okay and that he shouldn't worry about it. Whether that meant that it was already someplace safe, or—

One of the doors—the one with the electronic panel—slid open with a pneumatic hiss, and light from the outside came pouring in. Summerhill yelped in alarm and surprise, shielding his eyes on reflex, barely catching the silhouette in the doorway. It reached over toward the panel just inside the door, and then the bedroom lights switched on.

"Mr. Summerhill?"

"Katherine?"

For a long moment, Katherine stood there, slack-jawed. In place of her familiar black hostess' garb, she now instead wore a crisp, navy blue military uniform with gray and silver accents and insignia patches on her chest and shoulders. Also, where she'd reached in to turn on the lights with one hand, her other had gone to the large pistol at her hip.

That hand fell away, though, as she stepped into the room and hurriedly keyed the wall panel to shut the door behind her. She then turned to face Summerhill again, her stare still just as wide, mouth still open in disbelief.

"Mr. Summerhill?" she repeated. "Is that really you?"

"It's me," Summerhill assured her. "I'm guessing that's really you?"

Katherine paced around, the fingers of one hand combing through the curls of her blonde hair. Yet again she sized Summerhill up, then finally stood still and asked, "What the bloody hell are you doing in my cabin?"

168

"I'm really sorry," Summerhill said. "I know I shouldn't have run off on you like that. I was just so sure that it was the right thing to do, and... well, anyway, I came back to help you, like I promised."

"Came back to help me?" Katherine wandered over to the bed and sat down on the edge of it. "Help me with what?"

Summerhill bit his lip and fidgeted with his hands. "You know. With the Security Chief and the Consortium coming after you and all."

Katherine let out a familiar, sharp laugh. "Mr. Summerhill, that was almost five years ago. I haven't been in trouble for a long time." Her lips curled up into a quizzical smile. "Not that I don't appreciate the sentiment; you're just showing up a little late, is all."

Five years. After weeks and months spent hiking through the mountains, time had almost lost any semblance of meaning to Summerhill, but after having been rescued by Shoön, he'd expected that he would show up at the point in time he wanted, like it should have been a given. "So you don't need me?" His tail drooped and his ears laid out to either side.

"You're probably the last person I ever expected to see again, I'll say that much." Katherine pulled her side arm out from its holster and set it on her nightstand, then undid the top button of her shirt. "I don't suppose it's even worth me asking you how you even got here, eh?"

"I..." Summerhill looked into Katherine's face, and remembered her reluctance to believe anything he said back when they'd first met. Had she already lost her appreciation for the sense of wonder they'd found together inside the nevereef, where they'd bent reality with their minds and even gone back in time? "No, probably not."

"Oh, hey, don't be like that," Katherine said, and she patted the spot next to her on the edge of the bed. "I'm just saying, if you only came here to bail me out, it may have been a wasted trip." She smiled again, this time more honest. "It *is* a real trip to see you again, though, mate."

Taking a look around the room, Summerhill frowned. It was so spartan, devoid of any real touch of personalization or even personality. Lost sense of wonder, indeed. "So, you're military now, is that it?" the dog asked as he sat next to Katherine on the bed. "That's a bit of a change from cruise hostess."

"I wasn't always a hostess, remember," Katherine pointed out. "Though, all right, I'll grant you that military life isn't where I ever saw myself ending up, either. Still, it was the simplest way to ease myself back into a normal life."

Summerhill turned his head and looked at Katherine again, really searching her expression this time. She didn't look distant or guarded, but there was a part of her that struck Summerhill as sad—some part of herself that she wasn't even aware of. "How *did* you get away from the Consortium in the end?" he asked her.

Katherine's lips curled into a mischievous grin. "Oh, it was great. Turns out that the Chief was quite familiar with them, actually. When they showed up to apprehend me, citing their rules and regulations and whatnot, he interceded on my behalf." She looked almost proud, now. "He reckoned— and laid it out pretty firmly, I might add—that since the *Nusquam* was not actually *in* any defined reality at the time, the Consortium had no true jurisdiction while the ship was underway."

"So why didn't they just come after you again once the ship reached its destination?" Summerhill asked.

"Oh, I'm assuming they did," Katherine said. "As a fugitive from Consortium justice, I was to be subjected to 'any and all reasonable attempts at detainment' until I could be properly apprehended." She stretched back a little on the bed, her arms reaching behind her to keep herself propped up. "So, once their thugs left, the Chief decided that confining me to quarters counted as 'reasonable enough' in his book."

170

Summerhill felt a bit of admiration for the Security Chief, recalling Shoön's comment about 'selective interpretation' of the rules; he thought it an even further shame that the shapeshifting entity wasn't really the same type of dog-creature as himself. "And you got off the ship before it reached its next port of call."

"Precisely," Katherine replied. "And hey, one of the lifeboats had already been ejected under mysterious circumstances. What was one more to add to that?"

The convoluted loop of a timeline involving their original escape from the Consortium played itself out in Summerhill's head, up to the point where they were separated from one another. "So, then, how did I get out of my cell in the brig? Did you have the Chief shut down the power after all?"

The look on Katherine's face suggested that the memory Summerhill had just dug up was one that she'd either buried or simply forgotten. "Oh, right, that," she said. "Yeah, it looks like *something* caused an unscheduled reality breach over on the port side of the ship in the passenger section." Her nostrils twitched with a snort. "Knocked out power to a huge chunk of the ship. Full functionality didn't get restored for days."

Summerhill recalled his mad dash to reach the engineering section, hoping to be in time to cause the proper sequence of events to unfold as they were supposed to. He knew that he'd gotten distracted, but trying to recall details caused him to bump against a hole he had in his memory. "So... So you didn't need my help," he said, verbalizing his thoughts as he tracked back through them, "and then I left the ship, you left the ship, and five years went by and we never saw each other again?"

A crease appeared in Katherine's forehead as she looked at him. "Well, there was more to the five years than that," she said. "Compared to the impossible things that you see and do, though, I don't know if you'd find most of it all that interesting."

Ears back and tail limp, Summerhill wanted to say, *"You should know me better than that,"* but then he thought about the five years Katherine had been through since she'd last seen him. Even if her travels hadn't been impossible, and even if she'd lost that spark of adventure, she had to have gone through a lot, had to have experienced so much in the interim that the short time she'd spent with Summerhill had hardly amounted to anything at all.

Instead, Summerhill said, "I'm glad that you're all right. I was really worried about you."

The cabin was silent save for the ambient hum of technology. Katherine leaned forward and folded her hands together in her lap. The curls of her hair fell over one ear. Her body heaved with a long, slow breath that ended with a sigh. "You're like the weirdest guardian angel ever," she said at last.

"Well, I'm not an angel. I'm just a dog."

Katherine cracked a smile at that, which made Summerhill smile as well. "You know, I always used to dream that my life could be more like my granddad's stories." She sat back up, brushing her hair back behind her ear. "Now I think it's a bit too much like them."

There, for a fleeting moment, was that spark, that sense of wonder again.

The moment ended, however, as the intercom inside the cabin came on. *"Bridge to all hands. Prepare for FTL transition in one minute."*

Summerhill's ears pricked up. "Katherine," he asked, realizing now his oversight in not finding out earlier, "where are we, exactly?"

"Roughly four light-years out from Alnilam."

"No, I mean like, this room, right here. Where are we?"

A familiar look of confusion came over Katherine's face. "This is the star cruiser *Ajax*. Science vessel serving with the Fifth Fleet." When Summerhill didn't respond right away, she added, "Are you saying you didn't know that?"

"How am I supposed to know?" Summerhill asked. "I just showed up in your bedroom."

"Well, how are you here if you don't even know where you are?"

"I don't know! It doesn't work that way. I'm not sure how it works."

"Well, if you don't know, how am I supposed to know?"

Summerhill shook his head. "I never said you had to. I just came here to find you because I wanted to help you, but apparently I missed by a few years."

"God, everything about you makes my head hurt, sometimes." Katherine sighed, rubbed her temples with her thumb and middle finger, and then said, "And I also just realized that you're an alien creature intruding aboard a military vessel. That's going to be fun to explain."

"Does this mean you're going to throw me to Security again?"

"Technically, I *am* Security, this time."

"Oh, great. You get to cut out the middleman."

Now Katherine rubbed at her temples with both hands. "Mr. Summerhill, please, give me some more credit than that. It's not like I—"

Katherine froze. Not just Katherine, though, Summerhill realized a moment later, but everything: the flow of air through the cabin, the blinking of the lights on the wall console, even Summerhill's own heartbeat. No, not quite frozen—just slowed, so much that the world was moving at an infinitesimal, barely perceptible degree.

Then the room and everything in it took on a distinct shade of blue. It was a bright blue, a very familiar blue. Something tickled at the edge of the dog's mind, something playful and prodding, but also unnerving.

He could have sworn he'd heard a voice say his name.

"—forgot everything you did for me."

Summerhill stared back at Katherine, who had snapped back into full motion. "What was that?" he asked.

"What was what?"

Before Summerhill could clarify, the walls of the room seemed to expand, and he and Katherine appeared to shrink together with the bed. The dog's stomach felt queasy, and then reality itself snapped back to its proper proportions with a tangible, audible twang.

Katherine lurched, and she reached out to grab Summerhill, who was reeling even harder. She managed to snatch him by the wrist to keep him from falling off of the bed. "Ah, that. That was the FTL transition. I'm guessing that was your first time?"

"No," Summerhill said. "I mean, yes, it was, but not that. Before that."

"Before what?"

"Everything went blue, and you seemed to stop," Summerhill explained. "I thought I heard someone talking."

Katherine chuckled. "I was talking to you, silly. The relativity shift can be really disorienting. It plays tricks on the mind sometimes. Some species deal with it in different ways. Maybe yours doesn't handle it so well."

Whatever had happened before the transition had only happened to Summerhill, then. Maybe it was simply a natural bit of disorientation, like Katherine said, but he doubted that. This had felt too real, too coherent somehow to just be a trick of the mind.

Not that the state of his mind was a great thing to go by. He had to be allowed to trust his gut sometimes, though.

When it came to arguing points like this, Katherine tended to be hard to convince. And after five years of relative normalcy, their past experience together might not even do all that much to help Summerhill's case. Even if she had called him her guardian angel. Should that have been a more comforting thought?

"I know what I felt," he said, willing himself to believe it. "And it—"

He was interrupted as the cabin's intercom chimed in again. *"Bridge to Warrant Officer Tinsley. Can you report your current status?"* The voice was different from the one that had spoken the FTL warning. This one was male and terse, and reminded Summerhill of Katherine when she got into a bad mood.

Katherine leaned over to her nightstand and depressed a small button built onto the top of it. "This is Tinsley," she spoke aloud. "I'm just in my rack. Duty shift ended at seventeen-thirty."

The response from the bridge was delayed several seconds; when it finally came, the terse voice had lost a lot of its authoritativeness. *"Tinsley, Hermann says that his project started going haywire a few minutes ago, and he asked us to contact you."*

Summerhill shot Katherine a questioning look, but she appeared just as confused. She pressed the button again and replied, "Bridge, I'm not on Hermann's team. What does he want me for?"

"No, I know that, Katherine," the voice said, now much more personable, if also resigned. A sigh came through the intercom before the followup. *"Hermann just asked if you could provide a status update as to your current situation."*

"What situation?" Katherine asked. "If Hermann wants to talk to me, why doesn't he just contact me directly?"

There was another pause in the conversation before the intercom came on again. *"I'm just relaying the message as ordered, Tinsley. Can you provide a status update?"*

Katherine stared at Summerhill for several seconds, eyeing him, assessing him. A lump formed in the dog's throat, and he tried to beg her with his eyes not to turn him in again. Not after all this time. Not after all they'd been through together.

Closing her eyes and hanging her head, Katherine pressed the intercom button. "No 'status' to report, bridge. I'm just enjoying off-time in my rack. Tell Hermann if he has something important to ask me that he can—"

"Tinsley, this is Hermann," a new male voice said. This one was sharp, cutting, and it carried a distinct note of

panic—well-disguised panic, but panic nevertheless. *"What's going on right now?"*

Summerhill's pulse started to race. Somebody, somewhere on the ship, was convinced that something unusual was going on, and he and Katherine were right in the middle of it.

"There's nothing 'going on,' Hermann," Katherine replied. "I'm just in my rack."

"Are you alone?"

Katherine made eye contact with Summerhill. "Yes. Why?"

Hermann muttered a curse under his breath without cutting his end of the line. *"Tinsley, something punched a hole in the resonance field, and that hole is right in your quarters. We may have an intruder, and if you're alone, that means it's something we can't see."*

Summerhill choked down that lump in his throat. Katherine was still staring at him. The game was up, then: someone knew that he was there, and they were going to come looking, and Katherine was going to get pulled into it one way or another.

"Hermann, if there's a security risk to the fleet, then someone needs to inform the Admiral," Katherine said.

"Already done, Tinsley," Hermann replied. *"He's issued a fleet-wide alert. I expect we'll be dropping out of FTL very soon."*

Sure enough, before Katherine even had a chance to respond, Summerhill felt the very space inside the cabin shift, a sort of pressure that made it feel like he was being squished in upon himself like a sponge being wrung out. Then, once again, there was the twanging sensation of everything snapping back to normal.

Katherine looked aghast, and her finger came away from the nightstand intercom. With one hand, she did up the front of her uniform, and with the other, she reclaimed her pistol. "This doesn't look good, Mr. Summerhill."

"What do you mean?" Summerhill asked. "Should we not be stopping?"

"I don't think we should have been jumping in the first place. But that's not even the biggest red flag." Katherine stood up and breathed deeply as if recomposing herself. "A fleet-wide security alert has been issued."

"That does sound bad."

"Worse," Katherine pointed out. "I *am* Security, remember?"

"Right."

"And I didn't get his alert."

It took Summerhill a moment, but then the thought registered, and his eyes widened. "Oh. This doesn't bode well for either of us, does it?"

Katherine looked over her firearm, making sure it was loaded before holstering it at her hip. "No, it very much does not." Turning away from Summerhill, she rummaged through one of her drawers, sifting through personal effects that the dog couldn't see. He wondered if her orange-and-blue necklace was in there, or if she was allowed to wear it under her uniform.

Resisting the urge to angle his head to sneak a look, Summerhill wrung his hands together. "So, what do we do?" he asked. "Do we run again, like back on the *Nusquam*?"

"I don't think it's that simple this time," Katherine said. She paced back and forth in her cabin, her own fingernails digging into her hands, looking like they might draw blood. "I'm part of a military outfit. These are my people, not some bizarre law enforcement agency that I pissed off. We can't just shoot our way out."

"So we don't shoot," Summerhill said. "We just run, you and me. Get off the ship before they can find us."

Katherine shook her head, her exhaled breath coming out as a growl of frustration. "You don't get it, Summerhill," she snapped. "I don't have anywhere to run to anymore. I've lost too many homes already, and I'm tired of always having to..." Her words drifted off, and her pacing ceased, and she just looked at Summerhill, her expression blank.

She was thinking about turning him in, Summerhill knew. Worse, he couldn't blame her for wanting to do it. Whatever was going on here, whatever had caused this fleet to distrust Katherine, it all came down to him. Somehow. Not on purpose, but still somehow.

He'd come here to help her. He'd ended up doing the exact opposite. Way to go.

No, Summerhill wouldn't let Katherine come to harm because of him. He'd abandoned her once before, and through no help of his, she'd found some way of getting back to her feet. He couldn't let himself ruin that.

"Katherine, I—"

The room went blue again, the cessation of movement and sound even more awkward and jarring than the first time it had happened. Katherine froze, as before, the look in her eyes somehow even more accusing in the enduring stillness and silence.

"*Summerhill?*" The voice echoed inside of his head. "*Summerhill, lah, I thought that was you!*"

Despite time being slowed to a near halt, Summerhill's mind seemed to be working normally. He tried to place the voice, lilting and musical, but like so many other things, he couldn't be sure if it was supposed to be familiar or not. Moving his muzzle was impossible, and so he tried to respond by forming his thoughts into words. "*Yes, that's me. Who is this?*"

There was the brief impression of laughter, followed by, "*Oh, curious, curious! Lonely little Summerhill finally managed to escape.*" A series of clicks bounced around inside Summerhill's head. "*Naughty dog, let out without a leash.*"

Summerhill's mind scrambled, trying not to sacrifice the clarity of his words in his rush to reply. "*You know who I am? You know where I'm from?*"

"*Oh, no love, lah? Curious indeed. But oh, looks like there are other things in store for you right now. Will have to talk more later, naughty dog.*"

The blue tinge over the cabin lifted as Summerhill's mind cried out for the other consciousness to wait. Instead, an actual cry escaped his open muzzle as time shifted back to normal.

Katherine flinched at the sound, and her hand shot to the holster at her hip. She then bit her lip and breathed in and out through her nostrils. If she'd been wary of Summerhill before, she was even more so now after what must have looked to her like a random outburst.

He started to mouth an apology—started to, because before any words came out, there was a bright, painful flash. It blinded him, his vision going solid white, and then the sound of machinery, the floor underneath his feet, and the air against his fur all vanished.

 # TWENTY-THREE
INTERROGATIVES

There had been bright light when Summerhill lost consciousness, and now there was bright light again as he was returning to it. He couldn't tell if his eyes were open or closed, but he could tell that they stung worse than they'd ever felt—no, the Plain of Ice had been worse, but this was a close second. His stomach churned with nausea, and his head hurt even more than the time he woke up in...

...in where? Where had that been?

Wildflowers. An orange sun. Dirt and grass beneath him. Where?

As he drifted closer to full wakefulness, Summerhill was quite aware of the hole in his memory. He could feel the edges of it, as if a hole had been cut out—no, not cut out, but *torn* out, ripped and frayed, uneven, with tiny bits of the picture still left behind. Those sharp edges hurt, as if they were cutting into other memories adjacent to them.

At the near end of that memory gap was a chasm of emptiness and a giant wooden door, and on the far end was Katherine and the *Nusquam*, but in the middle, there was—

Katherine! There was no time to try to sort out this quandary with his missing memories. Katherine was in danger, and he'd been trying to think of a way to help her. If only he could sort out the buzzing in his ears and the light blinding his vision, he'd figure things out from there.

"His eyes appear to be focusing."

"Can he hear us?"

"I think so. He's—look, I just saw his ear twitch!"

"Careful, now. We're not sure what he might—"

Voices, all overlapping, analytical and overexcited, echoed in Summerhill's ears. As his hearing returned, so too did his eyesight. Both were still oversensitive. A halo of hazy color throbbed at the edges of his vision as the bizarre picture before him slowly took shape.

A man, human like Katherine, but with darker skin and less delicate features, stood with his face inches from Summerhill's. He lacked hair at the very top of his head, and what hair he had on either side was peppered with gray. His eyes were intense, his gaze calculating and emotionless as he stared at the dog, looking him over in calm silence.

The man wore a uniform, only vaguely reminiscent of Katherine's. It was dark blue, with trim of vermillion and silver, and his chest and collar both bore elaborate insignia. Behind him, standing in diagonal rows like a flock of birds, other uniformed humans anxiously waited for Summerhill to do something.

Summerhill was standing upright, somehow. He wasn't sure how he'd been unconscious without falling over, but his feet were firmly planted on the floor, and his sense of balance was fine despite the disorientation he'd been experiencing. Standing unconscious? How long had he been here?

As the spots of light faded from Summerhill's vision, the canine saw that some of the optic distortion remained. He was behind a layer of glass or some other translucent material that kept him separated from the humans. Turning around, he discovered that he was encased in some kind of cylindrical tube that ran between the floor and ceiling. Behind him was a baffling jumble of computers and display monitors and other high-tech gadgetry the likes of which he'd never seen, even aboard the *Nusquam*. Off to either side of the chamber there were rows of consoles, manned by uniformed technicians, some of whom were focused on their monitors, and others who were instead staring at Summerhill.

He was naked, he realized. Either these people had taken his clothes off before sealing him in this tube, or whatever had zapped him out of Katherine's cabin brought him and him alone. Regardless, being on display to a room full of people as he already was, the nudity didn't help his self-consciousness.

Slowly, the dog lifted one hand-like paw and touched it to the barely visible surface of the tube, then pressed his palm flat against it. It had to be some kind of advanced synthetic polymer, as it was far too sturdy to be glass, thin as it was.

There was a quiet, collective gasp from the assembled men in uniform. The darker-skinned one in front held up one hand to silence them, and then he looked intently at Summerhill. "Can you hear me?" he asked.

Summerhill nodded his head, his palm still pressed to the surface of his invisible cage.

The man raised an eyebrow. "Can you understand me?"

"Yes," Summerhill replied.

Raising his eyebrow further still, the man turned back to look at his colleagues, then cleared his throat and addressed Summerhill again. "How about now?"

"Yes."

"Interesting. And now?"

"Yes."

Another murmur rose up among the assembled viewers. Many of them looked shocked, but others looked delighted. The one in front (Summerhill decided he must be the leader) said, "Let the record state that the being has demonstrated an understanding of English, Korean, and Rigelian."

Summerhill tapped on the partition and then waved sheepishly to the uniformed men. "Excuse me," he said. "I think there's been some kind of misunderstanding here."

The leader began to walk around in a small circle in front of Summerhill's containment area. Off in the wings, scientists and technicians busily observed readouts and pressed buttons. "What do you call yourself?" the leader asked.

"My name is Summerhill. And if I could just—"

"Where do you come from?"

Summerhill sighed. "Oh, I wish I had an answer for you on that one. It's actually rather complicated, see, and I'm not—"

Again, the leader interrupted. "*What* are you? What is your race?"

"I appear to be some kind of dog. Maybe I'm part coyote or something?"

"Why have you come here? What is it you're after?"

"Well, as I've been trying to say, I think there's been some big misunderstanding here," Summerhill said. "You see, I had somehow wound up at what I think was the beginning of time, and I was trying to find Katherine, and I ended up in her quarters, but—"

"So you *are* acquainted with Warrant Officer Tinsley." The leader's voice was grave, and only now did he stop to pause and consider, at last ceasing his rapid-fire questioning. He turned to indicate one of the technicians behind him. "Inform Hermann that his suspicions were correct, and give him authorization to contact me directly if there's any further change in the resonance field."

Summerhill chewed his lip. "I promise, whatever you think is happening between me and Kath—Warrant Officer Tinsley, it's not. I mean, I don't know what you're thinking, but whatever it is, it's not that. Honest."

"How did you get inside our fleet? Through what means did you—"

"Admiral Choi," another one of the humans interrupted. He looked younger than the leader, his skin lighter, his uniform's regalia less elaborate, his face framed with eyeglasses. "Sir," he added with a quiet clearing of the throat. "The being's vitals have ramped up drastically. Heart rate and breathing rate are both elevated, and—"

The leader—this Admiral Choi—turned to the bespectacled man and looked him in the eye as he said, "Thank you, I can see that just fine myself."

"I realize that, sir," the younger man said. "I only wanted you to be aware that it's very likely that our—"

"I understand the ramifications, Ensign. Please do not voice tactical concerns in front of the creature."

Summerhill tapped his claws against the tube. "I said my name is Summerhill."

The Admiral ignored him, and kept his attention on his subordinate. He didn't glare, but there was a severity to his look that made the other man shrink pitifully back into his seat. With that taken care of, the Admiral turned to face another of his assembled staff members. This one was tall, bearded, with broad shoulders, his uniform bearing the same gray and silver accents as Katherine's. "How prepared is Security to deal with the creature at this point?" the Admiral asked him.

"Hi," Summerhill said, waving from within the tube again. "Look, you've just demonstrated that the creature can understand you perfectly. Maybe you don't need to talk about me like I'm not here?"

The bearded Security officer looked back and forth between Summerhill and the Admiral a few times, and hesitated to speak. "Well, sir," he eventually said, "assuming that the, uh, being—" He again looked at Summerhill, awkwardly cognizant that his every word was being overheard. "—assuming there's some sign that he's about to take threatening action, the vaporization array is ready to fire nearly instantaneously."

"Oh, now you're already planning to *vaporize* me?" Summerhill tried to throw his arms up, but the tight confines of his tubular chamber made him smack his forearms to a halt before he got them up past his chest. "If you're that convinced that I'm dangerous, ask your Warrant Officer Tinsley what she thinks about me."

Which, Summerhill realized all too late, may not turn out well for him. Katherine had been considering selling him out, he was sure of it, and if confronted directly by her superiors with the choice to save him or herself, he didn't doubt who she'd pick. Well, maybe she wouldn't tell the Admiral to go ahead and vaporize him, but the prospect of being trapped in an experiment tube for the rest of his life (what sort of lifespan did he even have, anyway?) wasn't exactly comforting, either.

"Oh, we fully intend to. And I'm sure that what she has to say will be most illuminating." The Admiral brought a hand to his chin and rubbed it as he paced around in that small circle he'd trod before. Here and there he would briefly raise one eye and fix it on his prisoner. The rest of the room was tense in their silence. Each footstep carried some great weight that everyone, including Summerhill, felt.

"Do you know where you are?" the Admiral finally asked.

"I'm apparently in some kind of tube," Summerhill replied. "In which I hope I won't be vaporized."

Pressing three fingertips against his creased forehead, the Admiral sighed, then said, "I have to wonder if this is all some kind of joke to you."

"You're holding me prisoner and threatening me with execution," Summerhill replied. "I'm taking you seriously, believe me. I'm just wondering why you're not doing the same."

"Then answer my question," the Admiral demanded. "Truthfully, not with flippant remarks."

Summerhill sighed and looked around. Since arriving in this reality, he'd only been in this tube and Katherine's quarters. He tried to detect any of the telltale vibrations that would suggest he was still aboard a ship, listening with his ears and eventually feeling a slight buzzing in his fur and through his bones, the sensations muffled, possibly by the tube. "Katherine said her ship was called the *Ajax*." He made sure to look the Admiral in the eye. "But she also said that it was a science vessel. So, if you're the Admiral, I can only venture a guess that this is your flagship."

The officers murmured, and Summerhill tried hard to make out with they were saying, but in the excited hubbub, it was difficult to pick out individual conversations from the inside of the enclosure. The Admiral was either annoyed or bemused at the situation that Summerhill had created; he, unlike the others, remained quiet, and stared at the dog, dubious and mistrusting.

"My science team tells me," the Admiral said, raising his voice such as to squelch any remaining chatter, "that you shouldn't exist. That the very matter you're made of defies analysis." He locked his eyes with Summerhill's, and stayed very, very serious. "That you are not merely an alien, but that you cannot possibly be from this universe."

"And is that important somehow?" Summerhill asked. "Either way, I'm not from here."

"You recognize that this is a military installation; therefore you understand why I must demand an answer as to what you are doing here and why you have invaded one of our ships."

"Honestly, I was just trying to find Katherine," Summerhill said. "I thought that she was in trouble, but it turns out I was wrong. I didn't know about any fleet or military mobilization and I certainly wasn't aware of any vaporization array, so if we could just discuss this calmly, I'm sure we could work something out."

Standing behind the Admiral, the Security officer had turned his attention away from the tube and appeared to be looking at one of the monitors off to one side. The Admiral himself drew closer to Summerhill. "And how is it that you know Katherine Tinsley?" He clasped both hands together behind his back.

"That's kind of a long story, really. How about you let me out of here and we can talk about it over drinks? Something fizzy, if you have it."

The Admiral pressed his face close to the tube. "I'm not letting you out until I know for sure that this fleet is safe," he said, his stern tone brooking no complaint. "You will answer the question."

"Fair enough. Though I will point out that the extradimensional dog-creature is very naked right now, and that's making conversation with a man in uniform such as yourself exceedingly awkward."

A few of the officers chuckled at that, and more than one had to pointedly redirect their gaze. The Admiral shot a quick look over his shoulder to silence his men. Clearing his throat, he resumed his interrogation. "You admit, then, that you are not from this universe."

"I don't see the point of denying something your scientists have already told you is true," Summerhill said. "That, and to be blunt, they probably understand it a whole lot better than I do, anyway. I'm not even sure how I got here."

"You said you came for Warrant Officer Tinsley. That seems straightforward enough."

Summerhill thought about his discussion with Shoön, her returning the pocket watch to him, and his dream of the leaf-strewn river before suddenly appearing aboard the *Ajax*. "It's not as straightforward as you might think," he told the Admiral. "If it helps, I knew Katherine—Warrant Officer Tinsley—from a long time ago. Before she was a member of your military." Which was true, as far as he knew. There was no real way of telling how much of what she'd told him before had been an elaborate fabrication.

The synthetic material of the tube started to darken, and Summerhill's heart pounded with panic as he feared that the Admiral had grown tired of this game and had decided to just go ahead with the vaporization. A moment later, though, the rest of the room went dark as well, tinted the same shade of blue that Summerhill had seen when time had frozen back in Katherine's quarters. Sure enough, the hubbub of the officers and their advanced equipment went silent, and the Admiral, his Security head, and the rest of his underlings went still.

"*Oh, Summerhill, something strange is coming, lah.*" It was the same lilting voice as before, and despite the nominal warning, it sounded distinctly amused. "*Your fault? Probably your fault. Naughty dog.*"

Anger rose in Summerhill's chest. If he could have gritted his teeth, he would have. Instead, he imagined doing it as hard as he could. "*Why is everyone trying to accuse me of something terrible when I haven't even done anything?*" he demanded.

"Because if the problem is just my being here, believe me, I'll leave."

The voice clucked a few times, then said, "Not sure you'll have the chance, lah. But stay alert, yes? Naughty dogs are clever dogs."

"Do I even know you?" Summerhill asked. "Because you sure seem to know me, and if you're going to keep insulting me, I—"

"Oh, Summerhill knows Royeyri, yes, yes. And Summerhill can trust Royeyri. Hopefully." There was another clucking laugh.

Summerhill uselessly tried to will his hands into fists. Since time had only slowed but not stopped, there was the very barest measure of progress, and that would have to be enough to satisfy his aggravation. "Look, if you can help me out of this mess, then help me. Otherwise, can you please get out of my head?"

"Tut, Summerhill, tut. Just sit tight—well, not that you have much choice at the moment!" Chuckling then faded into silence, and the blue ambiance began to lift from the room.

Royeyri? Should that name have rung a bell? Summerhill tried to search the hole in his memory for some sign of it, but as he suspected, there was only frustrating emptiness with too-vague, tantalizing clues that led nowhere solid.

Neither the Admiral nor his crew reacted as if anything were amiss. "Why don't we see what Tinsley herself has to say about the situation, shall we?" the Admiral said. He turned on his heels and nodded to his Security man. "Bring her in."

The Security officer brought his hand near his collar and said something too quiet for Summerhill to hear. Seconds later, a door on the far side of the room slid open, its two halves disappearing into the bulkhead to either side.

Two armed guards brought Katherine in. They were dressed like Katherine had been when Summerhill had first seen her over on the *Ajax*. Katherine herself, however, had been stripped of her uniform. She wore a white, sleeveless tee underneath a dark olive tank top, and her hands were bound behind her back. Her head hung low as she was marched in, but she looked up when one of the guards kicked the back of one of her boots as they presented her to the Admiral.

She looked at the Admiral, then past him to see Summerhill in his prison tube. A gesture from the Admiral, however, made her snap back to attention.

"Admiral Choi, please," she said. "I can explain. I just—"

"Oh, you will explain, Tinsley. You're right about that," the Admiral replied dryly. "You will also speak when spoken to. Am I quite clear?"

Katherine's head fell again. "Yes, sir."

For the space of several intense heartbeats, the Admiral regarded Katherine in silence, and though Summerhill couldn't quite see his face from this angle, he had no trouble picturing the dispassionate look in the older man's eyes as he tried to assess his lowly underling. "This creature," he said at last, without even bothering to indicate Summerhill with so much as a nod, "claims to know you." Only then did he look back, meet Summerhill's eye, then turn back to Katherine. "An entity from outside this universe—something unprecedented, something that no human being has ever encountered before in all our history—claims to know you, on a first name basis, no less."

He straightened his collar, then paused for a moment before going on. "And Specialist Hermann tells me that your mere presence, on multiple occasions, has caused anomalous distortions in the resonance field that his experiment is producing. A field which—"

"Sir, with all due respect, it was you who had me transferred from the *Agamemnon* to the *Ajax*," Katherine said. "I couldn't possibly—"

"I did not ask you to clarify your orders, Ms. Tinsley," the Admiral countered, and though his voice was sharp and clipped, he didn't quite snap. He took a deep breath, rubbed at his forehead, and began to pace in a circle around Katherine.

"We have a very real security breach here amidst our fleet, and a risk to civilization itself that may well be incalculable." He stopped after completing a full circuit around her. "And somehow, you, a young woman from one of the colonies, is smack dab in the middle of it."

Even from a distance, Summerhill could see Katherine swallow. She looked up at the Admiral, her face pale and her eyes wide. She shook her head, the curls of her hair falling down over her forehead. Her throat rippled again, and her chest heaved as she gathered enough breath and composure to speak. "Sir, please, it's not what you think."

"I don't know what to think, Tinsley." The Admiral's voice was flat. He again brought his hands behind his back. "Enlighten me."

Katherine nodded several times in succession. "Of course, sir. It's... Well, it's a long story."

The Admiral turned an eye to Summerhill again. "So I hear. Entertain me."

"I hope you like good stories, then, sir," Katherine replied, half of a smile cracking through onto her face. "First, the fact of the matter is that I'm actually from the year—"

Ambient speakers in the room sprang to life. "Nestor *to* Achilles, *priority one emergency channel. Our FTL support system just overloaded and—*"

"Achilles, *this is* Philoctetes. *We've lost main power throughout the ship. Sensors have—*"

"*—and are currently venting air into space. Repeat, this is* Menelaus—"

Just as abruptly, the jumble of distress signals went silent. The Admiral whirled away from Katherine and turned to one of the ensigns seated at the row of consoles. "Get me Royeyri," he barked. Gone was his stern lack of emotion; now he exuded the passion of command after three simple words. "Find out what the hell is happening out there."

At the mention of Royeyri's name, Summerhill jerked back in surprise so hard that he smacked the back of his head hard against the wall of the tube. While his skull was still ringing from the impact, the lights in the room flickered, and the speakers crackled back on.

"*This is Vessel Three-One-Two-Two-Four Prime of the Transdimensional Spacetime Integrity Enforcement Consortium.*" The words were gurgled and distinctly inhuman, but still wholly intelligible. "*Your vessel harbors a fugitive from justice. Surrender your prisoner to us immediately or we will have no choice but to use force.*"

TWENTY-FOUR
EXTRADITION

"Intruding vessel," the Admiral bellowed, showing no open fear even as most of his assembled men had faces wide with shock, panic, or disbelief. "This is Admiral Donovan Choi of the Fifth Fleet, Kentaurus-Procyon Hegemony. You are currently in violation of our space, and I demand—"

"*Your demands are inconsequential to us, human, as is your so-called sovereignty.*" The sinister, disembodied voice carried the faintest notes of contempt, as well as something else that Summerhill couldn't quite place due to the bizarre, alien tonality of it. Impatience? Urgency, perhaps? "*Consortium law requires us to give only this initial request for compliance.*"

The Admiral made a chopping motion with his hand across his own neck, then turned to the ensign at the communication terminal. "Do we have an ident on the vessel? Make, known designs, anything?"

"No, sir," the ensign said, shaking his head. With more trepidation, he added, "Royeyri claims he doesn't recognize it, either."

Lights and computer consoles flickered again as the ship lurched to one side. Summerhill lost his footing, but given how narrow the confinement tube was, he was unable to fall. His hands scrabbled at the smooth, curved surface as he tried to regain his balance, but before he could, the entire ship shook once more, sending him off balance again.

A muttered curse slipped from the Admiral's lips, the first sign Summerhill had seen of him not appearing completely in control. "What's the status of the fleet?" he snapped as he hurried between different stations, checking various readouts over crew members' shoulders.

In the midst of the chaos, Katherine stood there, forgotten by the Admiral and the crew. Summerhill could see the whites of her eyes as she looked at him, her face silently pleading with him for—something. What could he possibly do, though?

The communications officer stared at his monitor. "All ships reporting moderate to major damage, sir," he said. "Our own defense grid is down, and our backup FTL is fried. *Agamemnon* and *Philoctetes* claim they're dead in the water."

Another jolt rocked the *Achilles*, and the bearded Security officer shouted into the communicator at his collar, his words drowned out by a series of explosions that echoed through the bulkheads. One of the nearby consoles started to blare an angry-sounding alert. The Admiral pushed the station's crewman out of the way, then jabbed at the keyboard to silence the alarm. From deeper in the ship, Summerhill could hear the stampeding of hurried footsteps and people calling out orders.

The ship stopped shaking a few moments later, making the sounds of controlled panic louder and more distinct. Summerhill managed to get back upright again, bracing his body in place with his arms pressed against the sides of the confinement tube. Though the tension in the room was still palpable, military efficiency had taken over, asserting as much control over the situation as possible.

"Admiral, the vessel has ceased its attack," the ensign announced. "Communications are down. Sensors show that all our ships have suffered extensive damage, but are still intact. No casualties reported from aboard *Achilles* itself."

The Admiral drew himself back up and straightened the front of his uniform. "Where the hell did these bastards even come—"

A pinpoint of light blazed into existence over by one of the walls. The assembled crew in the room turned to look at the glow, which shimmered in the air with no obvious source. It then extended into a perfectly straight line through the air, parallel to the floor. With a sound like a thunderclap, space itself appeared to tear open as if along a seam formed by that line of hovering light.

The shape it formed was an oval, longer along the horizontal, its sides blunted. It reminded Summerhill of one of the viewing screens back aboard the *Nusquam*, only there was nothing physically there, only a window of nothingness which soon coalesced into an image projected to the entire room.

The creature in the viewing window was covered with a gnarled, glistening, wet-looking carapace. It had four legs, hindquarters extending behind itself, ending in a segmented tail that twisted slowly from one side to the other. Lacking any real torso, it instead had shoulders that served as the origins to both its forelegs and its arms, the latter ending in hands of four claw-like fingers. Its head was shaped vaguely like a walnut, complete with the seam running through the middle of the shell. Six shiny black eyes, three on either side, peered out from under horny crests that mimicked the appearance of eyebrows.

Its mouth was a comparatively tiny set of slavering mandibles that dripped as the creature spoke. "We will not be ignored, human. In the name of the Consortium, we demand that you relinquish the prisoner to us at once."

Several of the humans flinched and recoiled at the sight of the thing, some going so far as to cover their mouths in shock. The Security officer drew a pistol that looked identical to the one Katherine had worn earlier. He drew a bead on the creature, but the Admiral hastily stuck out his hand, silently ordering his man to stand down.

The Admiral glared at Summerhill, then turned to face the six-eyed creature. "Before we extradite our captive to you, we would ask that you let us know what he has done." After a short pause, he added, "Merely to satisfy our own curiosity."

The six-eyed creature turned its huge head to look at Summerhill. It lacked eyelids, and so it didn't blink, making even a brief glance feel like a penetrating stare. It clacked its mandibles, more thick liquid slurping down out of view, and returned its attention to the Admiral. "This being is unknown to us," it said. "We request the surrender of the one you call Katherine Tinsley."

"Tinsley?" With that single word, the Admiral's facade broke, however briefly, and Summerhill saw just how out of his element the man was, facing a being like this in the wake of his fleet being ravaged. "What's she got to do with any of this?"

"The joke's on you," Katherine called out, raising her head high despite her hands being clasped behind her back. "You've come all this way to find me, but I don't even have your precious modulator circuit anymore. I got rid of that a long—"

The alien creature's mandibles dropped further away from its face and spread apart, the only obvious change of expression it was capable of displaying. "The hyperspace modulator circuit is immaterial. Consortium agents will recover it via temporal manipulation, in due course. You have been found. Your people will turn you over to us or face further reprisal."

Even trapped inside his tube, Summerhill could feel the air of bristling anticipation pervading the room. People exchanged furtive glances, everyone wanting to voice any number of thoughts, concerns, suggestions, or fears, but none dared speak while the being from the Consortium had the floor. The Admiral looked at Katherine, studying her, but she ignored him, keeping her eye turned toward her alien accuser instead.

"Tinsley, explain this," the Admiral ordered, but before she had any time to respond, he turned to the viewing window and addressed the alien again instead. "What do you want with her? As her commanding officer, I demand that you tell me what connection she has to you."

"You are in no position to make demands, human," the alien replied. "Katherine Tinsley stands accused of three counts of temporal violation of Dimension Three-One-Two-Two-Four, two counts of existential integrity violation of

195

Dimension Three-One-Two-Two-Four, one count of home dimension desertion relative to Dimens—"

"None of that was my fault, and you know it!" Katherine's face was white, and her skin appeared stretched taut over her face. "Besides, how is that any different than what you yourselves do, hopping around time and space willy-nilly to do as you like? Admiral, please, you can't let them take me, I beg of you."

Summerhill tried to pound on the wall of his tube, but there was so little room to move his arm that all he could muster was a weak, ineffectual slap of his palm against the smooth surface. Nobody even seemed to be paying attention to him anymore, not even Katherine. That made the standing by and watching helplessly even harder to bear.

The alien rolled its half-dozen eyes and looked off to one side, its attention fixed on something not visible through the viewing window. It made a wet, throaty noise, and Summerhill couldn't guess what sort of emotion that sound was supposed to convey. "Ah," it then said, sounding eerily like one of the humans in tone for just one syllable, "we have further localized the source of the local spacetime anomaly. Human vessel, registration given as *Ajax*. History lists this vessel as conducting research on technology not permitted to your civilization in the current time frame." One of the alien's clawlike appendages reached over, out of view, and there was a single click. "Local spacetime infractions have been corrected."

The ensign at the communication console spoke up again. "Admiral, the *Ajax* is gone." Summerhill could hear the restraint it took to keep his voice steady.

The Admiral quickly stepped over to the ensign's station, shoving Katherine out of the way as he did so. He leaned over the junior officer's shoulder and stared at the monitor. "Impossible," he breathed, but the look in his eyes confirmed what the ensign had already said. He stood back up and faced the alien, the look in his eyes as cold as his voice. "This is an act of war. I demand that you—"

"You may demand nothing. We have tarried long enough here. The record will show that Katherine Tinsley was forcibly extradited without formal consent. A requisite demerit for this noncooperation will be noted on your civilization's record." The alien snapped its mandibles back together, cutting free a dangling dollop of thick saliva. It pressed some other button or switch that was out of view.

A glowing white ring formed around Katherine, roughly in line with her waist. It looked much like the line that had grown into the viewing window. Katherine bit back a nervous shriek as she watched the ring coalesce and grow brighter, and then she looked toward the tube.

"Summerhill! Summerhill, please, do something! Don't let them take—"

And then, Katherine was gone. The image of the six-eyed alien was gone. The room was silent save for the sound of machinery and equipment. Summerhill tried yet again to pound or punch or strike at the tube surrounding him, but all he could do was slap his soft palm against the translucent material, accomplishing nothing beyond making a pathetic thumping sound. His body started to shake, and he slumped back with a dull whimper.

Once several seconds had passed, the ensign made a throat-clearing sound to break the silence before announcing, "Admiral, the Consortium vessel has disappeared."

The Admiral sighed and paced aimlessly back and forth. He clasped his hands together behind his back and kept his head bowed. "Get on the short-range wireless. Alert all ships to the situation, and get status and recovery reports," he ordered, his tone muted. "I want repair updates every twenty minutes." He drifted over towards an empty chair and settled into it.

The crew went back to work, noticeably discomfited. Some of the officers stared at Summerhill again, and after a few moments of sulking, the Admiral joined in, too.

"What was that thing?" he asked. "Where did they take her?"

Summerhill couldn't keep his snout from curling up into a snarl. "Why should I tell you anything? Are you going to suddenly believe the things I tell you now that you're the one licking your wounds?"

If the Admiral was perturbed by that barb, he made no show of it. "Not to quote our six-eyed friend, here, but I don't think you're in the position to be picky, Summerhill. That's your name?"

"And I don't think you're in the position to be snide. What do you want me to do? Get Katherine back for you so you can finish putting her on trial yourself?"

The Admiral locked eyes with him. He wasn't in the mood to joke, but neither was Summerhill in the mood to back down just because some naval officer thought he could retain control of a situation he'd already lost control of.

"You know Tinsley," the Admiral said. "From before this, somehow. I'm not sure how, or what that means, or even if you're an entity capable of having feelings for individuals who aren't of your own kind. But she seemed to want you to try to help her. She'd want you to cooperate with me."

"Oh, don't act like you guys were best friends all of a sudden." Summerhill was glad that he was incapable of punching the tube. "You clearly didn't know her very well, and if the last few minutes are any indication, you didn't trust her, either."

The Admiral shot to his feet. "As of a few minutes ago, the Kentaurus-Procyon Hegemony is at war with this Consortium, as far as I'm concerned. My men have been murdered, and an officer under my command was abducted from aboard my own flagship." Anger smoldered in his eyes. "You have some connection to all this, and so help me God, I am both very capable and very willing to hurt you if you think you can toy with me, dog."

"I don't have anything to do with this!" Summerhill cried. "I'm just..." He bit his lip so hard that he thought he might bite it off. "I'm just a dog who wanted to save one of my friends.

Because that's what Katherine is to me. That's why I came here." He locked eyes with the too-proud Admiral, trying to see if he could appeal to his sense of... Mercy? Understanding? He wasn't even sure what he should want right now. "And maybe if you'd listened to me earlier instead of showboating, I could have done something."

On some sick, twisted level, this whole venture made sense in retrospect. He'd asked Shoön where he was supposed to be, and when she told him that was his choice, he'd thought only about getting back to Katherine, to save her from the Consortium. It had been his fault that he hadn't been more specific, hadn't thought about the real where and when he wanted to go. Because here he was, at a different where and when, and Katherine had needed saving from the Consortium. And Summerhill had failed.

"I'm sorry," he said to the Admiral. "And I know you probably think that this is somehow my fault, but I don't even care. I just want you to know that you're not the only one here who's kicking himself for just standing here without doing anything."

The look that crossed the Admiral's face was hard for Summerhill to read in the handful of seconds he had to see it. It looked as though the Admiral was going to say something, but before he could, one of the doors—the same one that the guards had brought Katherine in through—opened, and a peculiar creature walked into the room.

Shorter than a human by about a third, it looked like some strange cross between avian and mammal, with a body covered in something that looked like something partway between feathers and fur, blue and soft. Its face featured a prominent beak-like protrusion in front, as well as large, intelligent eyes, and its head looked too big for its small body. It too wore the uniform of the fleet, modified to fit its inhuman body.

"Navigator Royeyri," the Admiral said with some surprise. "What brings you down here?"

The creature did not respond right away, but instead took its time to assess the state of things. No, not 'it'—one of the ensigns had referred to Royeyri as male. Without so much as moving his body, Royeyri craned his head in unnatural ways that made Summerhill's neck hurt just to watch it, the birdlike creature apparently capable of turning his head almost completely around. He silently snapped his beak, peered into Summerhill's eyes, then turned his attention back to the Admiral.

"Commotion. Calamity." He clucked a narrow, dark tongue against the edge of his beak. "Royeyri thought Admiral Choi needed checking up on, lah."

Again, with the rest of his body staying stock still, Royeyri turned his head around to look at Summerhill. "Also, powerful creature here, Royeyri felt. Powerful, *dangerous* creature, yes."

Royeyri's voice was definitely the same one Summerhill had heard in his head while time halted. His diction was somewhat off, but that may have been a result of his speaking the human tongue despite not having a human mouth. Earlier, Royeyri had said that Summerhill could trust him.

But trust wasn't something that Summerhill was feeling much of right now. Telling the superior officer present that he was "powerful and dangerous" didn't do a lot to sell him on the idea that Royeyri was on his side.

The Admiral turned one eye to Summerhill, but resolutely refused to show any fear despite Royeyri's warning. "What about the ship that attacked us? Have the Syorii run across vessels of that type before?"

Royeyri shook his head with sharp jerks. "No, no. Very unfamiliar, that one was. Unfamiliar, scary, too powerful. Best avoided, yes." He lifted a limb, some sort of cross between a wing and a true arm. An accusing finger indicated Summerhill. "This one, though, Royeyri knows, lah."

"The dog-creature?" the Admiral asked. "He and Tinsley seem to know each other. Somehow."

Royeyri's beak-like snout curled into a semblance of a wicked smile. "*Really?*" he cooed, drawing the word out for several seconds, clicking his tongue in rapid succession at the end. "So, so very curious, that is! Lots to learn from this one, yes. Capture it, study it. So much to find out, Royeyri is sure!"

Once more, Summerhill tried to pound on the tube, but only succeeded in bumping his elbow painfully as he tried to wind his arm up. He muffled his bark of discomfort as best he could, then growled out, "I don't know what he's talking about, Admiral. I swear to you that I am not here to threaten you or your fleet. All I want is to save Katherine—"

"Lies and trickery, lah, that's what this one's good at. Trust Royeyri, Admiral. Trust Syorii knowledge and wisdom. Best to rid yourself of the risk, especially now, yes?"

The Admiral was looking weary. He sighed, rubbed at his forehead, then turned his head so that he could keep an eye on both Summerhill and Royeyri at the same time. "What do you propose we do with him, then? Stun him and eject him out the nearest airlock?"

The clattering of Royeyri's beak was probably his species' equivalent of a cackling giggle. "Oh, such a waste that would be!" he crooned (really, Summerhill thought the bird-creature was enjoying the situation far too much). "Like Royeyri said, capture it, study it, learn about it."

A rough snort came from the Admiral. "I don't think he'll be particularly cooperative on that account, really."

Royeyri waggled his fingers and twirled his wrist. "Oh, leave that to Royeyri, lah. No problem. No problem at all."

TWENTY-FIVE
STOP

The next moment hung there indefinitely.

There was the vaguest sense of blue—not the hopeful blue Summerhill had seen in his other self's eyes so very long ago, but a nauseating, unkind blue. It wasn't visual—nothing was visual anymore—but it was *there*, present, oppressive, like the edges of a too-small universe ready to collapse in on itself

Nothing at all was clear. Nothing was happening, at least not completely. There was no Royeyri anymore, no Admiral and only kind of a Summerhill. The dog felt a wave rising up through his torso, rising and rising and rising upward, but never cresting, only getting higher and higher and higher. At the same time, he had taken a breath, and the air was stuck in his lungs with no way for him to exhale it.

Thought was no longer a conscious thing for him. His mind was locked into a hazy state between asleep and awake. Perception was only ever half-real. He couldn't hear words, only remember the impression that someone had spoken; he couldn't see images, only sense movement out of the corner of his eye, always colored in that same shade of blue, always frozen, never actually happening.

In his half-sleep, Summerhill had half-dreams, nothing strong enough to feel real. Half-images, a pocket watch that tracked time that never passed, engraved with words that didn't exist. Half-people, an otter he didn't remember, a girl forever on the run from a crime that hadn't occurred. Half-reality, where nothing was clear enough to bleed into what now passed for his thoughts.

And to Summerhill, poor Summerhill, a creature who had only just come to realize how connected he was to the stream of time, it was pure agony to be trapped in a state where time itself no longer existed. He needed so badly to feel the next moment, just as badly as if he were dying of thirst and needed a drink of water. It was always almost right there, the refreshing coolness of it so near his tongue.

Never there. Always almost there. One moment, then the next. That's all he needed, that simplest of things. It was like listening to a record skip, hitting the same few words over and over and over without moving on to the next line of the song.

Royeyri had spoken to the Admiral, right before...

Royeyri had spoken to the Admiral, right before...

Royeyri had spoken to the Admiral, right before...

Summerhill was only ever at right before. Blue. Immobile. Indefinite. Right there in his pocket, and yet simultaneously a thousand realities away, an antique pocket watch had stopped, the absence of its ticking a heartbreaking thing.

Then, some time later, at some later point that was impossible to define or describe, the blue faded away with alarming gentleness, and the next moment finally came.

TWENTY-SIX
REDRESS

Royeyri was the first thing Summerhill noticed when the world finally started up again. It took a few bleary seconds before he realized that Royeyri was the only thing still there from before his sense of time had gone awry.

Gone were the Admiral, his men, the confinement tube, and the *Achilles*. Instead, there was a sparsely decorated living room. The lights were turned down low, but the furniture itself—low tables and round chairs without backs—had an ambient glow of its own. The floor beneath Summerhill's feet vibrated, and a quick look around revealed two windows, one to either side, both showing nothing but a field of stars and empty space.

Even looking around like that made Summerhill quite dizzy, and Royeyri was quick to move, stepping forward, catching hold of one of the dog's hands and helping to set him down on one of the cushioned chairs before he fell. "Easy, lah, easy," Royeyri said, voice soft and hushed.

Once Summerhill was safely seated, Royeyri's chuckled through the large nostrils in his wide beak. He shook out his winglike arms, then paced in a wobbling circle around the chair. "That's it, Summerhill. Nice and calm, yes. Royeyri knows what he's doing, yes, see?"

The act of sitting down made Summerhill feel less lightheaded, but now his stomach felt queasy. He doubled over with pangs like those of hunger, and his ears folded back to block out even the barely audible hum of the ship's idling systems. The symptoms of weakness and oversensitivity then began to abate, if slowly.

"What happened? Where am I? Where did everyone go?"

"Admiral would have done something very stupid, Royeyri knew. So, Royeyri had to step in, save the day. Ta-dah! And now here you are."

Summerhill lifted his head back up and looked at Royeyri, whose beak-snout was curled up into a proud grin. "That doesn't explain anything. I hope you realize that."

"One thing at a time, lah. Genius thinking takes time to explain, no?"

"Genius thinking?" Summerhill withheld a snarl. "You call telling me to trust you and then selling me out to the Admiral 'genius thinking?'"

Royeyri cackled, hopping from one clawed foot to the other as his beak snapped and his tongue clicked musically. "Lies and trickery, that's what that was! See, Royeyri is clever, too. Clever like Summerhill, naughty dog, all escaped from his prison and dropping in unannounced!"

Summerhill tried to push himself to his feet, but he nearly pitched over, and instead fell back on his rump, pinning his own tail. It was then that he realized he was still naked, as he'd been inside the confinement tube on the *Achilles*. Embarrassment combined with his fatigue and frustration. "You keep saying things like you know me." His voice had shifted into a whimper. "You're acting like I should know more about you than I do, and it's... it's driving me crazy, okay? So can you please start making sense?"

The energetic mammal-bird went calm and still, a soft whine of his own escaping his warbling throat. "Summerhill really doesn't remember Royeyri, does he? Oh, such a shame, lah! Back to the way things were before, yes. Sad, sad, lonely Summerhill, all alone."

The Admiral and his ship were gone. The Consortium was gone. Nobody was threatening to vaporize him anymore, and so while Summerhill wasn't sure he could trust Royeyri, the immediate danger was past, and that had to count for something.

"Tell me about my prison. Are you talking about the World of the Pale Gray Sky?"

Royeyri did a little hop and landed with both feet facing forward. "Yes, yes!" he chirped. "Empty skies, empty buildings! Vast, vast, neverending emptiness and just Summerhill in the middle. Summerhill *does* remember!"

Remembering that much was simple, and the churning fear in Summerhill's gut told him he was remembering it all too clearly, the isolation and solitude, the oppressive loneliness and the lack of meaning. "I remember being there. But I don't remember how I got there. And I don't remember you."

Royeyri clicked his tongue. "Summerhill doesn't remember," he said, shaking his head, not in dismay so much as confusion, as if this was the first time he'd been presented with this simple concept. "Summerhill could never remember things before, either, lah."

Summerhill shook his head. "So, wait," he said, holding up a hand, trying to will a nascent headache away. "You used to know me. At some point before I can remember now. And even then, I didn't remember anything about my past?"

The mammal-bird nodded his head. "Summerhill had problems remembering much of anything, lah. Very often, Royeyri would visit Summerhill as promised, and Summerhill would have forgotten all about Royeyri! So sad!" He gave his winglike arms a brisk flap. "Every day the same for poor Summerhill. So hard for Royeyri to explain that things change, not always the same."

While Summerhill still had no clear memory of Royeyri, the time spent in the World of the Pale Gray Sky was becoming real again. He remembered back when he had no sense of the passage of time, no concept of one day ending and another beginning. "Having visitors should have been remarkable," he said, as much to himself as to Royeyri. "I don't recall ever having something exciting to look forward to."

"Oh, sometimes Summerhill would be waiting, yes, all eager, tail wagging." Royeyri let out a nasal chuckle, then turned to look out the window as a flicker of motion passed outside the window, but Summerhill hadn't seen what it was. "But other times, Summerhill would be lost in his thoughts, again. Lost and trapped, too sad to open up, too sad to think or dream."

Summerhill shut his eyes and tried to remember anything like this. The jagged outlines of the hole in his memory were there, but the miniscule fragments contained nothing of the World of the Pale Gray Sky, as far as he could see. No, if he'd forgotten Royeyri, he'd done it a long time ago. "When was this, anyway?"

"Not so long ago, lah," Royeyri said. "No, not so long. Only decades, by this reckoning. Not sure how time passes for Summerhill."

How long had it even been since he'd left the World of the Pale Gray Sky? A day or two aboard the *Nusquam* and inside the nevereef, months in the dying world of mountains and snow, plus however much time had passed during the gap in his memory. That span of time couldn't account for all the things Summerhill knew. He was sure there had to be something else.

"I met myself," he said, looking Royeyri right in the eye. "Do you ever remember seeing more than one of me on your visits? You said sometimes I'd seem sad, and other times I'd seem happier. On some visits, did I have gray eyes, and others blue eyes?"

Royeyri hummed and turned his head almost completely sideways. "Not sure, lah. Royeyri never saw Summerhill physically, see. Not completely."

"What do you mean by that?"

"Syorii go places." Royeyri held his arms up, and his feather-fur ruffled as he gestured to the room around him. "Not with matter, but with self, you see?"

Summerhill's ears went back. "I don't, no. Sorry."

If Royeyri was offended, he just laughed it off. "Summerhill understood before. But Summerhill seems to forget things, lah."

The dog's ears flattened out to either side and his tail, already motionless, drooped lower. "Syorii is the name for your people? I heard the Admiral call you that, too."

"Yes, yes. Many Syorii with the humans. Kay-Pee Hegemony, very powerful, needs Syorii as navigators, see."

Summerhill thought about what he'd seen aboard the ships of the Admiral's fleet, and the technology they possessed. "They *need* you as navigators? Why's that?"

"Like Royeyri said, Syorii go places, see through space and time. Syorii see obstacles and accidents before they happen. Human computers, only see things at speed of light. Not fast enough, tut tut. So, Syorii navigate. Humans get to traverse space, and Syorii get to go with them in body instead of just mind."

"You can go places with your mind? Does your mind actually leave your body?"

Royeyri tilted his hand from side to side. "Go places, see places; hard to distinguish. Other places are hard to get to. Requires great concentration and spiritual purity."

"But you have this ability. And you can go to other worlds, like the World of the Pale Gray Sky?"

Royeyri nodded. "Some places are scary and dangerous. Some places are wonderful and exciting. And some places are sad and lonely." With that, he offered a sympathetic smile to Summerhill.

Summerhill chewed one of his claws in thought. "But you have some ability to teleport your bodies, too, right? I mean, otherwise, how did we get here?"

"Teleport? Syorii have no ability to—" Royeyri paused, his beak freezing in mid-sentence as his eyes went glassy with confusion. Then, he lifted up a limb as if in triumphant salute to himself and broke out into a very avian cackle. "Oh! Oh, ho, ho, Royeyri sees, he does!" He did a little jig, hopping back and forth from one foot to the other. "Summerhill only sees a blip and a flash and then—bing!—here with Royeyri again."

A sinking feeling started to form in Summerhill's belly. His ears stayed flat, and his words shook with trepidation as he spoke. "No, it wasn't like that at all, actually. I felt like I was going to be stuck and trapped forever." Not entirely unlike the World of the Pale Gray Sky, really. "Why, what did you do?"

"Royeyri used cunning and ingenuity and patience, lah." The Syorii knocked himself on the side of the head with his knuckles. "Admiral was on-edge, scared, unsure. *Mistrusting.*" He seemed to delight in saying that last word. "Summerhill, strange creature, naughty dog, obvious threat. Summerhill had to be stopped! So, Royeyri stopped him." The bird-creature's wrist turned in a circle again.

Summerhill's throat had gone tight. "Stopped how? I don't—"

"Stopped everything!" Royeyri chirped, again showing some pride in what he'd done. "Stasis. Shut down Summerhill's mind, Summerhill's body, made it all come to a halt. No more threat, no more problem."

"Stasis?" Summerhill's heart was racing. His mind was scrambling with panic, the edges of his perceptions already bristling with nervousness at something his conscious mind was still piecing together. "You had me frozen? For how long?"

"Not long. Made sure that Summerhill was in good health, first. But ah, tut, tut. Of course, Summerhill would be unchanged. Royeyri, very skilled, very clever."

There was more movement outside one of the windows. This time, Summerhill clearly saw the form of some kind of spacefaring vessel pass by. Against a backdrop of pinpoint stars, however, there was no way to gauge how large or how far away it was. "Well, I'm guessing we're not still in the fleet, since they were dead in the water. Unless they got things up and running again."

Royeyri chuckled and nodded. "Oh, yes. Took many hours, but ships fixed. Very, very large repair bill after returning to base! Oho, top brass, very upset, lah."

"So we already made it back to base, then?" That sounded better than floating helplessly through space, but Summerhill was still worried. "What about the Consortium? Does the Admiral have any leads on where they took Katherine?"

"Admiral Choi?" Royeyri tilted his head to one side, and then the other, looking as though he didn't comprehend what he was being asked. "Oh, Admiral Choi is dead, lah."

The indistinct anxiety Summerhill had been feeling congealed into full-on fear and dread. "Dead?" he squeaked. "Was it the Consortium? Did they kill him for—"

"Oh, no, no," Royeyri interrupted, waving both arms. "Consortium did not kill Admiral Choi. Admiral Choi was killed by—how did humans say it?" He clucked his tongue and shifted his weight back and forth, wobbling as he thought. "Ah, yes, yes! 'Inexorable march of time!' Inexorable march of time killed Admiral Choi."

"Wait, so he just *died*?" This wasn't making any sense. "How? When?"

Royeyri counted with jerking motions of his fingers that were too fast for Summerhill to keep up with it. "Twenty-three months ago? Yes, that sounds right."

"Royeyri, that's almost two years!" Summerhill could barely hear himself think as his rushing pulse pounded in his ears. "You kept me in stasis for two years?"

"What? No! No, no, no," Royeyri assured him. "Thirty-six years."

"*Thirty-six?*" Summerhill's jaw hung open after he blurted that out.

Royeyri looked unfazed by this announcement of his, and he only shrank back a little bit at the dog's shocked outburst. "Thirty-six," he confirmed. "Not long."

Summerhill's claws dug so hard into the fabric of his seat that they punctured holes through it, and the canine had to hold on tight to keep from reeling forward. "Not long?" he barked. "What happened that it took you over three decades to get me out of there?" Oh, this was no good. This was no good at all. How long did humans live? Was Katherine even still alive?

"Three decades, long for humans, lah, not so long for Syorii or for Summerhill," Royeyri said with a dismissive wave of his wing-arm. "Scientists took a lot of time studying Summerhill. Kept trying, kept poking and prodding, never learned anything useful. Couldn't make sense of interdimensional matter structure, had no way to detect vital signs because vital signs had been paused." He hopped up and landed daintily on his toes. "And they never suspected that Royeyri had been behind it all, because Royeyri is a genius!"

"Thirty-six years," Summerhill muttered. He was having trouble coming to terms with the reality of it. "They studied me in stasis for over thirty years?"

Royeyri nodded. "Studied and learned nothing. Eventually decided to transfer Summerhill from Rigil Kent headquarters to science station at Eta Vulpeculae. And who gets put in charge of transfer but Royeyri himself! So, now, Summerhill is woken back up, escape complete!"

"Yeah, complete after thirty-six years!" Summerhill clutched the sides of his head in his hands and rocked back and forth atop his chair. "You said that was a long time for humans. How long do humans live?"

"Hard to say, hard to say," Royeyri said. "Sometimes fifty years, sometimes a hundred." He paused for a moment, for the first time showing some sort of empathy for Summerhill as regarded what he was saying. "Summerhill is worried about a human? Not Admiral Choi, tut."

Thirty-six years. Given the life expectancy Royeyri had cited, that meant that Katherine would have been waiting half a lifetime for Summerhill to come back for her. Hell, she'd almost forgotten about him after just five years, last time.

And this all assumed she was still alive at all, which, given the way the Consortium seemed to treat her, was a dubious prospect.

Royeyri seemed to put some of the pieces together on his own. "Ah, Katherine," he said, closing his eyes for a few seconds. "Yes, the human from another time, taken by Consortium on the day Royeyri re-met Summerhill. Royeyri remembers her."

Summerhill slumped. His head was hurting, and his stomach gnawed at itself. "She's gone, now. I came back to help her and I couldn't. They took her and I didn't have a chance to save her."

"Ah." Royeyri tucked his head closer to his chest and crossed one foot over in front of the opposite leg. "Yes, thirty-six years, probably too late, in that case."

With his palms pressed in against his temples, Summerhill sighed. "It's not your fault. You didn't do it on purpose." He rubbed away his headache as best he could, then looked back up. "Thanks for getting me away from the Admiral and his fleet, Royeyri. I'm guessing from the sound of things that you haven't run into the Consortium at all since then?"

Royeyri shook his head. "Just the one time, lah," he confirmed. "Syorii know things, many things, that humans don't. Know of species, cultures, civilizations that humans have never encountered, but Consortium was new. Once and only. Probably for best. Very dangerous. More dangerous than Summerhill."

A halfhearted smile appeared on Summerhill's face. "Well, at least I don't have to worry about anything thinking I'm a threat anymore." But what did he have to worry about anymore? Katherine was gone, and Royeyri didn't actually know that much about Summerhill's past after all. Now it was pretty much just him, turned loose upon this new universe, having escaped the brief danger that had crossed his path.

Maybe Shoön had given him his new beginning after all: a clean slate, a fresh start, a world of possibilities without baggage or responsibilities. If he wanted to, he could remake himself completely; other than Royeyri, nobody knew who or what he was, and nobody expected anything of him. There had been some bumps, sure, but those were over, and now he was faced with nothing but pure opportunity.

But if that were the case, why did he feel so hollow and anxious, sitting here in the cozy cabin of Royeyri's starship, with that whole universe open to him?

No, he didn't feel hopeful or optimistic *or* free to do what he wanted. None of this changed the fact that he was still Summerhill, with an unknown past, a hole in his memory, a missing pocket watch from someone special, and a friend who had begged him for help. That was no clean slate.

He stood up and walked over to one of the windows and looked out into space. Here and there, he saw the distant flickering of other ships moving against the blackness of the universe. In all likelihood, Royeyri had brought him out of stasis near some sort of transit corridor. Maybe there was somewhere he could go, somewhere specific, if only he could think of it.

Closing his eyes, Summerhill looked into his own mind and tried to examine the frayed edges of his crudely removed memories. There had to be something useful there, some sort of clue that might guide him towards a larger purpose than just selfishly wandering off to embrace this would-be *tabula rasa* he'd been presented with.

Wildflowers. An orange sun. A purple sky, dirt and grass, the babbling of a stream. Wind. Wind and the scent of someone he knew and didn't remember.

Wildflowers. An orange sun. A purple sky and, somewhere in the distance, the words *"You and I made a commitment to each other."*

An orange sun. A purple sky.

A flustered fellow who looked for all the world like a river otter in a tuxedo.

The last rays of sunset were fading, marking the horizon with a band of bright orange, like a strip of distant fire.

"It's kind of a long story."

Summerhill's eyes snapped open. "Rydale," the dog called out, whipping around to look back at Royeyri.

Royeyri tilted his head and trilled a wordless sound of confusion.

"Rydale," Summerhill repeated. "Is there a planet Rydale somewhere?"

"Rydale. Rydale, Rydale, Rydale." Royeyri repeated the word with different pitches and intonations, as if he were trying on a number of slightly different jackets. "Not sure. Not familiar. But lots of planets have lots of different names." He gestured to one of the doors leading out of the cabin. "Could always check astrogation charts, lah."

"Then that's what I'll do," Summerhill said. "Because I need to find this place and get back there." He started to walk off in the direction Royeyri had indicated, then stopped, looked down, and let his tail droop. "But, um, in the meantime, would it be possible to get me some clothes?"

 # TWENTY-SEVEN
Delineations

For two days, Summerhill searched the databases and star charts aboard Royeyri's ship.

It was an arduous search, too. The Kentaurus-Procyon Hegemony was only one of several starfaring civilizations that inhabited known space. They had very detailed records of their own space, fairly comprehensive records of the space occupied by their allies (such as the Syorii), and more nebulous details about areas of space far beyond their own reach, observed only through telescopes or described by hearsay from sources of dubious repute.

In none of these records could Summerhill find any mention of a planet called Rydale, with an orange sun, a purple sky, and a population of sentient creatures that looked like river otters who walked upright. Even if the Hegemony knew it by a different name, surely those three facts were enough to narrow down the planet he was looking for.

It seemed, though, that if this planet was out there, then neither the humans nor Syorii nor anyone else in the records had ever been there.

Royeyri kept Summerhill clothed and fed during that time, but he learned early on to stay out of the dog's way when he was actively going through the charts and records. Whatever Royeyri did in his spare time, Summerhill neither knew nor concerned himself with. The ship kept running and the food kept coming. That was good enough for him.

On the morning of the third day (night and day were simulated by ambient lighting changes in line with the ship's Hegemony chronometer), Royeyri brought Summerhill some breakfast, but this time, stayed and lingered after dropping off the food.

The fur on the back of Summerhill's neck prickled with annoyance. The dog was willing to give the Syorii only a few seconds of pointed silence in which he could bow out and step away gracefully. When the mammal-bird alien didn't take the opportunity, Summerhill turned his head just enough so that he could see Royeyri over his shoulder, out the corner of his eye. "What do you want?"

"Summerhill is still having no luck searching, is he?" Royeyri wrung his hands together, the feathers covering his winglike arms shifting and rippling. "Perhaps it would be best if Summerhill found someplace else to go, instead, yes?"

Summerhill hunched forward and balled both of his hands into fists. He had, since the night prior, resorted to manually going over paper star charts, rolled out onto the floor so that he could kneel down and scour them inch by inch. "There isn't anyplace else to go. I have to get to Rydale."

"Royeyri understands, yes." He clucked his beak and looked around the observation lounge warily. "In the meantime, however, Royeyri thinks—"

"What?" Summerhill snapped. "What does Royeyri think?"

Royeyri hung his head and scuffed one clawed foot against the floor, clear of any of the star maps. "Royeyri thinks that going somewhere—anywhere—would be preferable to staying here." His beak snapped weakly at empty air again. "Should also point out that, technically, ship is AWOL from Kay-Pee Hegemony, too."

The map was a mess of pinpoints indicating solar systems, curved lines representing starlanes, and shading that showed localized nebular density. The mishmash stared back at Summerhill, mocking him with their overabundance of information and complete lack of answers. "Then let's go," he said, his eyes glued to the charts at no point in particular. "Let's move, fly, whatever. We can look for Rydale that way." Dammit, where was this other version of him, the one that already seemed to know what he needed to do?

216

"Not so simple, lah," Royeyri said, his throat warbling with an apprehensive coo. "Finding an uncharted planet, very difficult, very time-consuming."

Summerhill scoffed. "We can take our time, then. The way I see it, you owe me thirty-six years."

The Syorii's clawed feet were beginning to scuff noisily against the floor. "Taking time, not the key issue. Thirty-six years probably *still* not enough time, if Royeyri and Summerhill don't know where to look, tut, tut."

"Then we'll look as long as it takes!" Summerhill cried as he pushed up onto his feet and spun around to confront Royeyri. "Don't you understand? I don't *have* anything else but this!"

"Then maybe Summerhill should find something else," Royeyri suggested quietly, not making eye contact.

Summerhill clenched his fists again, his claws digging into his palms. "I don't want to find something else. I want to find Rydale."

The Syorii sighed and hung his head, taking a few seconds to glance at the star maps. "Very difficult," he repeated. "Probably impossible."

"We can find it. You said you can send your mind out of your body, right? That's how you see obstacles and plot faster-than-light travel?"

"Well, yes." Royeyri nodded. "Issue is with range, though, see?" He flapped a wing towards one of the observation windows. "Royeyri's mind can only go so far for so long. Royeyri's ship, same thing."

Summerhill pressed the heels of his hands against his temples. He made a concerted effort to swallow an angry growl before it could escape his mouth. "Then we'll draw up a plan," he said, trying to keep both his voice and his state of mind even and level. "What sort of range are we talking about? I mean, your traveling mind found me in a different universe, and your ship—"

Orange sun. Purple sky. Otter standing on a hillside.

"It's a ship that breaks the rules of reality and flies between different universes. You think it can't travel in time, too?"

Summerhill nearly fell over as the shock of the idea hit him. His legs wobbled, but by wagging his tail and wheeling his arms he kept from tripping over the map printouts at his feet. "I've got it!" he yelped, stumbling a bit more as he dropped to his knees and started tossing charts aside as he looked for something he *knew* he'd seen. "I know where to go!"

Royeyri hopped up into the air, winglike arms flapping as he went up and came down. "Summerhill remembers where Rydale is, lah?"

"I don't need to find Rydale anymore," Summerhill replied, and he snatched up one of the printouts from the spread-out pile and held it up triumphantly. "I've got a better idea now."

"Better idea? Better than the only idea Summerhill had?"

The dog smiled. "I know how to save Katherine," he said, and he showed the star map to Royeyri. "I need you to take me to the Orion Nebula."

 # TWENTY-EIGHT
PILGRIMAGE

The trip to the Orion Nebula, Royeyri warned Summerhill from the outset, would take several weeks. It was a journal of over a thousand light-years, most of it long stretches of faster-than-light travel through deep space, where there would be very little to see or do. Or the rare occasions they could rest and resupply at way points, they would have to be quick and subtle.

"Stolen Hegemony starship," Royeyri explained. "Manifest indicating 'dangerous biological specimen.' Not good to get found out, lah."

True to Royeyri's word, time spent off the ship was minimal. Summerhill never saw the surface of any planets, but he did get to go aboard space stations or larger cruisers that Royeyri's tiny ship would dock with. Some of the places they stopped at seemed like legitimate travel outposts, the stations carrying various amenities for travelers and explorers, such as food supply stores, entertainment centers, lodging, and even places of worship. Other stops were seedier, sketchier, the clientele and proprietors alike visibly of a less honest bent: pirates, mercenaries, illicit traders and their ilk.

On the inside, the nicer space stations looked indistinguishable from well-kept buildings, the only obvious indication that they were even in space being the open bay windows that looked out onto the cosmos. They were clean and bustling, though never anywhere near full to capacity. Very few of the travelers, even in the better areas, seemed terribly happy with their lot, and when Summerhill asked Royeyri about it, the Syorii simply responded with a vague comment about the rigors of deep space taking their toll after a while.

If anything positive could be said about the dens of ill repute that Royeyri stopped at along the way, it was that the folks there at least seemed to be in better spirits. Much of that, though, was due to their being drunk or having just bilked some sucker out of all his money with some shady deal or rigged card game.

The vast majority of the people Summerhill saw were humans like Katherine. An alien would occasionally be present in some crowd or another, but there was nothing like the menagerie of different beings aboard the *Nusquam*. Summerhill kept his eyes peeled for any otter-like creatures from Rydale, but he never saw any. Only once did he even see another Syorii, and Royeyri had apparently carried out their entire exchange telepathically before Summerhill had a chance to meet the fellow.

For the bulk of the journey, however, Summerhill and Royeyri were alone aboard their little ship. To keep busy, the dog spent much of his overabundant free time on the ship's computers, mainly reading up on things like the history of both the human and Syorii civilization and cultures. The details of much of the high-level politics were difficult to understand without better context; the Kentaurus-Procyon Hegemony was only one of many human governments that existed now, to say nothing of factions who held allegiances to states or organizations that no longer legally existed.

New Zealand still existed, though, and it seemed much as Katherine had described it so long ago: a tiny little island nation on just one planet (which wasn't even part of the Hegemony, it turned out), populated by millions of people, adding their own unique speck of color to the mosaic of human history. It was dizzying, really, to see just how much there was to read about even these minute aspects of human culture. Even with weeks spent in the depths of space, Summerhill had barely been able to scratch the surface of all the information at his fingertips.

He thought back to the World of the Pale Gray Sky, though doing so made his heart race and his blood run cold. There was no texture, no cultural context, no anything. It was just a city devoid of life, meaning, and even inspiration. Endless buildings, countless structures to go into and search through, and even so, that whole entire world contained less of interest than the information on one single computer terminal aboard one tiny starship piloted by a lone Syorii amidst a vast, inscrutable universe.

And how insignificant must even this universe be when set alongside the myriad realities represented by the guests aboard the *Nusquam*? Surely it was impossible for any one mind to accept and comprehend all of that, Summerhill thought. When he'd first made his way on board that fantastical cruise ship, he'd been impressed, sure, by how wonderful and diverse things were, but coming from his amnesiac background with so little judge against, he hadn't been able to appreciate how humbled and amazed he truly ought to have been.

While the encompassing truth of multiple realities were impressive, that didn't make the comparatively little things any less impressive, as Summerhill was reminded when Royeyri pulled the ship out of FTL and showed him the Orion Nebula itself.

Summerhill was struck wholly by the overpowering beauty of the nebula. It looked not unlike a flower, the swirling gases like petals blossoming outward in a stunning array of green and red and blue-violet. Darker gases formed the shape of a calyx, in the cradle of which blazed young, fierce stars. Summerhill gave himself over to the moment, transfixed by the majesty of the sight. Even the intractable Royeyri seemed impressed, for once.

From the ship's cockpit, the nebula looked close enough to touch, like something Summerhill could reach out and touch with his mind, to shape and sculpt and control like a flower made of burning fire floating through space. Royeyri then explained that Summerhill was actually looking at a region of space some twenty light-years across.

"Summerhill wants to find a drydock here?" Royeyri asked, as if just wanting to make sure, one last time, that the long trip out here did in fact have a point, even if it was a ridiculous one.

"This is where Katherine said it was. I can't imagine it'll be too difficult to find."

Royeyri just laughed and sauntered off back to the observation lounge. "Come," he beckoned. "Royeyri will search the nebula. If Summerhill is so smart and sure, maybe he can find some way to help."

The first several days of searching yielded no results. Royeyri would sit cross-legged in the observation lounge, spread his arms, and then his eyes would flash blue and his entire body would go limp. Summerhill would then spend hours sitting by him, his body unsettlingly cold and still without his mind at the helm. The Syorii assured him more than once that it was okay, and that his body naturally entered a state of drastically reduced metabolism while his mind was off scouring the nebula, but that still didn't change the fact that Summerhill felt like he was watching over a corpse, meanwhile.

Royeyri did complain that the nebula itself made it harder to search, something about the near absolute zero of empty space being much easier to 'see' through while his consciousness was on sojourn. Summerhill had nothing to compare the experience to, and so he just took the Syorii's complaints at face value, though after a few days of nothing at all turning up in their search, he was starting to get frustrated with the excuses.

The Syorii insisted on a regular, systematic search pattern, but something about that adherence to regularity made Summerhill grow rapidly impatient. The dog pored over the ship's maps of the nebula and spent hours staring out the different viewing ports. He continued to see the nebula as a flower; the overall shape formed the petals, and inside that would be the stamens growing up from the center. He picked out stars to be the anthers sitting atop those stamens, and he drew up search plans that involved following the trails of gas and dust that made up the filaments. Royeyri protested what he considered a highly unscientific and irrational approach, but Summerhill pointed out that they were looking for a time-traveling cruise ship so that he could rescue a waitress from New Zealand from the interdimensional space police, and taken in that context, further debate just seemed futile and a little silly.

A few days later, at the tip of the third such stamen, Summerhill and Royeyri came across a brown dwarf. After coming back from one of his out-of-body trips, the Syorii finally reported something unusual.

"Quite strange, yes. Like a bubble, but not a real one. More like a sphere of glass. Yes, blown glass, like humans and Syorii make! Except not glass. Something less tangible but more impassible."

"What is it, then?"

"Familiar," Royeyri replied. "Like the curtains that separate this place from other places. Other places, like where Royeyri first met Summerhill."

Summerhill looked out the window; from here, the tiny star wasn't even visible to the naked eye, but it was out there, somewhere. "Can you take us there?"

"Royeyri can do that, yes." The Syorii hung his head and cooed to himself. "On one condition, lah."

"What's that?"

The mammal-bird turned his large, round eyes back up at Summerhill. "Don't make Royeyri go with you."

"You don't want to come?"

Royeyri shook his head.

"Oh, come on. I thought you had this grand sense of adventure. You know, guiding ships out past the frontier, exploring the unknown, sending your mind to other universes and all that."

"This time is different. Royeyri very close to retiring, see. Big pension. Probably big hazard pay, too, for having ship overrun and taken over by dangerous Summerhill." The edges of his beak-like snout curled up.

Summerhill laughed. "You're going to go back to the Hegemony and tell them I hijacked your ship?"

"Only until Royeyri bravely took it back!" The Syorii clucked his beak and tongue and did a little hop. "Tragically, strange alien dog specimen got away, lah. Royeyri has to return empty-handed, probably discharged from service, forced to retire many months early."

The dog smirked. "You're a little sneak."

Royeyri held up his arms and tapped himself on both sides of the head at the same time with his knuckles. "Genius thinking. Lies and trickery." He winked. "Royeyri gets by."

TWENTY-NINE
TERMINUS

Whatever the 'barrier' Royeyri had described was, it wasn't anything visible. What was visible, slowly drifting through the nebula in far orbit of the brown dwarf, was the drydock.

From a distance, it appeared as little more than a rusted-out, floating platform. There was no activity around it. There was no *Nusquam*, nor any other ship. The dock appeared to be abandoned. But Summerhill wasn't ready to give up hope yet. After all, the technology that had gone into the *Nusquam* was beyond anything that he'd seen on any of his other adventures, and this 'barrier' Royeyri insisted was there might have been obscuring the truth.

"Just pull up alongside and let me out," Summerhill told the Syorii as he looked out the cockpit window. "I'll take it from there."

Royeyri shook his head. "Don't have a vacuum pressure suit that'll fit Summerhill on board, tut."

"It's okay." Summerhill walked over towards the airlock. "I don't think I'm going to need one."

"Royeyri isn't so sure about that, lah."

"I'll be fine." He opened the outer hatch to the airlock and stepped inside, and the door spun shut automatically behind him. "I didn't come all this way just to turn back because I didn't have a pressure suit."

The world went slow and blue. *"Are you sure?"* Royeyri asked, speaking directly into Summerhill's mind.

"I'm sure. I'm Summerhill. These things seem to have a way of working out for me."

Before Royeyri broke off the psychic connection, Summerhill felt the sensation of the Syorii wishing him good luck more than he heard any specific words. The blue faded, the world resumed, and the wheel for the airlock's outer hatch began to spin.

There was a hiss as the air escaped the airlock, and then the hatch swung open. Summerhill, unperturbed, stepped out onto the dock, heedless of the fact that there might not be any heat or atmosphere, and shut the hatch behind him.

Yes, there was heat and an atmosphere, though not much of either. The air was thin, but breathable, and though it was cold, it was nothing compared to the world of mountains and ice. Summerhill rubbed his hands up and down his arms and sides to fend off the initial chill. So long as this search didn't take very long, he'd be fine.

The drydock itself was less elaborate than Summerhill had imagined. It really was little more than a metal platform floating in space, several kilometers long. A few small buildings adorned its surface. Piers jutted out from the side of the platform facing the star, spaced at regular intervals, with a large gap where it looked as though one of them had long since broken free and drifted off into space.

Summerhill had hoped that some kind of shield or veil— perhaps the mysterious 'barrier' Royeyri had mentioned— had hidden the drydock's true appearance from sight, but that theory was off the table now. At some point, this place might have been bustling with machinery and personnel, but now it was just an abandoned ruin floating through the Orion Nebula.

If the buildings had ever been labeled, they didn't bear those labels anymore. Still, something must still be functioning on this relic somewhere. Some kind of technology was giving this decrepit hunk of metal a gravity well and a breathable atmosphere and a radiation shield. Either that, or Summerhill was more immune to the laws of physics than he thought.

As Summerhill walked along the length of the platform, Royeyri's starship broke away and made a turn towards open space. Before the ship flew out of sight, Summerhill looked up and saw Royeyri through the cockpit's viewports, along with the astonishment on the Syorii's face as he looked back at the dog standing on the platform without a spacesuit. All Summerhill could offer him was a smile and a wave.

He'd miss Royeyri's help, that was for sure. Still, the Syorii had done more than enough just bringing him here, and asking him to sign up for a mission to rescue a stranger was too much.

The far-off miniature sun was about the size of Summerhill's fist in the gas-backdrop sky. Somehow the sight was sad, and it made Summerhill long for the brilliant sun of Rydale and the sweeping expanse of wildflowers or the mountainside vistas of his imagined New Zealand to replace the flat run of rusty, irradiated metal. He'd been left with literally one place in this whole universe to go, and it had to look like this. At least the nebula was pretty?

He approached one of the mooring points that jutted out from edge of the platform, pointing towards the brown dwarf. Imprinted into one of the metal plates, right along the edge, were the words *S.S. Nusquam – Mooring Point #2*.

This was definitely it, then. This was, or had been, the *Nusquam*'s home port of call. Here, people had once worked on a ship that could break the barriers between universes and move through time. Now it was a barren hunk of metal orbiting a sad excuse for a star.

The computers aboard Royeyri's ship had put the estimated age of the universe at somewhere around fourteen billion years. In that time, how many civilizations had risen and fallen? How long could this drydock have conceivably been floating out here without anyone remembering it? Thousands or even millions of years was entirely plausible, which was well before the age of human and even Syorii space travel.

In that case, how had Katherine gotten here? *When* had she gotten here? She'd mentioned selling off the circuit she'd stolen from the Consortium to get passage here, so where and when did Katherine even come from? When it came down to it, Summerhill knew so little about her.

That wasn't going to stop him from trying to save her, though.

This empty, abandoned place was Summerhill's only remaining lead. If the *Nusquam* wasn't here anymore, he'd find out where it went. Or he'd figure out where to find another ship like it. Or he'd learn how to build a reality jump drive himself if he had to.

Summerhill continued his exploration of the spacedock. The doors to the first few buildings he checked were shut fast. There might have been a way for him to force them open, but he didn't feel like expending that much energy yet. For all he knew, he'd be stuck here for a very long time. Oh, he might be lucky, and the *Nusquam* itself might have temporal scanners or alarms that would detect him here, interloping, out of place and out of time. Or perhaps he'd be waiting centuries for interstellar archaeologists to discover this dilapidated relic of a lost civilization, leaving him to his solitude within the beautiful flower of the Orion Nebula.

Other than tugging on doors and panels that wouldn't budge, there wasn't much for Summerhill to do beyond walk back and forth along the length of the dock, looking for any other signs of writing, anything to give more information as to what this place had once been like. He found the occasional logistical label here and there, but not much else. He spent what must have been hours inspecting different nooks and crannies, covering every inch of the platform and the buildings atop it.

The only structure he was able to get inside was an old storage shed that had been thoroughly emptied out. Its walls and floor were caked with dust, and when his passage kicked it up, it was carried away by the thin, circulating atmosphere. Perhaps after he cleaned it out, the shack would make for a place to sleep.

In the meantime, Summerhill was going to have to at least try to get into some of the other buildings. He'd stay here and wait for as long as he had to, but he'd rather find something to speed up that process. If nothing else, these people had built the *Nusquam,* and so maybe they also had ways of preserving food for eons.

First, though, he just wanted to rest. He walked out onto one of the mooring points and sat down with his feet dangling over the edge. He looked down, idly amused by the slow swirling of interstellar gas. It could prove helpfully hypnotic, he decided.

He stretched his arms out behind him, his fingers and palms running along the uneven metal surface. The whorls of the nebula encouraged him to stare and relax. His mind added music in the form of half-remembered tunes he'd heard on various stops along his journey with Royeyri.

The beat in his head fell in time with the swirling of the gases. It was pleasantly natural the way that rhythm emerged, and Summerhill smiled to himself, kicking his feet as he hummed. After a while, the beat became the hauntingly familiar sound of the antique hunter-case pocket watch's ticking.

And then that ticking stopped.

On some instinct he didn't fully comprehend, Summerhill whipped his head around. From around the corner of one of the platform's smaller building stepped a short, slender woman. She looked human, but, like Summerhill, she appeared totally oblivious to the fact that she ought to have needed some kind of environmentally sealed suit and not just the violet (and revealing) cocktail dress she wore. Her hair was straight, and ran all the way down to the middle of her back, jet black except for the fierce and bright cardinal at the ends.

"You're not supposed to be here," she said, her voice clear and loud despite the minimal atmosphere.

Slowly, Summerhill got to his feet. "I apologize," he replied, his own voice carrying just as well. "I was just... waiting."

"Not for me," the woman replied. She strode towards him, slowly and purposefully. She wore heels, a vibrant purple to match her dress, and each step clicked and clacked with the intensity of a stabbing dagger as she drew nearer. "I'd know if you were expecting me."

"I wasn't expecting anything quite so soon, to be honest. I'm sorry if I've disturbed you, but there really isn't any way for me to—"

The woman chuckled, her laugh sharp, but not quite sinister. "I understand," she said, and left the matter at that. She stepped right on up to Summerhill and smiled. She was nearly as tall as him, her skin quite fair, her features angular and clipped. "You don't need to make excuses for me."

"Er, thanks. Though they're not really excuses. I'm honestly just kind of stuck here until someone comes to get me."

The woman reached out and touched him on the shoulder. "No one's going to be coming to get you, Summerhill," she said, and the canine's ears perked straight up at the use of his name. "But that's okay. Don't worry."

With a casual twirl, the woman turned around and walked a few steps away. "Can you feel it, Summerhill?" she asked, motioning with both hands to the empty space platform. "Thousands of people over the ages putting so much of themselves into this place. Can you feel their echoes? Can you smell them in the air, taste the memories on your tongue like I can?"

Summerhill swallowed. "I can't say that I can. This place just feels empty to me. Dead." That last word rang and echoed within his own head. As the woman turned to face him again, he looked her in the eye, and understood who and what she was. "The End," he said softly.

"Arasiel." The woman bowed her head in confirmation. Then she laughed again, and this time she was definitely amused and not anything close to sinister or menacing. "I'm surprised to see you here, though I suppose in a way, I probably shouldn't be."

Just to see if he could, Summerhill tried his hardest to feel the things that Arasiel said she felt about this place, but it remained cold and empty and devoid of anything. In fact, now the deserted platform felt more miserable than ever before. "I shouldn't have come," he said. "I made some sort of mistake, didn't I?"

"I wouldn't say that," Arasiel said as she drew closer to him again. "But you can't stay here much longer, I'm afraid."

Summerhill felt his throat tighten. "I didn't figure as much." His voice dried out as he looked into Arasiel's face.

"If she finds out I stole you from her," Shoön had said, *"she'd be quite cross with me."*

Arasiel touched her hand to Summerhill's chest, and even through his shirt and his fur, her touch was cold like ice. "That's not what I mean," she said. "This isn't the End—not yours, at any rate. Not yet. I'm not here for you."

"You're not?"

"I'm here for this place." A playful smirk appeared on her ruby red lips. "Though it is so, so tempting to collect you, as well, while I'm here." Her nostrils flared as if she were a fellow canine trying to drink in his heady scent.

Summerhill's smile of relief faltered. "Well, I'm glad to hear that you're not here for me. But why are you here, though? Why now?"

"Because this place's End is coming," Arasiel said. "It's a very old, very powerful place, and I need to see it with my own eyes, to drink it all in with the rest of my being. Its time is marked, as it always has been."

"What's going to happen?"

Arasiel strode along the very edge of the platform, with no sign that she was worried about falling off into the endless abyss. "The short version," she explained, "is that a violent stellar event took place many, many years ago." She looked up into what was, for lack of a better term, the sky above. "The powerful wave of force and matter it generated has been slowly making its way here ever since, and very soon now it will destroy this little but once very important spacedock."

"There's no way to stop it?" Summerhill asked.

"No. But even if there were, why should I want to? The End comes to all things, Summerhill. *All* things." She eyed the dog playfully and headed back in his direction.

She set a hand on his shoulder and turned him to face the run-down buildings that lined the dock. "Look at this place," she said. "It was here that a civilization constructed a means of crossing realities—of breaking the rules of reality. It was here that those people forged their dreams. It was here that the lucky few came to board that magical ship that took them to different times, different places. It brought them nothing less than the impossible."

Her fingers stroked along Summerhill's upper arm, purple-colored fingernails making furrows in the fur. "And in a matter of hours, it will all be destroyed. All that history, all those memories and dreams, reduced to mere dust on the stellar breeze. And it will be wonderful."

Summerhill gazed upwards. He could see no sign of any impending catastrophe with his naked and untrained eyes, but had no reason to doubt what Arasiel said was true. "Why will that be wonderful?" he asked.

Arasiel hummed as her cold touch ran back towards Summerhill's chest. "I would love it if you were capable of experiencing that moment with me, so that you could see the answer to that question yourself." Then she leaned up onto her toes and whispered into the dog's ear. "But as powerful a creature as you are, you aren't powerful enough to survive something like this." Her lips brushed the short-furred edge of that ear. "Not yet."

"Well," Summerhill said, shivering from both the cold and his internalized nervousness, "I'm not sure what I can do, then."

"All you can do," Arasiel said, "is not be here when the time comes." She settled back down on her feet and peered up into Summerhill's face. "When *your* time comes, I'll let you know." Her other hand cupped the side of the canine's muzzle, and she stroked it with the same sort of loving reassurance that

Shoön had shown him before. "You will be quite the splendid prize, but I dare not pluck you from the stream before you wash up on the far shore."

With that, Arasiel brought her lips to Summerhill's, and she kissed him. It wasn't a deep kiss, but there was a subtle passion to it nevertheless as her lips worked against his without any urgency or rushing. Her icy aura spread through Summerhill's snout, into his head, down through the rest of his body. It was like dying, and it made Summerhill yearn for the comfort that would come with the cessation of his existence, never having to struggle, never having to worry, never having to feel pain or sorrow or despair ever again.

Smiling with satisfaction, Arasiel drew away from the shuddering dog and let her hands slip away from his body. "Goodbye for now, Summerhill. I'll see you...well, someday. I won't ruin the surprise."

While Summerhill was still trying to think of an appropriate response to that, Arasiel struck forward with both arms, her palms flat and outstretched, and shoved him in the chest. He had no chance to regain his balance, despite flailing his arms and lashing his tail, and then he fell backwards, right off the edge of the platform, plummeting downwards.

He was acutely aware of the fact that there shouldn't be a gravitational force to make him hurtle down away from the drydock. Before the illogic of the situation could override his conscious thought process, the whirling gas of the nebula overwhelmed his vision, and everything starting getting brighter and brighter before a world-shattering boom hit his ears.

THIRTY
FREEFALL

The boom was still echoing through Summerhill's skull when the rush of air kicked in. It whipped and whistled, like a kettle that was right at the cusp of boiling. The bright swirling of the condensed nebula was now a mere afterimage on his eyes; it lost all color and went pure white, replaced by a much brighter light that came in at the edges of his vision and blinded him.

After several seconds, his eyesight returned. The blinding light was a glorious yellow sun, which was pitching and spinning out of control.

No, it was Summerhill that was pitching and spinning out of control. He tumbled through the air, head over heels, ears over tail, over and over again in a dizzying freefall. Above him was blue sky, the sun, and billowy clouds. Below him was a vast landscape, devoid of buildings and other structures. There was only the light green of fields, the darker green of trees, blue lines as rivers and blue dots as lakes.

Summerhill stuck out his arms, and the wind resistance caught him off guard in the way it made his arms briefly snap up. He untucked his legs next, and tried to tilt and tip himself this way and that to keep from spinning out of control. It was tricky, but manageable, and soon he'd oriented himself so that he was horizontal to the ground, limbs splayed, tail whipping in the wind, eyes fixed straight downward.

There was nothing to give any sense of scale, and so he had no real idea how long it would take for him to hit the ground. Minutes? That was his best guess. Terrain features were slowly yet steadily growing larger and more detailed, and as beautiful as everything was, Summerhill's sense of wonder was starting to fade, replaced with the very real fear that there was no way that he was going to survive a fall from this height.

Was this what Arasiel had in mind for him all along? No, that didn't feel right. She was coy and charming, and she played by a set of rules that Summerhill didn't quite understand, but it didn't seem like he was supposed to die here and now. She was clearly relishing the thought of his existence coming to an end, and she'd shown both regret and patience that his time wasn't sooner.

That meant that he wasn't going to die here. And if the wasn't going to die, then he just needed to find out what he *was* going to do.

There was a twinkle in one corner of Summerhill's vision. His eyes moved to track it, and his breath caught in his throat at what he saw: the blazing blue light he'd once seen so long ago, streaking across the daytime sky with all the vibrant clarity of a shooting star leaving a trail across the curtain of night.

No, it was even brighter than that, more real, more permanent, and it was moving away, so, so fast. On instinct, Summerhill reached for it, but the jerking of his arm caused his body to spin out of control again. Having lost sight of his prize, he flailed as he tried to reorient himself, but his panic made doing so even more difficult.

He couldn't have come this far only to fail now. He hadn't jumped through so many hoops, gone to so many places and done so many strange things only to fall out of the sky now. He hadn't crossed dimensions, cheated death, and explored parts of himself he never knew existed just to *lose* in the end.

It was like Arasiel had said: there were people, people like him, who had been out there, who had taken the chance to reach for their dreams, and who had seized nothing less than the impossible. The builders of the *Nusquam* had constructed a craft that sailed between realities; the hero from the mountains had set out to cross the Plain of Ice to save a dying world; a girl named Katherine had left her humble home, traveled across the universe, and escaped interdimensional law enforcement more than once.

Summerhill kept himself steady. He balled up his hands into fists, he bit his lip, and kicked at the air with his legs. This made him spin forward more than he'd intended, though, and in mid-tumble, he felt a sudden weight in his shirt pocket shift and then fall free.

A small metallic disc spun in a shimmering golden blur, reflecting sunlight off its surface as it dropped out of reach, falling faster than Summerhill. It took the dog a few seconds to focus his eyes on it, and a few more to realize what he was seeing, but when the ticking hit his ears over the sound of the wind, all doubt was gone: it was his antique pocket watch.

Nothing less than the impossible. Cruise ships didn't actually sail to other realities, heroes couldn't escape death forever, Katherine had never been seen again, world-spanning cities didn't exist to house just one person, timepieces didn't appear out of thin air and dogs couldn't fly.

Summerhill thought back to when he and Katherine had been stuck inside the nevereef, forcing their minds onto reality. He tried to find focus, to pull his thoughts together and find whatever part of his spirit or will he needed to call on, but panic kept taking over in its place. His arms flailed and his legs kicked as he scrambled in an attempt to fall faster before the watch dropped out of his reach.

Whether it was a matter of aerodynamics or sheer determination, Summerhill managed to close the gap by a few key inches. Swinging with an outstretched hand, he finally got his fingers to bat against the edge of the spinning watch, slowing it down enough so that on his next pass, he was able to snatch it up. Somersaulting once more in midair, the dog brought the watch up in front of his face so he could read the words engraved on the hunter-case: *To One of My Favorites.*

He came out of that somersault and stretched himself out into a perfect dive. Just holding the watch in his palm, feeling it tick and knowing that it was real, filled him with renewed vigor and resolve. He gripped it tightly, then gritted his teeth, hoping and imagining and finally *believing* that his force of will was stronger than the force of gravity.

Breaking free of his plummet, he swung back upward in a terrific arc, rocketing back into the sky, the trees and rivers below shrinking away as he spared a look down. Laughter erupted from his muzzle as the wind whipped through the fur on his face, blowing his ears back and pulling his tail out like a streamer that trailed behind him. He twirled and spun, the air whipping around his body, carrying him aloft and propelling him forward as he reveled in how it felt to fly.

He'd seized nothing less than the impossible. He'd made what he wanted out of reality, just like he and Katherine had once done as a team, sharing something special for so brief a time. Summerhill was alone now, but he'd find Katherine, he'd rescue her, and together they would experience the impossible together all over again.

First, though, there was the matter of the blue light. He knew it was the same light that had drawn him out onto his journey in the first place. Now he needed to follow its lead once more.

He scoured the sky until he relocated the beam of blue light racing amongst the clouds. As Summerhill sped up to chase after it, it sped up in turn. He tried to anticipate its movement and abruptly changed direction to intercept it, but the light veered off in the exact opposite direction he'd been expecting.

It seemed to be aware that it was being followed. Summerhill focused even harder on flying faster, but the light kept stringing him along. It took him on an exciting series of twists and turns and high-arcing loops like it was playing a game a tag all across the sky.

This was a game Summerhill was determined to win. If the blue light wanted to toy with him and lead him someplace, he was happy to play along, but one thing he wasn't going to do was concede defeat.

After several exhilarating minutes of cat-and-mouse, the light flared up in brightness by an order of magnitude and shot toward the ground. Summerhill raced after it, losing sight of it for a moment amidst the trees before he spotted the obvious point of impact: a blazing blue rectangle of light emanating forth from the trunk of a large tree. He slowed down, braking himself with his limbs against the air, then slowly wafted the rest of the way down to the ground. He settled on his feet and shook out his mussed-up fur, his heart still pounding in the aftermath of flying.

While he waited for his pulse and breathing to calm down, Summerhill looked at the pocket watch in his hand. Its ticking was like a gentle heartbeat, in a way, steady and regular, reassuring, like resting an ear against someone's chest. He gazed at the gold-plated surface, ran the pad of his thumb over the inscription, then popped the case open.

Where once there had been only the burnt-out edges of an old photograph, now the inside case held a picture of Katherine, her blonde curls spilling down over her ears, the leather cord of her pendant visible against her neck. The sepia tone did nothing to diminish her hopeful smile.

After closing the pocket watch and sticking it back in his pocket, Summerhill looked up at the tree before him. Blue light radiated from the frame of a door set within the trunk.

Standing next to the door, exactly as Summerhill had expected, was another version of himself, irises glowing with the same blue that came from behind the door in the tree. This other Summerhill looked back at him, smiled, and nodded with silent approval.

Before Summerhill could ask any questions, his other self said, "Find Katherine. Make sure you stick with her and everything will be fine." And then, in the literal blink of an eye, he was gone, the same way he'd disappeared so long ago.

There had been no grand revelation. Summerhill was no closer to discovering the truth behind who this other self was, but it didn't matter. He still felt a reassurance he hadn't felt since he'd first left the World of the Pale Gray Sky, invigorated with a sense of purpose that he was sure he would live up to.

Katherine. She was out there, in some reality, at some point in time. She'd begged Summerhill to do something to save her, and that's just what he was going to do.

With some trepidation, Summerhill wrapped his fingers around the doorknob. When he turned it, there was the simple sound of a lock coming undone, and then the glowing blue light shone through the door itself, illuminating a distinct and complex pattern in the wood grain, similar to the one in the door that led to the world of ice and mountains. The antique pocket watch was still ticking faintly in his ears as he pushed the door open and stepped inside.

THIRTY-TWO
COSMOLOGY

A flat surface almost like a pane of glass stretched out underneath Summerhill's feet, reflective like a waveless ocean that had gone still and silent. The dog stared down at it with apprehension before a few hesitant steps proved that it would support his weight just fine despite its fragile, delicate appearance.

The perfectly smooth surface sparkled as if sprinkled with glitter, but this was merely an illusion, created by the reflection of the sky full of stars above. Summerhill lifted his head to gaze up at it. Not only was it full of stars, it was full of planets, of nebulae, of entire galaxies, impossibly close, whirling and wheeling about at equally impossible speeds on any cosmological scale.

Summerhill turned in a circle and looked, the flat plane under his feet stretching out forever in every direction, the whole of the universe hanging in the sky above. Galaxies seemed to sparkle as stars within became novae and supernovae. Every time he blinked, entire civilizations rose and fell, worlds were born and died, stories were told and then lost forever.

To try to comprehend it all would be maddening. Time moved too quickly. Summerhill was too far away. But it was all there, really there, playing out for him like some kind of wonderful and tragic cosmic play. He marveled at the enormity of it all, at the humbling sensation of having even this fraction of all creation pouring into his eyes. He despaired as it impressed upon him his own insignificance, and he wept with joy at the sheer beauty of it all.

And this was just one universe out of what might be, as far as Summerhill knew, an infinite number of universes. He could launch himself into the stars above, into just one of the many galaxies passing by, and still never get to see or experience everything there. What he was looking at now was pure potential.

With one leg, he kicked off of the surface of the horizontal plane and let himself float. Time wheeled on by, so fast to his perceptions, countless stars continuing to burn while countless worlds continued to orbit around them. Summerhill could make this his very own celestial playground, wandering his way through reality, changing and altering that reality, ignoring any and all ties and responsibilities and acting on whim alone if he so chose.

The haunting skyscrapers of Summerhill's memory shot up at the edges of his mind. He now understood the World of the Pale Gray Sky, its purpose and its form and its function. The cosmos he was floating through now represented the tiniest fraction of what he might one day be capable of, there mere sight of which inspired him and filled him with a drive and a yearning to explore, to create, to experience. It was the very antithesis of the dull, lifeless oppression of his old life.

If the things he could do were based on the strength of his thoughts and his resolve pitted against the rules of reality, the World of the Pale Gray Sky, with its monotony, tedium, and isolation, was the perfect way to lock that down. Summerhill could think of no better way to quash his imagination and potential, to strip himself of his power to change rules, to change worlds.

It was so perfect, in fact, that the simplest explanation he could think of was that he must have been the one to put himself there in the first place.

He didn't know when he'd done it, nor did he know why— but then the when and the why and the how weren't important right now. What was important was that, if he had been the one to imprison himself, then it only made sense that he was the one to give himself the reprieve he'd earned, however retroactively. Cause and effect were reversed, it was true, but he knew, in that moment as he drifted slowly through space, that past-Summerhill, all alone in the World of the Pale Grey Sky, would grow to learn this lesson of responsibility he was learning now.

Besides, Katherine was in trouble, and he was the only one who could help her, which meant that past-Summerhill couldn't be allowed to rot away inside the World of the Pale Gray Sky for a dismal eternity. That poor, lonely dog needed to be set free so that he could grow, like a flower, weathering sun and storm, joy and hardship, and mature into the individual he was here and now.

That left figuring out a way to go back into the past, and into another reality, and Summerhill had just the idea. He took one last look at the nebulae and star clusters surrounding him and reminded himself that he wouldn't be where he was now if he hadn't already succeeded in doing what he was about to attempt.

That didn't make the prospect any stranger, but it gave him hope, along with the courage to try, and those were the things he needed more anything. The key pieces of the puzzle did all add up: the knowledge of the future, the perfect shade of glowing blue, and the ability to be someplace without actually being there.

"*Royeyri,*" he thought as loud and as clearly as he could. "*Royeyri, are you out there? I need your help.*"

 # THIRTY-THREE
MISALIGNMENT

Passing stars had their light shift towards blue before the myriad galaxies stopped spinning. Summerhill stopped floating as well, his mind taken into the link with the Syorii.

"Royeyri, is that you?"

The inside of Summerhill's head vibrated with a curious hum. *"This is Royeyri, yes,"* said a familiar voice. *"But who is this, lah? Curious dog, floating alone in space. Very unusual."*

"Royeyri, it's me, Summerhill. I was wondering if I could get your help with something."

The humming took on an even more peculiar tone. *"Summerhill? Royeyri doesn't know a Summerhill. Knows summer, knows hills, but no Summerhill and no dogs in space."*

Summerhill had been hoping that his desperate thoughts would reach Royeyri through time and space. Apparently, however, he'd reached across time in a direction he hadn't expected. *"Wait, Royeyri. Hold on. When are you?"*

"Royeyri is now! When else would Royeyri be?"

"I—Okay, maybe that was a dumb question. So you're saying we haven't met yet?"

The Syorii laughed, the disembodied sound made more sinister given that Summerhill couldn't see him. *"Royeyri seems to have met Summerhill a few moments ago. Greetings, strange dog in space!"*

Summerhill wanted to shake his head or roll his eyes, but could do neither. *"Yes, hi. Look, this is going to sound strange, but—"*

"Already sounds strange, lah. But strange is fine! Royeyri likes strange."

"Right, no, I get that. Anyway, I need you to trust me on something. See, I already know you."

Royeyri's phantom chuckling rang in Summerhill's ears again. "*Oh, clever dog, naughty dog! Bending time and making friends in addition to floating through space. Summerhill is like Royeyri, in a way.*"

"Um, sure, thanks. Anyhow, I'm going to, er, think at you, and try to prove that you and I have a history of working together and helping each other out."

"*Oh, Summerhill has already been thinking that, Royeyri sees,*" the Syorii replied, adding his distinctive cluck to the end of his words despite not needing to use a beak to communicate telepathically. "*So many marvelous adventures in store for Summerhill and Royeyri together!*"

In the back of his mind, Summerhill started to wonder how much this conversation was affecting his and Royeyri's personal timelines. "*Er, maybe you shouldn't look too closely at those,*" he said, just to make sure. "*But okay, the point is that we trust each other at this point in, um—look, where I am, you'd probably offer to help me.*"

Now the blue distortion over Summerhill's senses wavered with what had to be a giggle. "*Royeyri is listening. Floating space dog seems to have fun ideas, lah.*"

Fun ideas. Well, whatever got Royeyri to go along with his plan. "*I need you to take me someplace. To another place and another time. Can you do that?*"

"*Take you someplace? A non-Syorii someone to a different someplace at a different sometime?*" Royeyri's mental chuckle felt so real that he might have been floating right next to Summerhill in that moment. "*My, such a ridiculous idea! So ridiculous that Royeyri can't help but love it!*"

"*Too ridiculous to work?*"

More clucking echoed inside Summerhill's head. "*Royeyri isn't sure, but that hasn't kept Royeyri from doing ridiculous things before, lah.*"

"*All right. So long as you don't think it's too dangerous.*"

"Oh, never said it wasn't too dangerous, lah! Now, while Royeyri figures out how to do this, sit tight. Or float tight. Whatever Summerhill does."

"Wait! Royeyri, I haven't even said where or when we're going yet. It's a place called the World of—"

"Royeyri sees where Summerhill wants to go, yes, yes. Summerhill space dog thinks in distinct words too much when he doesn't have to. Inefficient."

Summerhill would have let out a sigh of exasperation if he weren't caught in the temporal slowdown of the mental link. "All right, I'm sorry. I just want to make sure I do this right, because if I don't get back to where this all started I'll never get to where it ends."

The blue tinge began to fade as time started to speed back up. "Wait! Royeyri, before we do this, I—"

"Yes?" Time crept to a halt once more as Royeyri brought the mental connection back. "One last question, lah?"

"You said before—in my before—that you met me in the World of the Pale Gray Sky, not floating all alone in space. Did I change that? Or was this always—"

"Perhaps this. Perhaps something different." Royeyri's voice clucked a few more times. "Lies and trickery. No real way to be sure with Royeyri."

ZERO
(RE)VISITING

The whiteness of the Beginning, which had once been blinding and unpleasant, was now merely confusing, because it was not at all what Summerhill expected to see. It took his eyes a few moments to adjust, and when they did, he was finally able to see the subtle corners and the shades of off-white and palest gray.

Shoön looked up from what she was doing, which could have been any number of things, near as Summerhill could tell. Much as had been the case the last time Summerhill had met her, she changed shape each time he blinked. As before, she was always the same young woman, but she was a young woman who always looked different.

"Summerhill," she said, a sly smile spreading across her mouth (which turned into a canine muzzle, at least briefly, partway through). "Three times in one lifetime. That's more than anyone should be here."

"For what it's worth, I wasn't planning on coming here," Summerhill replied. "How *did* I get here? Where's Royeyri?"

For only a moment, Shoön looked disturbingly like Katherine. She stuck a fingertip in her mouth, held it up in the air, and hummed. "Looks like you tried to play with time in a way you weren't quite supposed to. Something about wanting to get back to where things all started, was it?"

Dipping his head and folding his ears back, Summerhill offered his obeisance. "I'm sorry. I didn't think anything like this would happen. And I'm sorry if my being here is against the rules," he said. Then, his ears sprang back up as he got an idea. "But wait, if I was trying to get back where it all started, then maybe you're the one who helps me do that!"

Shoön's appearance had ceased shifting; now she was a canine creature superficially similar to Summerhill, with

246

features that were both more slender and more human-like. "My job is to send people along on their way. I'm not really sure what else you expect me to be able to do."

"But that's exactly it," Summerhill said. "I want to go back to my beginning. To make sure everything starts the way it should."

Shoön looked deep into his eyes. "You mean start over?" she asked.

"Kind of. I know more about what happens between now and then, and I think if I go back I can help myself get on track, and make sure I don't make mistakes or—"

"Summerhill," Shoön interrupted, "let me tell you a little bit about how time works."

"I understand that this is the beginning. Of everything and everyone."

Shoön rolled her eyes, half-playfully, half-impatient. "Let me do the talking here. Trust me, I know way more about this than you do."

Summerhill flattened his ears again and tucked his tail between his legs. "Sorry, Shoön."

"It's okay," she said, patting him on the shoulder. "Sit. Make yourself comfortable." As he sat, so did she, almost but not quite leaning against him. Even her presence alone was reassuring. "Now, hopefully this explanation will sort things out for you."

"All right. But really, if you just need to tell me, 'It's against the rules for me to start you over,' I'll understand."

One of Shoön's fingertips was suddenly at Summerhill's lips. "Shush. You're here because you want help with something, and so I'm going to give you what you need instead of what you want."

With a quiet sigh, Summerhill rested his head against Shoön's shoulder, and she put her arm around him. "I'm listening," he muttered.

"Time," Shoön began, "is like a stream." Her fingers brushed along one of the dog's ears. "People are like leaves that float across the surface of that stream."

She straightened Summerhill up and used her hands to make gestures as she spoke. "My job is to set those leaves down atop the stream, and let them get carried away by the current. And those are inexorably pulled down the stream once they leave my hands."

Summerhill squared his shoulders and listened intently. "Now, a lot of times," Shoön continued, "these leaves will clump up for a long time, and sometimes they'll split apart, and maybe they'll come back together and maybe they won't." Summerhill could see it all with perfect clarity in his mind, as if the words themselves were somehow turning into mental images. "Sometimes, a leaf will get caught in a little eddy, and it might swirl around and stop flowing downstream, but it's always only temporary. After a time, the leaf keeps moving, and eventually, all leaves wash up on shore, some sooner than others."

"And then your sister wanders the shores and collects them," Summerhill said.

Shoön smiled. "That's exactly right. The basic rules are pretty simple."

"It makes a lot of sense," Summerhill agreed. "Especially the part about equating me to a leaf floating along the surface of the water."

A sweet grin spread across Shoön's face. "Ah, but Summerhill, you're not one of the leaves." She scratched him under the chin as he whuffed in confusion, then tapped him on the nose.

"I'm not?"

Shoön shook her head. "No. You're one of the little silver fish that swims under the surface." She wiggled her fingers as she moved her hand back and forth. "You can slip downstream and you can head back upstream and sometimes you can leap out of the water entirely for brief periods of time."

Summerhill opened his mouth to speak, but didn't know what to say. Something in Shoön's words conferred unto him the profoundest sense of relief, but it was such a subtle thing that he couldn't identify why that was.

"So you see," Shoön continued, "you don't need me to pluck you from the stream and dump you back in someplace else. You can swim there all on your own."

There amidst the whiteness, Summerhill felt a great intangible weight lifted from him. He didn't know what else to do, so he put his arms around Shoön and hugged her slight frame close to him and nuzzled at her shoulder. "Thank you," he said. "I think I understand now."

Shoön hugged him back, then gently drew back away from him. "And that's all I wanted for you, Summerhill. Do you think you're okay getting back out there now?"

"I think I am." Summerhill got to his feet and brushed himself off. He smiled at Shoön again, and felt a little tug deep in his chest. "Before I go, though, can I just ask you one more thing?"

"Of course you can."

Summerhill swallowed. "The last time we met. When you brought me back here instead of just letting your sister find me." The image of Arasiel's eager smile filled his mind. "Why did you really do that?"

Shoön looked into Summerhill's eyes, wearing a textbook enigmatic smile. "Because, Summerhill," she said as she touched a hand to his chest and leaned in to plant a kiss on his cheek. "You were always one of my favorites."

Warmth spread through Summerhill's entire body, originating from the spot where Shoön's lips had touched him. "Thank you," he replied. "For everything."

Taking the dog's wrist in one hand, and squeezing his paw in the other, Shoön led Summerhill off to a barely visible corner, around which he could hear the burbling of a freshwater brook. "And thank you for giving me the chance to see you twice more," she said. "My sister would be quite jealous."

I wouldn't be so sure of that, Summerhill thought, but he kept it to himself. "Goodbye, Shoön. I'm going to miss you."

"Go. You need to get back to swimming, or you won't be able to breathe, you silly dog."

With that, Shoön gave him a pat between the shoulders, then shoved against his back, pushing him around the corner, towards the source of the stream.

 # THIRTY-FOUR
REDEFINITION

Royeyri was nowhere to be seen or felt, but that wasn't surprising. Given Shoön's fish analogy, it was probable that the Syorii's attempt to pull Summerhill through space and time was tantamount to trying to reel the dog in on a line, and in all likelihood, the metaphysical equivalent of that line had been broken. But Summerhill would worry about Royeyri later. The two clearly had a history that would work itself out eventually in some form or another. In the meantime, Summerhill was concerned not with the past, but with the future.

A row of skyscrapers, drab and familiar, stretched out before him. Their presence did not fill his mind with instinctual panic and chilling fear. No longer did they symbolize the death of hope and imagination; now he saw them as plants of stone and brick and metal growing from asphalt earth, plants that he had grown all by himself.

Outside one of the ground floor windows of the closest building, Summerhill stared at his reflection, searching his eyes for the telltale blue that he'd seen when he'd come to free himself before. But the face that gazed back at him had the same, dull, storm gray eyes he'd always had. There weren't even the barest flecks of other color there in his irises.

But how could that be possible? He'd distinctly manifested the blue eyes when he'd come back to find himself. Maybe he just couldn't see it, similar to how Katherine hadn't seen the blue hue over reality when Royeyri had spoken to him. Maybe that was farfetched, but he didn't have a better explanation for something he barely understood anyway.

Well, that detail would have to sort itself out on its own. For now, Summerhill was back here in his own past, and now his task was to help free himself by giving him the inspiration he needed to think. Where had he first spoken to himself without realizing it? It was that one tobacconist's shop, right?

Countless adventures, months of hopping across realities, trudging through snow, and traversing time and space still couldn't suppress what might well have been centuries of time spent in the World of the Pale Gray Sky, and so Summerhill still knew exactly where to go. At every intersection, his mind rebuilt its map of the city, and he made the most direct approach he could to the small tobacconist's shop, his steps increasing in speed the closer he got.

But then, when he rounded the last corner and indeed saw his past self leaning against the wall, he also saw the other version of himself who had been speaking with him. From this distance and angle, he couldn't see if this other self had blue eyes, but he didn't dare take the time to peer closer and check. Instead, he swung back around the corner, out of view, and began panting.

What was going on here? How had he come back in time to find himself, only to find that he was already—

Summerhill poked his head back around the corner. Now, the other two versions of himself were walking down the street, toward the park where Summerhill remembered stopping to sit and think on a bench while talking to himself some more. Neither of them were looking back in his direction, affording him a few moments to stare dumbly without risk, and with each step they took, more doubts crept into Summerhill's head.

Clearly, he'd been wrong about his self-given reprieve—or had at least been wrong about the timing of it. Just who or what this other blue-eyed Summerhill was—be it a different future version of himself or something altogether different— was a mystery he'd have to solve later. For now, Katherine was still in trouble, and she still needed his help, regardless of whether he'd sorted out his own existential quandaries.

Turning and heading in the opposite direction of his two look-alikes, Summerhill brainstormed for options. Freeing himself was already taken care of, which meant that, for the time being, he could focus on rescuing Katherine. But how?

The World of the Pale Gray Sky had been his prison, but it had also been his own world. That meant that he made the rules—made them and could change them with no one's permission but his own, without having to break them.

He'd created the world, and he'd created it as a big, empty city. But not entirely empty—he'd populated it with buildings, with furniture, with vehicles, with all of the things that went into a city except for the people. Whether he'd fashioned it that way on purpose, knowing he'd someday need it, or whether it had all been a happy accident didn't matter. He scanned the rows of buildings closest to him, looking for one that might suit his purposes, and quickly found one: a tall, narrow office building, its faces covered with large panes of glass that appeared dim and lifeless due to the sunless atmosphere.

And here, trapped in the prison of his imagination, he knew precisely how to draw together enough focus. He headed for the office building, trotting fearlessly into its shadow. No longer would he be afraid of something he knew could not hurt him. This was the last this place would ever see of him.

Summerhill strode into the lobby of the building. There were spaces for a doorman, for a receptionist, several chairs in the waiting area, but no people. There was a directory with numbers, but no names listed alongside them. The lights were on, but no one was home. Summerhill headed for the nearest office and barged inside. Its door was unlocked; there was no one to have ever locked it.

Over in one corner was a large printer. Summerhill picked up a large stack of blank paper and tossed it down onto the desk. He sat at the desk, then picked up a ballpoint pen from a featureless mug. The cap came free with a crisp snap, the plastic nice and cool, the pen having never been used. Summerhill doodled a tiny flower in one corner of the desk blotter, just to make sure the pen worked. It wrote blue—not magic blue, but normal, office ink blue.

Satisfied, Summerhill pulled the stack of papers in front of him. On the topmost page, he wrote out, in big capital letters:

PROMISES

He looked down at the rest of the page beneath his makeshift chapter title. It was blank and inviting. Rife for imagination, not dead to it. He brought his pen into position, then paused for a few moments to come up with the right words.

Summerhill broke through the veil between realities and appeared aboard the Consortium vessel just in time to save Katherine from the agents who had abducted her.

He relaxed his thumb and forefinger, and the pen slipped free and rolled onto the desk. Then he lifted his hand up, extended his fingers, and slammed his palm down flat against the paper as hard as he could.

THIRTY-FIVE
PROMISES

Summerhill broke through the veil between realities and appeared aboard the Consortium vessel just in time to save Katherine from the agents who had abducted her.

She was still wearing the sleeveless tee and tank top she'd been dressed in back on the *Achilles*, and her wrists were still bound with the same cuffs. She was flanked by two guards, bipedal humanoids clad in black, like the team that had infiltrated the *Nusquam*. Both of them carried energy rifles at the ready.

The inside of the Consortium vessel looked very different from what Summerhill had expected. Given the strange six-eyed alien that had handled the negotiations with the Fifth Fleet, he'd assumed that the ship would be some kind of unpleasant insectoid hive, with organic passageways dripping with unidentifiable fluids and doors that operated like the valves of blood vessels. Instead, he was in a very sterile corridor in the shape of a perfect hexagon, the walls a very dark green, with complex circuits and cables that came into view briefly as various panels slid open and closed.

Katherine and her escorts were about thirty feet away. They were still facing away from Summerhill. His arrival apparently hadn't made any noise, and the three marched along at an even pace as if there was no cause for haste or alarm.

Well, that could be fixed. "Let her go!"

The three stopped and turned in unison. The Consortium guards brought their rifles to bear. Between them, Katherine froze as her jaw dropped and her eyes widened. Summerhill couldn't help but smile as her shock changed from disbelief to exhilarated hope.

"Who are you?" one of the guards demanded. "Identify yourself, immediately!"

Summerhill took a couple steps closer. The guards reaffirmed their grips on their rifles and kept their aim squarely on him. "My name is Summerhill," he announced, "and I'm here to escort Ms. Tinsley out of here."

"The human woman is a legal prisoner of the Transdimensional Spacetime Integrity Enforcement Consortium. She is being held on three counts—"

"Three counts of violating existential spacetime yadda yadda, yeah, I know the drill." Summerhill flapped his hand as he spoke and took another step. "I don't care what she did. She's coming with me."

One of the guards took a hand off of his rifle to touch a button on the side of his helmet. "Intruder alert in section Four-Two-One—"

The rest of the call was cut off by the sound of the other guard's rifle going off. Searing green fired from the muzzle of the gun, a lance of light and energy heading right for Summerhill.

Summerhill made no attempt to dodge. He stood his ground, and in the fraction of a second between the guard pulling the trigger and the energy beam hitting him, he brought his arm up, palm extended forward.

The green beam stopped about a foot from Summerhill's hand, changing at that point from a bolt of energy into an explosion of pink flower petals that raced past him and down the hall in a double helix. Heat washed over his face and body, but he forced himself not to flinch.

A second or two later, the rifle stopped firing, and the remaining flower petals billowed down the corridor and out of sight. Summerhill grinned, making sure to show his teeth, as he took another pointed step towards the two guards. "Feel like trying that again? Because I can do this all day."

That was a lie. Doing that once had been exhausting and demanding, and Summerhill knew that he'd only be able pull that stunt off once, maybe twice more before the effort drained him completely. Hopefully the Consortium agents wouldn't try to call his bluff.

They didn't, at least not right away, and in that moment of distraction, Katherine acted.

The guard who had made the emergency call still had one hand to his helmet, and he was caught completely off his guard as Katherine kicked the back of his leg from behind. He yelled and dropped to one knee, and then Katherine delivered a follow-up kick to his elbow, causing him to drop his weapon to the floor.

Summerhill rushed forward as the second guard turned to train his gun on Katherine, but before he could line up a shot, she had ducked well inside his reach to deliver a firm headbutt to his chest. The blow didn't take him down, but it did knock him off balance. Katherine used that opening to rush him back against the slanted lower wall of the hexagonal corridor, momentum knocking the wind out of the guard's chest and making him drop his gun, too.

The first guard reached for his own weapon, still on the floor, but Summerhill hooked his toes into the trigger guard and flipped the gun into the air. He caught it and pointed it down at the guard, trying his best to look the man in the eyes through his blank helmet. The guard stayed on his knees and held up both hands in surrender.

Somewhere in her tussle with the other guard, Katherine had gotten her cuffs wedged into one of the sliding panels on the wall. She turned and wrenched, gritting her teeth as she did so, and though she couldn't possibly have been strong enough to break those cuffs, the metal snapped apart with a sharp yank. She shook her arms out, then muttered a quick, "Much better," before grabbing the side of the guard's helmet and smashing it hard into the wall. She did this two or three more times until the man went limp and crumpled onto the floor.

"Oh, Mr. Summerhill," she said as she bent down to pick up the second rifle. "You've finally mastered the art of making a proper entrance." Striding up behind the guard on his knees, she raised her rifle, flicked a switch, and fired.

The green bolt struck the guard in the back, and he crumpled to the floor in a heap. "Oh, bugger," Katherine said, looking at an indicator set in the rifle's stock. "Looks like this thing's out of juice already. Just what did you do to it when they fired it at you?"

Summerhill ignored the question, his muzzle hanging open with shock. He shook his head to help recompose himself, and tried to avoid looking at the guard on the floor. "Sorry. I just—I've never seen anybody kill someone before."

"The Consortium's got enough to be mad at me about," Katherine said. "Don't need to add murdering one of them to the list. That was just the stun setting." She looked at the rifle again. "At least, I think it was. I don't exactly read 'Consortium' or whatever language this is."

Summerhill and Katherine then both looked at each other. Despite being disheveled and panting, Katherine looked excited, like she was riding an adrenaline rush and loving every second of it. Seeing that made Summerhill's tail wag, even though he was still acutely aware of his fear and anxiety from being where he was.

"Thanks for not taking five years to catch up with me, Mr. Summerhill," Katherine said. "So, how'd you manage to get here this time? Wait, no, don't tell me: it's a long story."

"Pretty much," Summerhill said, and then alarms started to ring through the corridor, emergency lights flashing. "It just always comes down to finding you and making sure I stay with you."

"Just like back when we first met, huh?"

"Yeah." Summerhill thought again about his trip back to the World of the Pale Gray Sky, and his mysterious other self giving him the impetus to find Katherine in the first place.

"Though remind me that, at some point, I still need to figure out why I even know to find you."

"Good to see you still make as much sense as you ever did. If it's all the same, right now I'm glad you came to find me at all. Figure out the small stuff later." Katherine then nodded down the hallway. "Come on. I'm guessing that however you got here, we can't get out the same way."

"Well, with just the right focus and a whole lot of determination, I can break through the boundaries between realities," Summerhill replied as he handed the other energy rifle to Katherine. "But it's pretty tricky, and more importantly, I don't know if I can take other people with me."

After giving the rifle a quick once-over, Katherine poked both guards with her feet to make sure they wouldn't be in pursuit anytime soon, and then brushed the curls of her hair our of her eyes. "Then I guess that means we're stealing an emergency craft and getting out of here that way." She then broke into a brisk job down the hallway.

Summerhill followed after her. "Are you sure they even have those?"

"Oh, I'm sure," Katherine called back to him. "This won't be the first one I've stolen from them."

"You seem to have a bad habit of stealing things." Summerhill had an easier time keeping up with Katherine's pace than he thought he would, his exhaustion from stopping the energy blast now washed away by his own endorphin rush.

As they approached a sealed door, Katherine looked back and smiled at him. "Isn't this just like old times, Mr. Summerhill? You and me, trying to escape the clutches of the Consortium while racing to the nearest escape pod?"

"Can we not make a habit of that, too?"

Katherine punched the door panel, and the six-sided door slid open with a few jerking motions. "Only if you stop making a habit of disappearing on me."

"Deal," Summerhill agreed, and then they were off down the next corridor. This one was wider, more imposing, the sound of the blaring klaxons louder and harsher in his sensitive ears.

"Stay on your toes," Katherine shouted, slowing down as they approached a hexagonal junction a couple hundred feet down the hallway. "And try to pay attention to signage. Near as I've been able to tell, the interior of Consortium ships and facilities don't need to follow the normal rules of three-dimensional space."

"And what does that mean, exactly?"

"It means that different pathways may not go the direction you think they go." Katherine drew the rifle into a firing position as she stepped to the edge of the junction and turned to look down one of the branches. "I guess when you're the ones who enforce the laws of reality, you're free to break them as you see fit." She then gave Summerhill an 'all clear' gesture with one hand and waved for him to follow.

He did, checking behind him as he went. Near as he could tell, the hallway they'd taken was going exactly the direction he thought, but he was willing to take Katherine's word for it that that might change. "So are these emergency craft likely to be well guarded, I take it?"

"Probably more so than usual. I really pissed the Consortium off good last time they had me as their guest."

"Great. So what's the big plan? Shoot our way out?"

"We've got a lot more firepower than I had last time," Katherine said. "May as well use it." The hexagonal corridor ahead sloped downward at what looked at a steep angle, but as she and Summerhill trotted along it, the incline appeared to level out; instead, now it looked like the way they had come was angling up to meet them.

The wall panels were opening and closing much faster now, too, and the klaxons and loudspeaker system kept broadcasting intruder alarms. "I don't suppose you have another, less violent solution in mind?"

"If this were a story of my granddad's, he'd want us to come up with something elegant and clever, I suppose. Tell you what: if another way out presents itself, I'll definitely consider that over a firefight where we're hopelessly outnumbered."

The hallway ended in a rounded cul-de-sac with a translucent colorless hexagonal pillar that ran from floor to ceiling. Katherine walked around to the opposite side and smiled with recognition at a holographically projected panel on its surface. There was a large series of buttons, labeled with pictographs instead of text. "What does this all do?" Summerhill asked.

"This is how we get to different areas of the ship much faster." Katherine's hand hovered over the buttons as she scanned them all for the one she wanted.

Some of the symbols had meanings that Summerhill could take simple educated guesses at, like the knife and fork for the mess area, or the row of three rifles for the armory. Others were much more esoteric, like the nine-pointed star with the clockwise arrow curved around it, or the three solid dots arranged in an equilateral triangle. Another button bore what looked like a stylized representation of the six-eyed alien's head.

Thankfully, that wasn't the button Katherine pressed; instead, she hit one marked with what looked like a pair of wings.

A chime sounded, and then the hallway leading away from the cul-de-sac changed. It was still a hexagonal corridor, but this one was much narrower, lined with indicator lights and devoid of the same shifting panels. "Come on," Katherine said, swinging the rifle back up into both arms. "This should lead to the flight deck."

She was already jogging down the corridor, and so Summerhill had no choice but to follow after her. "We're going to steal a ship right off of their flight deck?"

"Don't be silly," Katherine called back. "We're going to cause a catastrophic accident on their flight deck. That should hopefully set off their evacuation protocols."

"Hopefully? And what if it doesn't?"

"Hey, it's the closest thing I can come up with right now to an elegant and clever solution. Think of it as a work in progress." The hallway curved left and ended at another closed door. Katherine stopped in front of it. "Trust me. I can be pretty damn inventive when the situation forces me to be."

Summerhill chuckled. "Isn't that what leads to things like you becoming a hostess on a dimension-traveling cruise ship?"

Katherine made some kind of hand gesture above the panel that Summerhill couldn't make out, and the door slid open. "Hey, that worked out just fine for a few years. Right up until around the time you showed up, actually."

"The timing of that was a complete coincidence, and you know it."

"I'm not sure I believe in coincidences anymore after meeting you, Mr. Summerhill." The blaring of the klaxons was even louder now with the door open, the pitch lower and more hollow. "But hopefully that just means you didn't show up out of thin air to save me only to have us fail now."

The fur on the back of Summerhill's neck stood on end, and his ears folded back. "Actually, speaking of which, I'm kind of worried that we haven't run into any resistance yet in our escape."

After giving her energy rifle another quick check, Katherine smiled. "Maybe they got cocky after finally managing to recapture me. We just need to make the best of the head start we've got."

"Hey, you're the one who said they'd probably be on high alert because of you. I'm just saying."

Katherine set a hand on the dog's shoulder. "Hey. We're going to get out of here, Mr. Summerhill. Don't worry." She paused for a moment in thought, then reached around the back of her neck and pulled off some kind of chain necklace, which Summerhill hadn't seen before due to Katherine's hair and clothing covering it up. "Here. For good luck." She reached up and placed the chain around Summerhill's neck.

A pair of tiny, inscribed metal plates hug against his chest. "What's this?"

"Those are my dog tags," Katherine said. "Almost makes more sense for you to wear them anyway."

Summerhill wrapped his fingers around the tags hanging from the chain, and then he smiled. "I'll take all the good luck I can get right now. So, is the plan still to hit the flight deck as hard as we can and cause some mayhem?"

"Either hard or precise. Preferably both." Katherine took point again and led the way down the hallway. "Keep your eyes peeled for anything that looks like it might be really important. Or like it might explode."

"I still can't believe this is your definition of 'elegant.'"

"It's better than the idea I had before, you have to admit that."

"That's not exactly saying much."

Katherine gave Summerhill a gentle nudge on the shoulder with her fist. "For the moment, it's the only idea we have. But don't worry: with my ingenuity, this energy rifle, and your... whatever it is the thing you can do is called, we'll be fine."

Summerhill wanted to be able to say that they'd gotten out of worse situations before, but he wasn't sure how true that actually was. Besides, Katherine was right about needing to make the best use of their time, and stopping to concoct a more solid plan was a luxury they didn't have. "Okay. If I see anything that looks like it might explode, I'll be sure to point it out."

An eager grin spread across Katherine's face. "See, that's the spirit," she said, and she charged on through the open door into the adjoining hallway.

After a few dozen yards, this new hallway opened up into a much larger area. As Summerhill got closer to it, he could see that this was the flight deck that Katherine had mentioned. It was brightly lit, but there was little distinct that he could see from so far away, with the exception of a series of launch tubes on the far side, and the wing of what must have been some kind of plane or small starship.

"I doubt I'll be able to jury-rig any of the fighters," Katherine called out as she broke into a brisk run. "But maybe some of them might already be armed up and I can hit their exposed weapon payloads or something like that. Keep your eyes peeled."

Katherine made it out into the hangar first, with Summerhill right behind her. He didn't see what made her skid to a halt next to one of the fighters, however, until after he crashed into her.

Off to the right side of the flight deck was a tall gantry, atop which stood a dozen black-clad Consortium guards, all carrying identical energy rifles, all of them aimed right at Summerhill and Katherine. In the middle of those guards, nearly twice as tall as any of them, was the six-eyed alien who had spoken with the Admiral. Its segmented tail was curled up above its hindquarters, like a scorpion, the tip glistening in the bright light.

"Katherine Tinsley," it hissed, its wet, guttural voice even more unsettling in person than it had been over the viewing screen. "The Transdimensional Spacetime Integrity Enforcement Consortium has never been forced to execute a sentient being from your universe before the due process of a trial. Do not force us to sully our record."

Despite having twelve people with guns drawing a bead on her, Katherine looked remarkably composed, Summerhill thought. He helped her scan the hangar, looking for any obvious target. There were a number of additional small fighter craft lined up, seemingly ready for launch, but none of the various crates, boxes, and barrels piled in the corners and lining the walls had any obvious markings to suggest that they contained hazardous or explosive materials.

"You are outnumbered. We control your escape routes. Desist in this futile attempt to evade justice." The six-eyed insect creature's mandibles dripped more than before, the secretions both thicker and louder. The separate sections of those mouthparts looked creepily like a pair of hands being wrung together in vile delight.

Katherine gritted her teeth. She still held her rifle at the ready, and she looked like she might be ready to go down in a blaze of glory if the Consortium creature taunted her much further.

Summerhill wasn't going to give her that chance, though. He stepped up next to her, reached into his pocket, and pulled out the antique watch. "Actually, I think you're going to let us go."

All twelve rifles up on the gantry turned to aim squarely at the dog. The alien's six eyes focused on him, each in turn, unblinking. "Unknown creature, your being aboard this vessel is in direct violation of Consortium law," it said. "However, we are willing to offer a full pardon if you turn Katherine Tinsley over to us."

The pocket watch's ticking was very audible in the big, open hangar. Summerhill let it tick for a few more seconds, smiling all the while, before he responded. "You really have no idea who I am?"

"You are not listed in our records. Our quarrel is not with you."

"Your records? Your records that cover everything that you run into across all space and time in all different realities?"

"Correct."

"My name is Summerhill of the World of the Pale Gray Sky. Ring any bells?"

The six-eyed creature tilted his oblong head to one side. "You are not listed in our records," it repeated.

"You sure about that? I'm kind of surprised." Summerhill ran his thumb over the inscription on the outside of the pocket watch. "I mean, if Katherine's time and space violations have you this riled up, I can only imagine the sort of trial you'd put on for me."

An orange and green holographic screen appeared in midair beneath the alien's four-clawed hands. It started to type away, but Summerhill couldn't see the details on the screen from the floor of the hangar deck. "Our system does not recognize you," the creature announced. "You have done nothing to warrant Consortium attention."

"Maybe not yet." Summerhill held the pocket watch even higher above his head. "But I promise you I will. How often do those spacetime records of yours update, anyway? Pretty frequently?"

Next to him, Katherine shivered anxiously. She turned her head and stared at him out of the corner of her eye. "Mr. Summerhill, what the hell do you think you're doing?" Her hands shifted on the rifle grip. They glistened with sweat.

Summerhill stared back up at the gantry. He didn't know who'd put the Consortium in charge or where their authority came from, but he'd seen enough of their methods and actions to know that any reality would be better off without them. In his mind, he envisioned all of the things he was going to do to help bring the Consortium down after he and Katherine got out of here. He would be the fish in the stream, swimming with the current, against it, jumping out of it, doing anything to keep a step ahead of the game as he brought their agency down, piece by piece.

The holographic screen interface turned a bright red. Summerhill couldn't read any of the new words that had just appeared, but he recognized the image of his own face well enough. The alien creature let out a low-pitched, gurgling cry of alarm as a torrent of thick saliva spilled forth from its quivering mandibles. "Men!" it shrieked, waving its arm and making the holographic screen disappear. "Forget Tinsley! Orders are to neutralize the dog-creature on sight!"

"I really wouldn't do that if I were you," Summerhill yelled above the din as the dozen guards leaned further over the gantry and steadied their aim. "You take one shot and I press this button." He stroked the tip of his index finger over the button that opened the hunter-case.

"And what is that supposed to be, exactly?" the six-eyed alien demanded.

"It's a miniaturized singularity generator. The kind used by the otter-people of the planet Rydale in their war against the Akashic Realm." Summerhill was willing to bet that this agent didn't know every detail about every civilization across time and space without the help of a computer. "One touch of this button, and your whole ship will get torn apart."

Katherine was still staring at him, and the blank look on her face seemed to silently tell him, 'You know that's just a pocket watch, right?'

The six-eyed alien gurgled a laugh. "There is no such device."

"You sure about that?" Summerhill asked. "I mean, until your records updated just a few moments ago, you seemed pretty sure I wasn't anything to worry about, either."

"We could destroy you before you had a chance to activate the device."

"Yeah? Then why haven't you done it yet?" Summerhill asked. "Is it because you know what I can do with those energy rifle blasts of yours? All I need is to buy myself a fraction of a second, and *click*." He took a long stride forward. "And if your records on my activities are accurate enough, you know I'd sooner die than give up my freedom again."

Several seconds passed without either side saying a word. The pocket watch ticked away, the sound filling the otherwise silent hangar. Summerhill's left ear twitched as Katherine swallowed dryly.

The alien creature waved its arm to call up the holographic interface again. "We shall see," it said as it began typing.

Summerhill looked back over his shoulder, quickly gauging distances. "Yes we will," he said, and he tossed the pocket watch straight up into the air.

The twelve guards fired in almost perfect unison. Most of the shots went wide of such a tiny, moving target, and the one that did hit reflected off its spinning surface, ricocheting into the far wall.

More importantly, the other eleven energy blasts sailed right above Summerhill's and Katherine's heads and struck the fighter craft behind them.

The machine began to spark and fizzle, venting pressurized gases and liquids into the air. Warning lights and tiny alarm bells along the craft's surface started to go off. The alien up on the gantry let out another wet shriek, the noise wordless and horrifying.

The spinning pocket watch came back down, and Summerhill snatched it out of the air right as Katherine shoved him from the side, causing him to stagger a few steps before she pushed past him and grabbed one of his hands to pull him along. She swung him by the arm into one of the launch tubes, then dove in after him just as the fighter craft exploded. Hot air rushed into the tube, and the dog's ears rung and ached, but the two were safe from the impact of the explosion itself. The whole hangar bay itself shook, and then, a mere moment later, another of the fight craft exploded as well in a chain reaction.

For a moment, the flight deck went dark, and then the emergency lights came on. They alternated red and green, and whooping alert sirens rang through the open bay as the automated loudspeaker announced the disaster in a robotic monotone.

"Run!" Katherine shouted in Summerhill's ringing ears, and she helped haul him to his feet. They darted out from the launch tube, a few stray energy rifle blasts going well wide as they ran out of the hangar bay the same way they came in.

Except that when they crossed the threshold back into the hexagonal corridor, rather than finding themselves in the hallway back to the transport unit they had taken here in the first place, they instead came out into an alcove with half a dozen single-occupant pods lining the wall, their doors already open.

Katherine smacked Summerhill on the back. "That was brilliant, mate!" she hollered, her voice clearly cutting over the emergency sirens. "Not so sure about 'elegant,' but hey, whatever gets the job done."

Raising her energy rifle, she fired into four of the pods, frying their control panels. "I'm sure they've got more of these elsewhere on the ship," she said, "but why make it easier for them, right?" She then walked up to one of the pods and began giving it a look-over.

"So then, where are these going to take us?" Summerhill asked. "Can we control them?"

"Probably not well." Katherine wedged her rifle in between two of the consoles, into a space that looked designed for exactly that purpose. "Not that I'm an expert on Consortium technology, but I'm guessing these work similarly to the lifeboats on the *Nusquam*."

Summerhill frowned. "Meaning that they'll take the occupants wherever the on-board computer thinks they belong."

"I'm afraid so." Katherine patted Summerhill on the shoulder. "But don't you worry, Mr. Summerhill," she said with a broad grin. "If the world is as strange and nonsensical as I think it is, we'll run into each other again someday." She then leaned in and gave him a kiss on his furry cheek.

She turned back to the escape pod, then quickly spun back around. "Oh, and I need these back, actually," she said as she grabbed hold of the dog tags around Summerhill's neck. A quick yank broke the ball chain, and she stuffed the tags into her pocket before hopping into the pod.

"Thanks for saving me again, Mr. Summerhill," she said as she got comfortable against the support cushion on the inner wall of the pod. "I'll see if I can ever return the favor."

Before Summerhill could say anything, Katherine pressed a button on the console next to her right hand, and the door to the escape pod slammed shut. There was a bright flash, and then the socket for the escape pod was empty.

THIRTY-SIX
REMINDER

And so Summerhill was alone again. If he stood there waiting, though, he was sure to have plenty of company in the form of armed Consortium guards, so he shook off his feeling of dismay and climbed into the lone remaining escape pod.

After getting settled in, he took one last look at the pocket watch. A shadow danced over its reflective surface, and the dog looked up.

Standing in the middle of escape pod alcove was Arasiel, still in her purple dress and her purple high-heeled shoes. She puckered her bright red lips as she stepped up to the open escape pod.

"No," Summerhill breathed. "No, not now. I did everything right. It can't end here."

Arasiel rested one hand just inside the escape pod hatch. Even in shadow, the vibrant cardinal fringe of her hair was impossibly bright. "No, Summerhill. Not for you." She stroked the whiskers on one side of his snout, her icy touch making the fur all the way up his cheek stiffen. "But it *was* supposed to be the End for a certain someone else."

She didn't look angry, but somehow that made her scarier. "I... I'm sorry?" Summerhill offered. "I was just trying to—"

"I know what you were trying to do, Summerhill," Arasiel said, brushing her fingers alone one of the dog's ears, the chill of her fingertips just shy of painful. "Really, all you've done is delay the inevitable."

"If it's inevitable, then you shouldn't be mad."

Arasiel threw her head back with a brief laugh, then pulled away so that she wasn't leaning into the escape pod anymore. "Oh, Summerhill. What would ever make you think I was mad?" She brushed her bangs out of her eyes with her long

270

nails and stood perfectly upright. "I just wanted you to know that I'll remember you did this."

Summerhill set his finger against the button that launched the escape pod, but he didn't press it yet. "Well, then I withdraw my apology. Because I'm not sorry for trying to save someone."

The whole ship then lurched as the sound of a loud explosion reverberated from somewhere nearby. Arasiel showed no outward reaction except for a thin smile. "No apology necessary." Another series of explosions, weaker than the first, shook the ship in rapid succession. "Now I've got two prizes to collect someday, both of them so much the sweeter because of what you've done." She touched her fingers to her lips and blew him a kiss, her lipstick having stained her fingertips blood red.

With a casual twirl, she turned around, her long hair sweeping behind her. The next moment, she disappeared into thin air, and the ship began to list again.

That was all the warning Summerhill needed. He took a deep breath and pressed the button. As the flash of light overtook the escape pod, he had a very good idea of where it was going to send him.

 # THIRTY-SEVEN
GRATITUDE

It was late evening, with Rydale's orange sun shifted towards red as it hung low in the sky. The ocean formed a nice, placid horizon, broken only by a single offshore island.

The very first stars were visible high up in the sky, far away from the sun. Familiar patterns showed themselves, and Summerhill recognized this sky as the one he'd seen back when he'd lost track of himself inside the nevereef with Katherine. Maybe at some point in his distant past, he'd come here for some reason, and although he knew he might never find out whether that was true or not, the uncertainty no longer bothered him.

A large city filled up the coastal plain between the ocean and the gently rolling hills off to the southeast. There was still at least an hour of light remaining before true night, and so only some of the brighter city lights were on. Rydale architecture seemed to prefer buildings that were round instead of angular, short and squat, like cones that had had their tops sliced off.

From up here on the hillside, Summerhill could see almost the entire city. Down there, there were probably millions of otter-people, the scent on any crowded street likely enough to drive him into a frenzy.

Luckily, Summerhill didn't need to go down into the city, and he didn't need to deal with thousands or millions of otters. Just one.

He was out walking along the grass outside of the small house up here on the hill, a blue and purple truncated cone built next to a small stream. He hadn't noticed Summerhill yet, walking with his head down as he carried a bucket in one webbed paw. His path was carrying him up the gentle incline, though, so he was bound to run into the dog eventually. Perhaps literally if he didn't look up soon.

Having already collided with the otter twice before, Summerhill decided to spare him a third such incident. "Hello, Tekutan," he said.

The otter squeaked in alarm as he came to a halt, lifting his head up as he came out of his daze. "Summerhill?" His wide eyes twinkled in the faint light of dusk. "What are you doing out here? I thought you were back—" He trailed off as realization dawned. "You're not my Summerhill, are you?"

Summerhill had his hands stuffed into his pockets. "Have you been well?"

Tek set the bucket down and stepped closer, then stopped himself. "Is it, um, okay if I get closer?"

"I should be okay around just one of you. At least for a minute or two. So have you been doing all right? Sounds like you've, um, settled."

"Yeah. Yeah, we're good." The otter paced a few steps in either direction. "Sorry. Wow, this is really awkward."

Summerhill took a couple steps closer to him. "It doesn't have to be."

"Is something wrong?" Tek asked. "Is that why you're here? Did something happen? Or do you need to collect your other self back? Please, I know things were strange when we met, but—"

"Tek, relax, please." Summerhill set a hand on the otter's shoulder, and the touch of that fur made his body tingle with half-memories and full-urges he knew he had to ignore for now. He'd be okay for a little bit longer, though. "I'm just here to say thank you."

That clearly wasn't what the otter had expected to hear. "Thank me? For what?"

"For something you said to me the last time I was here," Summerhill replied. "You said something that gave me the key clue I needed to save my friend." The dog flattened his ears and let out a little chuckle. "I tried to forget you. Guess it's a good thing I didn't do a perfect job of it."

Tek scuffed one of his webbed feet at the grass. "Oh. Well, I mean, you're welcome, I guess." His toe tapped against the bucket. "Was this the same friend you mentioned before?"

"Yeah." Summerhill stared at the bucket, too, instead of at Tek. "Her name's Katherine. She's okay now."

"That's good." Tek paced some more, his breathing on the loud side. "I'm... I'm glad things worked out okay for you both."

"I also wanted to say that I'm sorry," Summerhill blurted. "If what I did hurt you or scared you or... I don't know. I don't remember much about our time together, but I recall enough to know that I must have really cared about you."

Tek turned to look back at his house down by the stream. "You *do* really care about me," he said. "Trust me."

Summerhill felt his chest grow tight. He wanted to grab the otter and kiss him, but he knew that would be a huge mistake, both because of the ensuing physical reaction as well as the confused and conflicted emotions that would come with it. "There's so much I want to ask. About what happened with me and you, and what's happened since I've been gone."

The otter's eyes glinted with moisture in the pre-sunset light. "You're wonderful," Tek said, and he sniffled away his tiny tears. "You've always been wonderful."

"I don't completely lose control of myself when I'm around you?"

"Depends on how I look at you and what I whisper into your ears when we're alone together." The otter let out a chuckle that was interrupted by a weak sob. "Sorry. That probably wasn't appropriate."

Summerhill shook his head. "No, it's fine." He gazed over at the house. It was weird to think that there was another one of him in there, right now, unaware of any of what was going on. "I wish I could know what he knows, about you and about us, but I get the feeling that if I did, I'd—"

274

"You'd never leave," Tek said. "There was a time when I didn't believe that, but now you—well, no. I shouldn't say."

"And you don't have to." Summerhill smiled, and gave Tek's shoulder another squeeze. Staying here too much longer was going to be a bad idea. "But I'm glad you're okay. Both of you."

Tek nodded. "Yeah. So am I."

"I should... I should get going." Summerhill looked back over his shoulder, at the copse of wide trees a few dozen paces away. "It was good seeing you again. I just... Maybe don't tell the other me that I was here? I get the feeling that'd just upset me."

The otter picked up his bucket. "I'd never want to see you upset. Especially because of something I said."

Summerhill thought of Tek trying to console the other version of him, and could easily visualize the otter's earnest tenderness as he reached out, caressed that other dog's cheek, and whispered plaintively while staring into his lovers eyes and—

"Tek," he asked. "What color are his eyes?"

"My Summerhill?" The otter looked curious and confused for a brief moment, but then he smiled, nice and bright. "The same as yours. The most beautiful and perfect shade of gray I've ever seen."

An answer that left more questions, but perhaps an answer that was for the best. Summerhill nodded in acknowledgment and took a few steps backwards. "Goodbye, Tek. I'm glad I met you."

"I'm glad I met you, too, Summerhill." Tek shook his head and smiled. "I don't know who or what you really are, but you're something special."

The otter traipsed back up the hill with his bucket. Summerhill watched him go for a little while longer before turning around and heading back to the trees.

The Consortium escape pod was nestled within, hidden just well enough by the flowering branches. The on-board power display showed that the pod didn't have enough juice left to activate its reality jump drive again, but Summerhill was pretty sure that wasn't going to be a problem.

He pulled the antique watch out of his pocket and held it up close to his ear, listening to it tick. Shutting his eyes, he rubbed the cool metal against his cheek; it was no worse for the wear, even after being shot by an energy rifle. Before putting it away, he opened the case, watched the second hand flick by, and then smiled at the sepia tone photograph of himself that looked back at him.

After taking one last deep breath of fresh Rydale air in through his nose, the dog reached up to pluck a vibrant blue blossom from one of the trees, and then he walked back into the escape pod. He knew that, if he concentrated hard enough, he'd be able to draw focus from the machine and what it was meant for, and only needed the briefest moment of pure concentration to be able to jump out of the stream for a little bit.

TWO
IDYLLS

Tek leaned his head back and hummed, his eyes open as mere slivers. The otter took a deep breath and let it out as a sigh of contentment. From this angle, the sheen of his fur did a lovely job of catching the brilliant orange hues of the setting Rydale sun.

The russet-furred canine slipped his arms down and tightened his embrace around the otter's chest, then planted a small kiss at the base of one of his small rounded ears.

This was the fifty-seventh time he and Tek had watched the sunset together (he'd been counting), and it still hadn't lost its charm. Rydale was a lovely place, and even here, on the outskirts of Tiadinara City with its millions of inhabitants, it was easy to get lost in the overflowing presence of unsullied nature. Rather than interrupt the view, the cityscape actually synergized amazingly well with it, twinkling spires against a backdrop of orange-purple that then lit up like high-intensity lanterns once the sky went to black.

That wouldn't come for the better part of an hour, though. Until then, Summerhill and Tek had their sunset to enjoy together.

"You know, you never told me," Summerhill said, murmuring into Tek's ear. "Rydale has barely mastered extrasolar travel. How did you manage to end up as a passenger on board a ship in the middle of nowhere?"

The otter tilted his head further back, looking at Summerhill upside-down. His contented smile became a mischievous smirk. "You never asked."

All around the two of them, the wildflowers were still in full bloom. Their scent always made Summerhill feel better at the end of a long day. Their petals were soft to the touch, soft like velvet, their colors seeming to change in the glow of sunset.

Tek's scent did wonders for his mood, too. The otter had initially seemed worried about letting Summerhill get too close, and had waffled and made excuses about irresistible urges, but his ability to protest had quickly run out. That scent did incite some nice urges, but they weren't anything that either of them seemed to mind.

Whenever they kissed, the effect was even more potent. If they kissed for long enough, sometimes Summerhill would feel his tongue start to tingle, and his mind would briefly play innocuous little tricks on him.

"Would you tell me?" he asked.

Tek scooted back along the grass, situating himself between Summerhill's legs with the dog's arms still wrapped around his torso. "It's kind of a long story."

The glow of the orange sun disappeared below the horizon, though the vibrant, cloud-streaked band of twilight would linger for some time to come before dusk turned into night. The scents of flowers and otter were caught up on the evening breeze and brought to Summerhill's nose. Stars began to pop out against the deep, dark purple.

Summerhill drew his arms even more protectively around the otter and looked out over the city, across the fields of Rydale, and at that beautiful sky beyond. He smiled, kissed his lover between the ears, and thought of how lucky he was to have been given a place such as this.

"Go right ahead," he said. "I'm not going anywhere."

 # THIRTY-EIGHT
Pioneers

Katherine stood next to her own powerless escape pod, right at the edge of a rocky precipice that overlooked a vast alien landscape. Light flooded the eerie valley below, light that was a greenish-yellow, coming from a swirling sun that took up a wide arc of the horizon behind which it was slowly sinking. Bizarre peaks rose against the strange-colored sky, not jagged or angular, but stringy, almost organic, looking like they'd been poured there.

Gas-bag creatures floated by, silhouetted in front of wispy purple clouds. Tendrils hung from their undersides, like the tentacles of a jellyfish. From down in the valley came the cries of other creatures, echoing off of the winding, twisting canyon walls that cut through the landscape like hastily made scribbles.

Deeper in the valley, in the shadows of mountains that looked like they were slowly melting over the course of a million years, were faint blue lights. From this distance, it was impossible to tell if they were natural, artificial, or something else entirely.

Katherine didn't turn around, but she spoke as though she wasn't the least bit surprised that Summerhill had appeared out of thin air right behind her. "You know, the last time I used a Consortium escape pod, the damn thing had the courtesy to drop me in the middle of a crowded space lane where I got picked up within minutes." She held one arm out and gestured to the alien valley below. "This? This is new."

"New can be good sometimes," Summerhill replied as he stepped up next to her. "Sometimes looking forward to the new is better than dwelling on the old."

"Now you really do sound like my granddad. Not that that's a bad thing, I suppose."

Summerhill twirled the blue Rydale flower between two fingertips, then held it up for Katherine. "Here. I brought you a souvenir."

Katherine took it, but she didn't look particularly impressed. She held it, examined it, spun it around like Summerhill had, and then eventually just started to chuckle, shaking her head. "Thank you," she said with an honest smile as she tucked it behind one ear. "It's beautiful."

From off in the distance came a shrieking cry as some kind of red flying reptile with a dagger-like beak speared one of the gas-bag creatures. A sound like a gunshot echoed through the valley as the gas-bag burst like a balloon.

"Part of me almost thinks the Consortium did this on purpose," Katherine said. "Let me escape to a booby-trapped escape pod that drops me on some alien hellhole planet in the middle of nowhere to live out my punishment with no hope of escape."

Summerhill smiled and patted her on the back. "There's hope of escape," he assured her. "I'm here."

"Oh, sure, *you* can escape." She stared back out over the landscape. "That still leaves me stuck here."

"I'd never leave you stuck here. You know that."

Katherine turned back to look at him, and she smiled again. "I guess you've helped me out of worse. Do you have any brilliant ideas, then?"

"Not yet. But we'll figure out something. We always seem to do better when we're together."

That made Katherine's smile widen, and she laughed again. "May as well get my gun, then. Looks like we're in for a long hike."

When she turned to head back to the escape pod, Summerhill stepped in against her side and stuffed his hands into her pants pocket. She cried out in surprise, but he drew out her dog tags before she could stop him.

The dog held them up to his face, the metal of the tags glinting in the light of the green sun. He jostled the metal chain, and then a third piece he hadn't noticed before dangled out from between the two tags themselves.

It was the small rectangular orange-and-blue pendant that Katherine had worn back on the *Nusquam* and during their journey within the nevereef. Now that he was seeing it up close for the first time, Summerhill could make out the intricate series of lines carved into both sides. After staring at them for a few seconds, he recognized the pattern as being the same style as the intricate wood grain on the dimensional doors he'd found. "What's this?" he asked.

Katherine's lips curled up into a proud grin. "That, Mr. Summerhill, is one genuine Consortium hyperspace modulator circuit."

"You mean the thing that they've been hunting you over all space and time to get back?"

"That's the one."

"You said you'd sold it!"

"I lied." Katherine winked, then grabbed it back from Summerhill, along with the dog tags. "I'm a liar and a thief. It's kind of what I do."

Summerhill thought back to the corridor outside the flight deck aboard the Consortium ship. "Wait, so when you let me wear your dog tags for good luck—"

"Hey, if we got split up, I figured it was better for the magic talking dog who can block lasers to have it."

"Uh-huh. And I'm sure it had nothing to do with making sure I'd take the heat if things really went to hell back there." The dog sighed, his ears pricking back up as another of the flying reptiles shrieked through a nearby canyon. "But wait, why'd you take it back when you could have gotten away from it forever by leaving me behind in the escape pod bay?"

Katherine grabbed the energy rifle out of the escape pod, then punched Summerhill on the arm. "First of all, I'd never have just left you there to get caught. I could have fried the last escape pod, too, if that had been my plan." She held the circuit and the dog tags back up. "And the reason I keep this,

Mr. Summerhill, is that as long as this is in my possession, I know for sure that there's a roughly five hundred year span in my universe where the Consortium can do bugger all. The trick is making sure that's the time frame I manage to get back to." She eyed the circuit as it caught the eerie light from the alien star. "And hey, I bet I could make enough money to buy an entire planet if I ever found someone I could actually fence this to."

Summerhill rubbed the sore spot on his arm and rolled his eyes playfully. "You know, I'm glad you consider me a friend."

"It's better than being an enemy of the Consortium all by myself." Katherine stuffed the dog tags back in her pocket. "Speaking of which, I'm dying to see what it is you do to them in the future that gets them as scared as they were back there."

"Hey, see?" Summerhill pointed out. "That's how you know for sure that we're going to get out of this."

"I know for sure that *you're* going to get out of this."

"And I'll always stick with you." Summerhill reached up and touched the flower behind her ear. "Which means we're getting out of this together."

Now Katherine was the one to roll her eyes. "Come on. We need to figure out how we're going to get down from here. Looks like it's going to be a pretty treacherous climb."

Summerhill stepped up to the edge of the overlook. "I can help us get down a lot faster."

"Ooh, can you create some kind of vine or tree or whatever? Because that would be—"

"Oh, no. I've got something much, much better in mind."

Katherine raised her eyebrow and lowered her rifle. "Why does that worry me?"

The dog turned around and offered Katherine his hand. "Here," he said, wagging his tail. "Let me show you how it works."

Slowly, Katherine's hesitation melted away, and her lips evened out into a trusting smile. "Right, then. What do we do, exactly?" she asked, putting her hand in his.

"Nothing less than the impossible," Summerhill said, and with that, he stepped off the edge, bringing Katherine with him.

About the Author

Born and raised just outside of Boston, Massachusetts, Kevin Frane spent time living in Japan before settling in the San Francisco Bay Area in 2002, where he has worked in video game localization in addition to his writing career.

His first novel, *Thousand Leaves*, was nominated for the Ursa Major Award for Best Anthropomorphic Novel for 2008, with the follow-up *The Seventh Chakra* nominated for the same in 2010. His novella *The Peculiar Quandary of Simon Canopus Artyle* was nominated for the Ursa Major Award for Best Anthropomorphic Short Fiction for 2010.